STINGER

STINGER

John Nichol

Hodder & Stoughton

British Library Cataloguing in Publication Data

Hardcover edition ISBN 0 340 75115 0
Trade paperback edition ISBN 0 340 76657 3

Typeset by Hewer Text Ltd, Edinburgh
Printed and bound in Great Britain by
Mackays of Chatham, PLC, Chatham, Kent

Hodder and Stoughton
A division of Hodder Headline PLC
338 Euston Road
London NW1 3BH

STINGER

Foreword

The CIA covertly supplied hundreds of Stinger missiles to the Mujahedeen in Afghanistan during the war with the Soviet Union. The SAS trained the Mujahedeen in the use of the Stingers, which wreaked havoc among Soviet helicopter-gunships, military and civilian aircraft.

At the end of the conflict an estimated 300–400 missiles remained unaccounted for. The US originally offered $3 million to buy them back. This was increased to $30 million when US Intelligence received information suggesting that Libya was attempting to purchase them. The ransom has never been paid and the whereabouts of the missing Stingers remain unknown.

One of the reasons for the panic that engulfed the US government after the downing of TWA Flight 800 in July 1996 was the fear that it had been shot down by Fundamentalist terrorists armed with Stingers.[1]

John Nichol
May 1999

---

[1]*Ghost Force: The Secret History of the SAS*, by Ken Connor (Weidenfeld & Nicolson).

Prologue

I sat silent as the blank screen of the briefing room filled with a grainy colour image of a 747 rolling along a taxiway, through a haze of heat rising from the tarmac. Side-lit by the setting sun, it thundered down the runway and rumbled into the air, its jetwash rattling the chainlink perimeter fencing and stirring a storm of dust and litter from the waste ground beyond the wire.

The camera tracked the jet climbing into the darkening sky, the smoke trails from its engines merging with the pall of smog hanging over the city. The towers of Manhattan were framed beneath the wing for a moment, then disappeared as the jet began a long turn south and east.

The neat grid of street lights flared into a brief, dirty smudge of light at Coney Island before the jet was clear of the land. Still holding the climb, it banked further east to follow the shore of Long Island out towards the open sea.

To the north of the jet I could see the twin tracks of the airport's main runways and the navigation lights moving across the sky with military precision, one line of jets dropping towards the north runway as another procession lifted off from the south.

The viewpoint abruptly changed to a camera somewhere on the Long Island shore. The rays of the sinking sun reddened the upper atmosphere, glinting from another aircraft wing in the distance ahead of the jet. Thousands of feet below were the winking navigation lights of a slow-moving transport aircraft and the lights of ships moving across the dark water.

The gathering darkness over the Long Island shore was pierced by the glow of bonfires at Fourth of July parties. Fireworks flowered in brief flashes of vivid colour, then faded to black.

There was a flash much bigger than the others and a white streak sped upwards towards them, bridging the distance to the jet in a heartbeat before exploding in a vivid ball of orange flame.

The jet was ripped apart in an instant, the cabin walls shredded by the blast. The heavier nose section broke away immediately and began a long tumble downwards. Still driven by the bellowing jet engines, the rest of the fuselage canted upwards and climbed a further 2,000 feet into the sky. The camera jerked wildly as the cameraman tried to follow the path of the jet, and the image was blurred by the shaking of his hands.

At around 16,000 feet the jet stalled and went into freefall. The camera lost it, overshot it, then tracked it again as it hurtled downwards. The sheer force of its descent ripped off the wings, and thousands of gallons of kerosene fuel ignited as they gushed from the ruptured tanks. What remained of the aircraft disintegrated as it hit the water and 50,000 gallons more spread in a burning slick across the water, as if the sea itself were on fire.

The crew in the severed cockpit survived the initial blast and remained alive throughout the three and a half minutes it took to fall the 14,000 feet to the sea.

Their terrified voices, almost drowned by the clamour of the cockpit emergency warning sirens, underscored the horror unfolding on the screen. I could hear the co-pilot repeating over and over again, 'Oh, God. Oh, Jesus. I don't want to die. I don't want to die.'

The pilot began to recite the Lord's Prayer. After a few words his voice faltered and died. The only other words he said were 'Fuck it,' just before his voice was cut off by an avalanche of sound.

The screen went blank as the final, thunderous concussion faded into the sibilant white noise of static, and I dragged my eyes away from the speakers relaying that cold, dead sound.

Chapter 1

Three weeks earlier – Afghanistan

Beyond the mountains to the north I could glimpse the beginning of the steppe, an ocean of grey dust that seemed to stretch into infinity. To the east there were only mountains and more mountains. The brown, parched summits below us were mere pygmies of a few thousand feet compared to the rank upon rank of serrated peaks that lay in the far distance, at the very limits of my vision. Permanently capped with snow, they towered far above the 10,000 feet at which we were flying.

As we cleared the next ridge I saw a few stick figures – shepherds, traders and nomads, following the threadlike tracks over the dusty hillsides towards the capital. It was now in sight, a mud-coloured sprawl that lay like sediment in the bottom of a bowl of hills. Across the valley floor lay a river of dust that ran to nowhere, disappearing into the sands of the great desert to the west.

The pilot glanced at me. 'We'll be on finals shortly. It's a rather steep descent . . .'

'Of course,' I said. 'Thanks for inviting me up here. It makes a change for me to be able to admire the view while someone else does the driving.'

I went back to my seat, passing the only two other passengers on the aircraft. A few minutes later the wing dipped and we began a steep, spiralling descent towards Kabul airport. From the corner of my eye I saw fierce white star-fires drifting away from us as the pilot punched out flares to decoy any missiles.

He levelled at the last possible moment and touched down with a jolt that rattled my teeth. The engines bellowed under reverse thrust and the aircraft slowed, its landing gear juddering over the cracks and ruts in the runway.

There were no announcements over the Tannoy as we pulled to a halt outside the terminal. The Pakistani steward threw open the door, gave a half-apologetic smile and disappeared into the flight cabin. I picked up my shoulder bag and walked to the exit. There was no flight of steps, only a wooden ladder held against the side of the aircraft by two impassive men in greasy overalls.

I climbed down and collected my other bag, which had already been taken out of the hold and dumped on the concrete. I glanced around. The airport looked as desolate as the battered city that surrounded it. A single Pakistani transport plane stood near the terminal, but the rusting remains of Migs and Tupolevs still littered the perimeter, a decade after the end of the war against the Soviets. Only one hangar remained standing and part of its roof had collapsed. Wooden scaffolding surrounded the remainder, but I caught sight of three helicopter gunships through the open hangar doors.

The terminal building was windowless, and its rust-stained, peeling walls were pocked with the marks of shell bursts and bullets. I walked inside. The baggage hall was unlit and the carousels and conveyors were silent and shrouded in dust.

At the far end of the baggage hall three soldiers armed with Kalashnikovs lounged around a table. They straightened at my approach, gave my passport a cursory glance, then began to go through my bags.

It was my first sight of the Taliban soldier monks. They were all young – in their late teens or early twenties at a guess – and all bearded. Their black turbans were folded into elaborate shapes like cock's-combs, with a longforked tail of cloth trailing down their backs. Their expressions were neither welcoming nor hostile, but the thick rim of black kohl around their eyes gave them a forbidding look.

I was carrying no magazines or tapes and my only books were a couple of dog-eared paperbacks – *Bleak House* and *Great Expectations* – but the soldiers seized them just the same. They exchanged comments in guttural Pushtu as they passed the copies between them, then threw them into a box at the side of the table. 'Forbidden,' one said.

I opened my mouth to argue, then thought better of it, shrugged and bowed my head. He handed back my passport, and I pushed open the sagging doors to walk into the harsh sunlight.

As I shaded my eyes I heard a familiar voice. 'Late as usual, Sean.'

Jeff's round, pale face was creased in its permanent expression of slightly pained surprise. There was a sheen of perspiration on his forehead, and as we shook hands his plump fingers felt clammy.

'What the hell are you doing in Kabul?'

'The same as you – flying a heli.' He turned to make the

introductions to the two people flanking him. 'Sean Riever, this is Dexy Turner.'

Dexy was a couple of inches shorter than I, but powerfully built, his arms rippling with muscle. 'Good to meet you, Sean. Don't let Jeff's proprietorial air fool you, he's only been here a few days himself.'

The accent was English – south London – and his smile was warm, but his eyes were perpetually alert. 'We'll be working together a fair bit, I head up one of the mine clearance teams.'

I turned towards the other member of the welcoming committee, a woman clad in an all-enveloping mauve burka. I could see only the glitter of her dark eyes through an embroidered mesh visor. 'And I'm Amica,' a disembodied voice said. The accent was local, but there was a trace of something else in there too. 'Welcome to Afghanistan.'

'Thank you,' I said. 'I'm looking forward to working here. Is that an American accent I can hear?'

'I spent some years there, yes.'

'Why did you come back?'

The visor of the burka swung back towards me. 'America was too materialist.'

Dexy laughed. 'That's not a problem you're ever likely to find here.' He led the way to a white pick-up with a local driver sitting at the wheel. 'Afghan Mine Clearance Organisation' was painted in red letters on the side. Beneath the name was the AMCO logo and a picture of a Kalashnikov with a red line through it.

'We allow no one inside bearing arms,' Amica said. There was the faintest hint of a smile in her voice.

'I didn't realise you and Jeff already knew each other,' Dexy said as we drove away from the terminal.

'I was paired with him when I transferred from fast-jets. He nursed me through my first few months of flying helis.'

Jeff laughed. 'Not really. I just sat alongside him, shut my eyes and prayed.'

'But how come you're working for AMCO?' I turned to Dexy. 'He's the only man I've ever met who wears a home-made poppy on Remembrance Day.'

Despite the sledging, Jeff's smile didn't fade. 'How much are you getting paid to work here, Sean?'

'What do you mean? I'm seconded; I'm getting my normal RAF pay just like you—' I paused. 'Aren't you?'

He shook his head. 'More fool you. I'm here for one reason only – the money. I'm on a hundred K, tax free, with a fat gratuity at the end of my three years.'

I glanced at Dexy. 'And are you a mercenary too?'

Dexy's tone was cold. 'I'm here to do a job that the Afghans either can't or won't do for themselves. I clear mines and try to train others to do so. I'm a soldier and I get soldier's pay, but no more than I could earn in the UK without risking my life every day to earn it. That all right with you?'

'Of course, I didn't mean to—' I paused. 'It's just I assumed everyone here would be a volunteer. I hadn't even realised AMCO had the budget to pay fat fees.'

'We don't,' Amica said, 'but if people have skills that we need and there are not enough volunteers to do the job, we have to find the money to pay the market rate for them.'

'And what's your job with AMCO?'

'I'm a medic, specialising in trauma. There's no shortage of that kind of work here. And I help with the administration—'

Dexy interrupted her. 'Amica runs the whole operation, but since the Taliban refuse to acknowledge the possibility that women might be capable of anything more than living inside a portable tent, we have to do the talking when they're around.'

I shot an uncertain glance at the driver.

'Relax,' Amica said. 'He's no friend of the Taliban. He used to run a tea-house and hostel when Kabul was on the hippie trail. He sold them food, a room for the night and the best marijuana in Afghanistan. Isn't that right, Panna?'

The driver grinned. 'Number one, far-out hash. Blow your fucking mind, man. You want some?'

I smiled. 'I'd never have guessed you'd spent time around hippies, Panna.'

'They were good times, man,' he said. 'Then the Russians ruined everything, and the Taliban are worse.' He hawked and spat out of the window. 'When they go' – he drew a finger across his throat – 'the hippies will come back and I'll be rich.'

'Are the Taliban that bad?'

The cool voice emanating from the mesh of the burka took on a harder edge. 'If anything, they're worse; but don't blame it all on us. They were formed in the Muslim seminaries in Pakistan, encouraged by the Islamic government in Pakistan, but funded and weaponed by their paymasters in Washington, London and Riyadh.' She gave a bitter laugh. 'Please don't judge all Afghans by what the Taliban do.'

I looked out of the windscreen as we jolted over the scarred and pitted road. On every side was a scene of utter devastation. For block after block, houses and buildings had disintegrated into piles of dust and rubble.

'This place is called Jade Maiwand,' Amica said. 'It's the worst area; the destruction here was almost total.'

'It's like Beirut,' Jeff said.

I shook my head in disbelief. 'It's more like Hiroshima.'

Nothing had been spared in the fighting. Schools and

hospitals lay in ruins, and even a mosque had been destroyed, its broken tiles and mosaics of lapis lazuli littering the ground like fallen petals.

Amica pointed to the wreck of another ancient building from which the stumps of huge stone pillars protruded through the collapsed roof. 'The Kabul museum,' she said. 'It had a fine collection of Buddhist relics. They've all been looted and sold by the Taliban.'

Beyond the wreckage I could see row upon row of roofless, fire-blackened houses climbing the hillsides, their walls pocked and pitted by gunfire, their empty windows framing only the sky.

The devastation was less severe near the city centre, but there were no grand buildings or broad avenues, just a jumble of shoddy buildings – drab concrete shells interspersed with rows of mud-brick shanties, propped one against another, like books on a shelf – and a cluster of footbridges spanning the muddy waters of the Kabul river at the city's heart.

None of the traffic lights worked, and the red and white booths from which police must once have directed the flow of vehicles were empty and abandoned. There was little traffic to control: only a few lorries and buses and a handful of ramshackle bicycles stirred the dust in the rutted and cratered streets. The only new-looking vehicles were the red Toyotas of the Taliban. They passed with their horns blaring incessantly, as pedestrians and other traffic took cover, pulling to the side to allow them through.

We took the road to the east, through another cluster of devastated buildings, but as we rounded a corner Panna braked suddenly. A rough barrier had been erected across the road, next to a dead, bomb-splintered tree. Six black-robed figures stood in front of it, Kalashnikovs at the ready.

Panna had been playing Indian movie music on the tape-player, a surreal soundtrack to the vision from hell unfolding around us. As soon as he saw the roadblock, he jabbed his finger on the eject button and slipped the tape under his seat. He shoved in another cassette and martial music began to blare from the speakers. 'Checkpoint music,' he said.

Amica shook the sleeves of her burka over her wrists and slid to the far side of the seat. 'If they ask questions, I will try to speak for us, if they allow me to do so,' she said. 'Some Taliban treat me as an honorary man, others refuse to acknowledge me. If they ignore me, it will be a chance for you to practise your Farsi.'

I'd been on a six-week intensive course in the language, but was far from fluent in it. My uncertainty must have showed, for Amica hurried to reassure me: 'Don't worry, it's a foreign language to them too. The Taliban are almost all Pushtuns. Show their leader the papers and give him every respect, however idiotic his requests or questions. To make him lose face in front of his men would be a very serious error. Don't react, and above all don't get angry.'

As the pick-up ground to a halt the leader of the Taliban group gestured with his Kalashnikov, ordering us out. His hair and beard were grey, but he was a powerful and imposing figure. The puckered line of a scar ran across his bony, hooked nose and through one eye-socket. The milk-white pupil stared sightlessly at us, but the other eye was hazel and hawk-sharp.

We stood in a row at the side of the vehicle as the Taliban searched the car. Amica was a couple of paces behind us, her head bowed. With the exception of their leader, none of them looked more than eighteen years old. They stared at us with baleful hostility from peasant faces with kohl-rimmed eyes and thin straggling beards.

One of them emerged from the car brandishing the cassette that Panna had hidden. He caught a loop of the tape on the tip of his bayonet, ripped it out and threw it to the base of the dead tree. The black ribbons of tape rustled in the wind.

The leader shouted a question at Panna. I heard the words *faranji* and *kafir* – foreigner and infidel. Panna's answer did not please the Taliban and he punched Panna in the face. The driver dropped to his knees, a thin trickle of blood running from the corner of his mouth. The leader uncurled a length of electrical flex from around his waist and brought it whistling down on Panna's back half a dozen times. Despite the pain, Panna neither flinched nor made a sound.

Dexy's face remained impassive. Jeff had tensed alongside me, and beads of sweat trickled down his forehead and dripped from his nose. I forced myself to remain still, but as the leader turned to look at me his eyes widened and he stepped towards me, pulling a wicked-looking curved knife from his belt.

I froze, my mouth dry with fear. The Taliban leader grabbed me by the hair and dragged my head downwards, forcing me to my knees.

'Wait!' It was Amica's voice.

The leader turned to stare at her.

'This man has just arrived from the West to help us,' she said. I could hear the tremor of fear in her voice. 'He is not yet used to our ways.'

The leader strode towards her as if he would strike her, then paused. 'Then I shall have to teach him.'

He began hacking at my hair with his knife, punctuating each cut with shouts and curses. The blade was blunt and my scalp burned as clumps of hair were torn from it by the roots. He carried on until the ground at my feet was covered in blood-stained hair. Then he put the point of the knife under my chin and forced me upright. He shouted at me again, pleased at the fear in my eyes, then pushed me away.

He kicked at Panna. 'Bring the *faranji* to the sports stadium tomorrow afternoon. They shall learn what it is to be a good Muslim.'

Jeff was shivering with fright, but the Taliban leader left him and Dexy alone. He glanced back at Amica standing by the rear wheel of the pick-up, her face averted, then motioned for us to get back into the car.

We waited in silence. Finally the leader made a dismissive gesture with his hand and the barrier was raised.

Panna started the engine and we roared off down the road, trailing dust. Jeff looked away from me, reluctant to meet my eye, but Dexy's gaze was level. 'Sometimes the hardest thing is to do nothing,' he said. 'But we can't jeopardise what we're here to do by trying to fight these guys, whatever the provocation.'

I heard a muffled sound. Behind the burka, I was sure that Amica was crying. I hesitated, then reached over and touched her arm. 'Are you all right?'

She started. 'I'm— It was seeing that man, Salan.'

'The Taliban leader?'

She nodded. 'He did not recognise me – how could he beneath a burka? But I knew him.' There was cold rage in her voice.

I waited for her to continue, but she was silent.

'You will have to fight me to get to him,' Panna said. 'He has shamed me, whipping me like a dog.'

Amica parted what was left of my hair to inspect my bloody scalp. 'We'll treat your wounds as soon as we get back to the compound. Yours too, Panna.'

He shrugged his shoulders, then cursed as the movement reopened the wounds on his back.

'What did he mean about learning to be a good Muslim?' I said.

'You'll find out tomorrow.'

We drove on, following the curve of the encircling hills, and halted at the gates of a compound ringed with barbed wire. Inside, I glimpsed a group of white vehicles and a huddle of dirt-brown buildings. Four Taliban soldiers guarded the entrance. From their posture and the direction they were facing it was obvious that their prime duty was less to keep others out, than to keep watch on those inside.

Two Asian men in ill-fitting linen suits stood nearby. 'Who are they?' I said.

Amica kept her voice low. 'Secret police. From the Pakistan Inter-Services Agency.'

The Taliban peered at our papers and handed my passport to the Pakistanis, who noted the details then returned it. Panna nosed the pick-up past them into the compound, weaving between baulks of timber laid across the ground as primitive tank or car-bomb traps.

We parked by a battered forklift truck. Four huge, grey rubber fuel bladders were lined up on pallets along the fence facing the entrance gates. Two sides of the compound were flanked by a series of low, mud-brick buildings. The space between each one was filled with neat stacks of boxes and equipment bearing the AMCO logo, but the rest of the compound resembled a junkyard. There were heaps of old, bald tyres, piles of rusting scrap metal and a mound of torn paper, cardboard, dead leaves and broken wood, weighed down by yet more scrap metal. A fire was smouldering in a rough depression scraped in the ground, heating a metal dome on which a one-armed boy was laying naan breads to cook. An oil drum, lying on its side and split lengthwise, was half-filled with grey, greasy water. I realised from the piles of cups and plates close by that this was the kitchen sink. The flies seemed to like it.

The main building was protected by mounds of sandbags, and every window was screened by heavy-gauge wire mesh. More rough baulks of timber shielded the doors.

'This was a former Soviet post,' Amica said. 'It was abandoned when the Mujahedeen overran Kabul.'

The interior was dark, musty and cool and looked more like a cell block; a series of tiny rooms, each one no more than six by ten feet, led off the single, long, dark corridor. There were no chairs, tables or even beds in any of them, just a low pile of rugs and a cushion propped against the wall. Personal belongings hung in plastic bags from nails hammered into the mud walls.

'Where is everybody?'

'In the minefields,' Dexy said. 'That's what we're here for – remember?'

I dumped my bags in an unoccupied room and followed Jeff and Dexy back outside. 'Where's the heli?'

Jeff pointed to what appeared to be a hillock of the same red-brown dust as the compound. 'Under that tarpaulin.'

'Jesus, how long have you had it buried?'

'Since the last crew quit,' Dexy said.

'What happened?'

He turned to face me, still with the same impassive expression. 'They got tired of being shot at.'

We moved the rocks pinning down the edge of the tarpaulin and dragged it off the heli, filling the air with dust.

'It's a corpse,' I remarked. 'No wonder you buried it.'

'The Mark I Hydra,' Jeff said. 'Also known as the flying brick. The Sovs introduced it when Boris Yeltsin was a teenager. It's primitive, grossly under-equipped and underpowered, but it's so easy to fly even you shouldn't have any problems.'

'Let's hope so,' Dexy said. 'I'm aiming to be in Konarlan by tomorrow night, if you crabs can manage to get us there in one piece.'

'Konarlan?' I said.

'It's a village a couple of hundred kilometres east of here. We use it as a forward base. There are so many people crippled by mines around there you couldn't even organise an arse-kicking competition.'

'What's the food like?' Jeff said. 'I've been in Afghanistan a week and I haven't had a decent meal yet.'

Dexy exchanged a glance with me. 'Is he always this insensitive?'

'No, he's usually worse.'

'You won't be getting gourmet meals up there,' Dexy said. 'Rice and spring onions, and a bit of fat or gristle on special occasions.'

Jeff sighed. 'It'll probably do me good anyway.' He patted the paunch straining against his belt. 'I've been piling on the lard recently.'

'You're in luck. They've got one of the finest dietary aids known to mankind here.'

'Don't tell me — dysentery, right?'

Dexy smiled. 'We'll have you three stone below your fighting weight before you can say "pass the pebbles" '.

Jeff gave him a suspicious look. 'What do you mean?'

'Didn't you know? Your piles are in for a treat. Toilet paper is strictly a metropolitan luxury. They don't use it in the rural areas, just pebbles or sand — or your fingers if you can't find anything else.'

Jeff winced. 'Thanks. Right now, that's what I really needed to know.'

I walked over to the heli and kicked the tyres. 'So, are we going to try and get this crate airborne?'

Dexy looked at his watch. 'Not today, I think. We're almost on curfew. Get some rest tonight and you can put it through its paces first thing tomorrow.'

'In that case,' I said, 'I'm for a brew. Where do we get one, or is there no tea around here either?'

'Two sorts,' Dexy said, 'black and green. I'll show you what passes for a canteen.'

He led me around the back of the main building and into a room sparsely furnished with cushions and low tables. The one-armed boy I had seen earlier was feeding the fire beneath the samovars with scrap wood. He paused to ladle sugar into two tin cups and filled them with black, astringent tea.

Panna was lying face-down on one of the tables, grimacing with pain as a woman cleaned the wounds on his back. She wore a khaki cotton shirt and trousers, and was tall and olive-skinned, with long hair as black and glossy as a raven's wing. She seemed to sense my scrutiny and glanced up for a moment, holding my gaze with her dark eyes.

Only when she spoke did I realise that it was Amica. 'I'll be finished with Panna in a minute, then I'll have a look at your scalp.'

'I'm all right.'

'The flesh is broken in a few places. If it gets infected you'll be no use to yourself or us for several days.'

Dexy and I sat sipping our tea as I waited my turn at the treatment table. 'What made you switch from fast-jets to choppers?' he said.

I looked up, surprised by the question. 'I wanted a change. Does it matter?'

'No, it's just that it's an unusual career move, that's all. Not many people get bored with fast-jets.'

'I didn't.'

'You were decorated in the Falklands, weren't you?' He saw the look on my face. 'AMCO in Geneva forwarded us a copy of your Cfile. Look, it doesn't matter. It's obviously a touchy subject, forget it.'

I hesitated before replying, fighting down the irrational surge of anger that I felt at his questions. 'Yes, I fought in the Falklands. It's not something I'm too keen to talk about though, if you don't mind. I lost— I lost a lot of friends there.'

'Is that why you're here?'

'In a way. I'd seen enough killing.'

He gave a grim smile. 'You've come to the wrong place then.'

'I mean—' I struggled to find the words. 'I suppose I just wanted to do something for the people at the other end of the gun-barrel for a change. Mine clearance seemed a good option.'

When I looked up, Amica's eyes were fixed on me. She flushed and looked away. 'Panna's patched up, I'll do your scalp now.'

Dexy drained his tea and stood up. 'I'll be in the compound,' he said. 'I can't bear to hear a grown man scream.' He winked and sauntered out.

I sat on the end of a table while Amica stood over me, frowning with concentration as she dabbed at the cuts on my scalp. I could smell her perfume and felt very conscious of her nearness to me. I tried to look up at her face, but she placed a cool, firm hand on my brow and pushed my head down again. 'Keep still, this won't take long.'

'Why did my hair make Salan so angry?'

She gave a sour laugh. 'The Taliban believe that devils nest in long hair.'

'But obviously not in long beards.'

She shrugged. 'There is no logic in the world of the Taliban, or only of the most twisted kind. They have banned cameras, television, music, chess – even flying kites.'

'Kites?'

'Kites were a national passion for us. The sight of a thousand multi-coloured kites swaying against a backdrop of snow-capped mountains and a sky of the deepest blue was—' She broke off and gave a slow shake of her head. 'No kites fly in our skies now, and there are no songbirds in our houses. All we are left with is the scent and colour of the flowers we nurture in our gardens. No doubt the Taliban will soon ban those as well.'

She stood motionless, her expression veiled, and I found it impossible to shift my gaze from that proud but haunted face. Then she concentrated once more on her work.

An uncomfortable silence grew between us and I was glad of the distraction when the boy brought me more tea. 'What happened to his arm?' I said, as he went back to tending the fire beneath the samovars.

'A mine.'

'Poor little kid.'

'There are thousands like him.' She stepped back and studied me in silence for a moment, as if trying to read something in my face. 'Come with me. There's something I want to show you.'

She led me back outside and pointed to a low building at the back of the compound. 'Come and see the other side of our work. We don't just clear the mines, we clear up after them as well.'

A piece of filthy, frayed hessian sacking hung over the doorway. As I pushed it aside, I was hit by a wall of heat. A legless boy pushed himself around on a wheeled wooden platform. He was loading plaster casts of arms and legs into an oven belching smoke and flames. The roar of the fire was drowned by the rattling din of ancient lathes. Behind each of these sat another amputee turning or trimming more limbs. Another group, all missing one or both legs, hacked with knives at threadbare tyres, fashioning sandals from the tread.

I tore my eyes away.

Amica's mouth was set in a thin hard line. 'This is one of Afghanistan's few growth industries,' she said. 'Some of these boys were wounded in action for the Taliban.' She shrugged. 'No one else pays any wages. Others lost their limbs on mines scattered in their family fields.

'Many of them were crippled when the Taliban decided to expel all foreigners, including AMCO. They said they could carry out their own mine-clearance programme. They first attempted to clear the minefields by sending their troops out to probe the soil. It was not a success; they were untrained in the work and many men were killed clearing a single large minefield.

'So then they sent boys like these crawling across the fields, pushing knives or sticks into the ground. No one knows how many were killed or wounded – probably thousands – before they relented and allowed us back in.'

We stayed only a few minutes in the building, but the sights that I had seen there stayed in my mind long after I lay down that night and closed my eyes, until at last I fell asleep.

The beginning of the familiar nightmare filled me with dread, but I was powerless to change its course or wake myself from it. It had been some time since the end of the war that had claimed the life of the woman I loved, but I was still haunted by the same painful memories and recurring nightmare. I saw green water slopping over Jane's face. She choked and spat. 'The chute. I can't get it free.' Seawater flooded her billowing parachute and it began to sink beneath the waves, dragging her with it. I saw the terror in her eyes and cried out, flailing at the water with my hands, but the waves kept carrying her away from me, just beyond my reach. More and more waves broke over her head. She spat the water from her mouth. 'Let me go, Sean. You've got to let me go . . .'

'No! I can't lose you now.'

Her face came clear of the water again, but her lips were already turning blue. She gazed into my eyes and I felt her hand brush mine. I lunged for her, but my fingers closed around nothing. She was already sinking as the parachute wrapped itself around her like a shroud.

'NO! NO! NO!'

I was awake, bolt upright, streaming with sweat. Jeff mumbled a drowsy curse at me from across the room, then went back to sleep.

I shivered as the sweat cooled on me in the night air. I slipped out of bed, towelled myself dry and pulled on my clothes, then walked out into the night.

Chapter 2

The mountain peaks rose above me, black against the starlit sky.
The sound of distant gunfire broke the absolute stillness of the
night. As my eyes grew more accustomed to the dark I realised
that I was not alone. Another figure was sitting on a rock, staring
towards the east where the faintest trace of blood-red heralded
the beginnings of the dawn. She stirred and turned towards me.

'Amica? I'm sorry. I hope I didn't startle you. I didn't see you
there at first.'

'Can't you sleep either?'

'Too many demons.'

She nodded.

We stood in silence for a moment, listening to the faraway
thunder of guns. Flashes of fire among the hills to the north
showed where the shells were landing.

'Are those demons what drove you to Afghanistan?'

'Partly.' I hesitated. 'I wanted to go somewhere as far – in every way – from the Falklands as I could: no Air Force, no complications, no women—'

I paused, embarrassed, but she smiled. 'It's all right, I won't take it personally.'

'I – I just wanted to go somewhere I could sink into my work for a while, do something so all-enveloping that it wouldn't leave me time to think, and so demanding that I'd just fall exhausted into bed every night and sleep till daybreak.' I paused. 'The plan doesn't seem to be working too well, does it?'

Her dark eyes searched my face. 'The Falklands must have been terrible for you.'

I began to bridle, feeling the familiar tide of anger rising inside me. I didn't want sympathy or concern or compassion. All I wanted was what no one could give me: Jane alive and well and back with me again. I felt tears stinging my eyes. I turned my head and walked a few paces away from Amica until I had control of myself again.

Amica waited in silence. I felt a sudden urge to unburden myself to this stranger, pour out my heartbreak into the darkness, but I stifled the thought as soon as it had formed. All that was keeping me going was the grip I kept on myself. If I let my thoughts dwell in that dark place that haunted my dreams . . .

'Yet you came to another war zone,' Amica said at length.

'I've seen enough killing, but I'd heard something of what mines have done here and I wanted to do something to help. I had to crawl through a minefield in the Falklands – they're all over the islands. They weren't laid to a plan; no one knows where they are or how many . . . But it's easy there, they just fence off the land and leave it. It's only fit for sheep-grazing, anyway.'

I saw the glint of a tear in the corner of her eye. There was another series of explosions and more flashes lit up the northern hillsides. 'My country has been at war for more than thirty years,' she said. 'In all that time, I cannot ever remember a night that was not broken by the sound of gunfire. Some say we have never been at peace throughout our history. When we are not battling invaders, we fight among ourselves. The Soviets are long gone, but the war continues, Muslim against Muslim. Perhaps it will never end.' She passed her hand over her face. 'You will understand as you see more of Afghanistan. As you look around, something will puzzle you. At first you will not even realise what it is. Then it will begin to dawn on you. A whole generation is missing. There are virtually no men between fifteen and forty. Some are away fighting for the Taliban or one of the warlords, but most are already dead.

'In the absence of their fathers, young boys must provide for their families. The women and girls cannot help them; they are confined to their homes, forbidden to work and banned from education after the age of eight. We're not even allowed to possess money – why would we need it when we're virtual prisoners in our own houses? Even there we're not safe from the mullahs. A woman is forbidden to wash when menstruating or for forty days before the scheduled date of a birth and for forty days after it. Can you imagine that?'

'I'd rather not,' I said.

'The boys do everything. They are builders, carpenters, money-changers, mechanics, smugglers, farmers, thieves, but even they are not too young to fight. The Taliban always need more soldiers, and if there are not enough men, then boys must do.' There were tears in her eyes. 'Christian rulers once sent the Children's Crusade to besiege Jerusalem. They were slaughtered in their thousands. Now Muslim children are sent to fight and die for their religion. The mullahs tell us that there is no holier death, but I cannot believe that Allah would demand the death of children as the price of faith.'

'And yet you are still a Muslim,' I said, 'despite everything that's been done here in the name of Islam.'

'Do you blame Christianity because the Catholic Church supported Hitler? Is the religion at fault because of what men do in its name?' She fell silent.

'Why do you stay in Afghanistan?'

'Because it is my country, because I hope to play a small part in changing it for the better, and because—' She hesitated. 'Because my husband is buried here.'

'I'm sorry, I didn't know.'

'How could you?'

'When did he die?'

'When the Taliban took Kabul.' Her voice had hardened and she looked away from me again, gazing towards the mountains.

I watched her for a while, then walked quietly away across the compound, leaving her staring into the darkness.

I cat-napped for half an hour, but woke with the dawn, an Air Force habit so ingrained that no amount of fatigue could shake it. I felt the stubble on my chin, but the thought of shaving with blunt razors and cold water for months persuaded me to begin growing a beard. I splashed ice-cold water on my face and walked to the canteen.

Breakfast was simple but delicious – grapes, green tea and discs of warm, fresh naan bread. Jeff arrived a few minutes later, bleary-eyed. I saw him wink at the one-armed kitchen boy and slip him a couple of crumpled Afghani notes. When he sat down opposite me, he had two boiled eggs on his plate.

'Didn't take you long to work out the system, did it?' I said.

'He'd get them for you as well, if you asked him. Twenty Afghanis a throw.'

'I'm the poor sap who has to survive on Air Force pay, remember. Anyway, I'm quite happy with my breakfast, thanks.'

'Enjoy it while you can, Jeff,' Dexy said, sitting down next to him. 'The only protein you'll be seeing once we get to Konarlan will be if you manage to catch a rat.'

I finished my breakfast and walked outside. Half the compound was still in shade, but I could already feel the heat of the sun as it rose above the mountains. I strolled over to the Hydra and began checking it, peering at the engine intakes and the landing gear and scanning the rotors for any sign of damage. Then I clambered into the cockpit and settled myself into the tiny, rock-hard seat. Jeff followed me a few moments later.

Compared to a Puma or a Chinook, the Hydra was rudimentary in the extreme. Much of the interior, even down to the grips on the flying controls, was bare metal. The backs of the pilots' seats were the only division between the cockpit and the cab. There were no seats in the back, just metal rings fixed to the walls at one-metre intervals, to which equipment – or passengers – could be attached. There was a winch and a mounting for a machine gun by the door, and twin guns in the nose, fired by the pilot.

The only instrumentation was an altimeter, an engine gauge, an air-speed indicator, temperature, fuel and oil pressure gauges and a warning panel. There was no radalt, no Head-Up Display, no computerised navigation system.

'As far as I can see, the only way to navigate is by holding a folded map on your knee. How did we come to believe for so long that the Soviet threat was quite so terrifying?'

Jeff looked up from the instruments. 'Because it suited everybody to believe it. The forces got more manpower and weapons – and more generals and air marshals – the arms manufacturers got more orders, there were jobs for spies, spooks, analysts and experts by the bucketload, and the politicians got to talk tough and strike macho postures without ever running the risk of their bluff being called.'

'It's good to see that your time in the Air Force hasn't blunted your idealism; it could so easily have turned you into a cynic.'

'So what's your explanation?'

I smiled. 'The same as yours.'

Dexy too had climbed into the cab. He leaned forward in the gap between our seats. 'Think you can fly it?'

'It's a helicopter, isn't it?' Jeff said. 'Of course we can fly it.'

I held up a hand. 'But first we'll need a couple of hours bumping around to get used to the control settings and the feel of it. After that we can take it anywhere you like, though we might need a little more practice before we go low-level.'

Dexy smiled. 'We'll save that for tomorrow then.'

'We're going to start her up in a moment. You're welcome to stay right where you are while we take it for a test-drive, but perhaps you'd be happier watching from ground level?'

'I've some stuff to do,' Dexy said a little too quickly. 'I'll see you when you get back.'

'What's the matter?' Jeff said. 'Don't you trust us?' We exchanged a private smile as Dexy scrambled down from the cab.

I pulled on the flying helmet and connected the intercom and radio cables. I ran my eyes over the instruments, then reached up for the starting switch. There was a whine as the turbine began to turn. The engine stuttered and belched black smoke, then roared into life.

Jeff checked for fuel and hydraulic leaks as I kept my eyes on the engine gauge. When it reached twenty per cent, I slid the lever from stop to ground idle and Jeff released the rotor brake on his side of the cockpit. The noise of the engine doubled and the blades began to turn. Their shadows passed over the cockpit with a slow swish like a scythe cutting grass, then accelerated to a blur as the noise grew.

I slid the levers forward again into flight idle and felt the Hydra lift a little on its springs. I released the brakes and eased the cyclic forward a touch. The response was more sluggish and the Hydra's controls slacker than the Pumas I normally flew.

Jeff and I ran through a final set of pre-flight checks, then I radioed Kabul control and announced ourselves in both Farsi and English. 'Kabul Centre, this is AMCO helicopter, seeking clearance for a proving flight.'

I was uncertain whether the centre would even be manned, but I was greeted at once in the precise English of a Pakistani air traffic controller: 'Roger, AMCO. Your destination?'

'Centre, we're returning to the AMCO compound here.'

'Roger AMCO, no traffic, you're cleared for take-off.'

I glanced across at Jeff. 'Here goes.'

He nodded. 'Shit or bust.'

I checked the sky was clear above us, then took a firm grip on the cyclic with my right hand and began to pull the collective lever slowly upwards with my left. The engine howled and the downwash sent dust, sand and debris scudding away across the compound. The nose lifted first, followed a fraction of a second later by the tail. It lurched upwards, swaying from side to side and dipping at the nose and tail as I adjusted the controls.

The heli plunged downwards as I pushed the cyclic forward a touch too far. I jerked it back at once, but the Hydra still hit the ground with a thud that made the springs groan, and then catapulted back into the air. I tried again, nosing the heli around within the tight confines of the compound.

Twice more I almost lost it as the unfamiliar travel on the controls undid me, but each time I recovered it quickly. Finally I managed to settle it into a relatively stable hover. I held it at twenty feet above the ground, using a notch in the hills on the horizon as a reference point to check attitude and stability, while I kept testing the response of the controls to minute adjustments of the cyclic and collective.

I paddled the left and right rudders to test the rate of turn, then raised the collective higher. The beat of the rotors quickened and the nose rose under the extra power. I pushed the cyclic forward a fraction to hold it at five degrees above the horizon and felt the vibrations through the fuselage change.

As we climbed higher, I saw the knot of guards outside the gate. The low sun cast long, thin black shadows on the ground beyond them. I stared at them, trying to read the shapes, then I dumped the collective and sent the heli plunging back towards the ground as shots rang out above the thunder of the engine.

'What the fu—?'

We hit the ground so hard that Jeff's helmet slammed into the roof of the cab.

I killed the engine, hit the belt release and was out of the heli in seconds, ducking under the rotors as they wound down. I kept the armoured steel hull between myself and the gates, in case the Taliban were still trigger-happy, then sprinted for the corner of the building.

Jeff joined me a couple of seconds later.

I peered round towards the gates. Dexy and Amica were already there, remonstrating with the guards. As we stepped out of cover, I glanced at Jeff. 'How does that hundred K look now?'

There was a catch in his voice. 'Not enough, not nearly enough.'

Dexy and Amica walked over to us. 'You guys all right?'

'I'm beginning to see why the other pilots left. What the hell was that about?'

Dexy gave a weary shake of his head. 'We had no authorisation to make a flight today.'

'We were cleared by air traffic control.'

'But not by the soldiers on the gate.'

'So they shot at us?'

Amica shrugged. 'It's the normal Taliban solution to a problem.'

'So what happens now?'

'We have to wait for authorisation, even though we already have blanket permission to fly within our defined areas. You may as well take the rest of the day off. Their commander, Salan, is otherwise engaged today, so we're going nowhere till tomorrow at the earliest.'

'I have to go to the bazaar,' Amica said. 'There's something we need. I must bring another woman with me. Why don't you come with us?'

'All right,' I said. 'I'd like that.'

Amica and her colleague appeared a few minutes later, indistinguishable from each other in mauve burkas. I peered at the mesh, trying to make out the features behind.

'Don't do that in the bazaar,' Amica said. 'Avoid looking at any women, even though they are veiled, and be very careful not to touch any. Even brushing against them is grossly offensive. You must also walk a few paces in front of us. It is forbidden for men and women who are not married to walk together.'

'Even with a safe conduct from the Taliban?'

She shrugged. 'It is not wise to put too much trust in pieces of paper, especially when most of the Taliban soldiers can't read.'

Despite his beating the previous day, Panna, chauffeuring again, produced another tape of Indian film music with a flourish and began to play it as soon as we were through the compound gates.

We drove in towards the city centre, past shelled buildings and ranks of rusting, sawn-off shipping containers that provided homes for families who peered at us from their dark interiors. 'We call this area Khair Khana – Container City,' Amica said.

Only a few figures moved through the desolate landscape. An old man and two boys, who could not have been more than eight, were working at the side of the road, using wooden forms to make mud bricks out of the dust and rubble that must once have been their house. Their faces looked back at us, stoic and impassive, their skin, hair and clothes so covered in clinging yellow dust that they looked as if they had grown out of the rubble.

A few moments later Panna pulled up at the side of the road. 'We'll walk from here,' Amica said. She handed me a thick bundle of grubby banknotes. 'We're making for the Street of the Scribes. I'll show you the shop. They sell rubber stamps ready-cut with Islamic texts and symbols. I want you to buy as many different ones as you can, every kind of paper and every shade of green ink they have.'

'Don't tell me,' I said. 'You're going to make your own greetings cards.'

She hesitated. 'The Taliban commanders and the local warlords all issue safe-conduct passes, like the one you're carrying. Many of the commanders and the vast majority of their foot-soldiers are illiterate, so the signature is often a thumbprint and the pictogram is as important for ID purposes as the script.'

'Why do we need to forge them when we're operating with the permission of the Taliban?'

She hesitated again. 'Sometimes we need to work in areas the Taliban want to keep us out of.'

'Doing what?'

'Clearing mines, of course.'

'What happens if we get caught?'

'I try not to think about that.'

After the silence of the near-empty streets came the noise and bustle of the bazaar. The gutters were choked with refuse and stank of raw sewage. Crowds of pedestrians pushed past, apparently oblivious to the stench. Many hobbled on crutches or were half-supported, half-carried by their companions.

We threaded our way along the narrow, twisting alleys. Women in blue, mauve and cinnamon coloured burkas stopped dead at our approach and turned their faces to the wall until we had passed them by.

The stench of animal and human dung and black, choking clouds of diesel smoke belched out by the ancient trucks mingled with wood smoke, incense, the aromas of fruits and spices, and the stink of decaying meat. The scrawny mule of an ice-seller dragged a cart laden with opaque blocks draped in wet sacking. Clouds of flies followed it, swarming on the water dripping slowly from the cart. Stallholders squatted on the ground, haranguing or haggling with passers-by. The people all looked pinched and thin and the goods on display were a threadbare collection – sandals cut from old tyres, second-hand cooking pots, empty bottles and used light bulbs. Pedlars and hawkers with ramshackle stalls, upturned cardboard boxes or sheets of crumpled paper spread in the dirt, offered cigarettes and gaudy plastic trinkets. Others sold cucumbers, radishes and tomatoes, grapes, mangoes and apricots, though few people seemed to have the money to buy. Only the gun shops were lavishly equipped, with an assortment of rifles, including some ancient Lee-Enfields dating back to the British Afghan wars, and rows and rows of Kalashnikovs.

I nudged Jeff. 'Each one of those represents a dead Russian.'

'Or an Afghan,' Amica said. 'The puppet government's troops were issued with them too.'

A nearby stall sold the staples of Afghan life – black and green tea, rice, sugar and naan bread. The price of a Kalashnikov was the same as a half-kilo of sugar.

The metal workers were clustered together at one end of the bazaar, announcing themselves by the din of hammers pounding on steel. An astonishing array of goods made from recycled metal lay on the stalls or in the dust around their feet. Some had been burnished until the metal shone. The dull surface of others still carried Cyrillic inscriptions, showing their Soviet origin.

Like virtually all the stallholders, the coppersmiths and metalworkers were young boys. So too were the money-changers. 'Inglisi!' one shouted, brandishing thick bundles of much used currency. 'You want Afghanis? I take dollars, pounds, marks, francs, rupees, dhirhans, Saudi ryals. I give you good rate.'

I smiled and shook my head.

We found what we were seeking in a long narrow alley off the main bazaar. A scribe sat cross-legged on the step, writing letters for a queue of illiterates waiting their turn with stoic patience. The shop was cramped and gloomy and every inch of the walls and ceiling was covered with merchandise. Among the tins and boxes were sheafs of yellowing paper, Chinese-made ballpoint pens and a few fountain pens which I'd already noticed people wearing as jewellery.

The shopkeeper, a wizened old man showing a mouthful of black teeth, greeted us with his hand on his heart, and immediately dispatched a boy to fetch tea from the tea-house.

I sorted through his stock, amassing a pile of rubber stamps, some blank, others ready-cut with different inscriptions from the Koran, images of crossed scimitars and Kalashnikovs and the wavering outline of the borders of Afghanistan. He shot us a suspicious glance as I lined up our purchases, but by the time we had done some half-hearted haggling, the amount we were paying had swept away his reservations.

Jeff suddenly gave a cry of triumph and reached into a sack propped in a dark corner near the back of the shop. He stood up, brandishing a half-dozen toilet rolls. They were of indeterminate provenance and yellow with age, and the paper looked as hard and brittle as parchment, but he added them to the pile of merchandise with the air of a man who had found the Rosetta Stone. I shook my head in disbelief.

'Laugh all you like,' Jeff said. 'I'm not wiping my arse on rocks if I can help it.'

The shopkeeper's beam broadened even more as he totalled our bill. We paid with a sheaf of Afghanis, drank the tea his sweating assistant had brought, and parted from him on a wave of mutual good wishes.

We pushed our way back through the crowded streets to the pick-up. Amica sat in silence for some time. 'Afghanistan used to be the cross-roads of Asia,' she said. 'In the bazaars of Kabul and Herat you could find the riches of the whole continent on display – porcelain and silks from China, spices from the east, pearls from the Gulf, furs, gold and diamonds from the Soviet Union, emeralds and lapis lazuli from Afghanistan.'

Her face was invisible behind the veil of the burka, but I could hear the sadness in her voice. 'What do we have now? Sandals cut from old tyres and cooking pots made from Soviet scrap metal. Only the arms dealers and drug-runners are thriving.'

She pulled the sleeve of her burka back to look at her watch. 'We must hurry, you have an appointment at the football stadium with Salan and his men. It would not be wise to keep them waiting.'

'What are they going to do to us?'

'To you? Nothing. They're going to make you watch what passes for justice here.'

'Public executions?'

She nodded. 'There's one every Friday.'

Chapter 3

We left Panna guarding the pick-up and joined the crowds thronging the streets towards the sports stadium. Signs in three languages credited the UN and German aid agencies with financing its restoration. The new concrete terracing and un-marked steel crash barriers were a bizarre contrast to the surrounding desolation.

The Taliban guard examined our papers. He laughed and I heard the word 'Salan' as he called to an officer nearby. The man nodded and moved away through the crowd.

I hesitated, unsure of what was to happen, but the guard waved me forward, shifting his gaze to the next person in the queue. As I slowed just inside the gates, I heard Amica's low voice behind me. 'Go to the right. Women sit in a separate section.'

The two women moved away through the crowd. It parted

before them, leaving a circumspect corridor through which they could pass. Jeff and I squatted on the bare concrete terracing, shading our eyes from the sun. The grass of the football pitch at the centre of the stadium was burnt brown and scarred with tyre tracks. A wooden stage had been erected, surrounded by banks of loudspeakers, as if a rock concert were about to take place.

Amica was invisible somewhere among the four or five hundred burka-clad women segregated from the crowd of at least ten thousand. Children moved through, selling drinks, cigarettes, sweets and bread, while Taliban soldiers patrolled the perimeter of the arena, using lengths of electric cable or the branches of small trees as whips.

A party of mullahs and officers strode out of the tunnel. Among them I recognised the hook-nosed profile of the Taliban commander, Salan. A roar went up from the terraces as if the Afghan football team were taking the pitch.

For the best part of an hour the mullahs took it in turns to harangue the crowd from the platform, their voices distorted by the loudspeakers. At length Salan raised his arm and the first victim was driven into the stadium in the back of a red Toyota. The crowd greeted him with laughs and jeers. A mullah read the charge-sheet as three doctors, surgical masks hiding their faces, mounted the platform.

Four soldiers held the man while a doctor injected an anaesthetic into his arm and applied a tourniquet, producing a scalpel from a black case.

The crowd fell silent, pressing forward for a better view.

The victim made no sound as the doctor sliced through the flesh around his wrist and then cut the tendons and snapped the joint. He passed the severed hand to Salan who inspected it minutely, then tossed it into the dirt beneath the platform. There was a roar from the crowd. The doctor bandaged the stump and the man, still mute, was driven away.

I felt sick. The use of the trappings of modern medicine made the barbaric ritual even more disturbing than if his hand had been severed by a sword.

Two more thieves were treated the same way before yet another red Toyota carried in the star turn, a man accused of murdering a rival in a dispute over a piece of land. The father of the victim was led on to the platform and asked whether he had it in his heart to grant mercy to the killer. He gave an emphatic shake of his head. 'If all the world's gold was given to me, still I could never forgive him.'

His speech was greeted with another roar from the crowd. Salan handed the old man a Kalashnikov. The murderer, still showing no apparent emotion, was forced to kneel. His hands were tied behind his back and a turban wound around his head, covering his eyes.

The victim's father stood behind him, raised the Kalashnikov and fired. His shot only hit the man in the shoulder. He slumped forward, writhing and screaming as blood sprayed out over the platform. The old man fired twice more, one shot hitting the stomach, the other missing altogether.

As he hesitated, Salan took him by the arm and dragged him forward until he was standing directly over his victim. Salan then took the rifle barrel and pressed it against the head of the still-screaming man. He stood back, barked an order and the old man fired two more shots. The body jerked and at last lay still.

There was a moment of silence as the echoes faded, and then bedlam – roars and cheers from the crowd, and a volley of shots into the air by the Taliban soldiers. The dead man's family scrambled to load the body into the pick-up and drove it out of the stadium.

A mullah made a fiery closing speech, shrieks of feedback adding emphasis as he threatened a similar fate to all criminals, traitors and enemies of Islam. Then the mullahs, Salan and the other Taliban officers marched down from the platform and disappeared into the tunnel. A soldier picked up the three severed hands lying in the dirt and tossed them into the back of a pick-up.

As the soldiers drove out of the stadium, men and boys ran out across the pitch. They clustered around the platform, examining the bloodstains in the dust and searching for the spent bullets that had killed the man.

Sick and shaking from the bestial display, Jeff and I allowed the crowd to sweep us along, out of the stadium and back towards the centre of Kabul. We leaned against the pick-up, waiting for Amica and her colleague, still not exchanging a word, but studying the faces of the people pushing past. Brothers, sons, friends and families hurried by, animated and excited.

When the women arrived, we drove off through the busy streets. No one spoke until we were back inside the compound.

As I walked away from the pick-up, Amica caught my arm. She studied my face for a moment. 'There are even worse sights to be seen here, Sean. Adulterers and unmarried couples are stoned to death, gay men are buried alive under a pile of rubble.' She shuddered. 'No one deserves to die like that.'

'Not even Salan?'

A shadow passed over her face. 'Not even Salan,' she said, but they were hollow words.

She turned away and with a sweep of her arm took in the amputees' building as well as the stadium, still visible on the skyline. 'The terrible things that you see here can affect people in one of two ways. Some are hardened, made cruel and indifferent to the suffering of others. The rest—' She broke off for a moment. 'People like you, I hope, try to do something, however small, to make a difference.'

I shook my head. 'People like me are cowards when faced with a regime built on oppression and cruelty. We are the good Germans, the people who look the other way and pretend they cannot see.'

She took my arm, her fingers digging into my flesh. 'No. You are not like that. But like me, you must bide your time, even if that means standing silent as you are humiliated or as another victim is whipped defenceless at your feet.' She released her grip. 'Our turn will come.'

At first light the next morning we began loading equipment and supplies for the journey to Konarlan. I helped Dexy stack helmets with toughened plastic visors, thick, steel-reinforced gauntlets, long, thin metal probes and riot shields into the cab.

Then he walked to a low stone shed near the gates. It was covered with an earth mound, leaving only the steel door exposed. 'The magazine,' he said. 'We told the Taliban we'd site it near the gates so they could keep an eye on it. Actually we decided that if it was going to go up, it might as well be as far from us and as close to them as possible.'

He unlocked the door and passed me a stack of boxes of charges and rolls of detonator cord. 'Don't drop the heli while we're carrying these, will you?'

'Only if the Taliban drop it for me.'

We finished loading inside an hour, and I topped up the tanks from one of the grey rubber fuel bladders at the far side of the compound. The whole of the morning was then taken up by trying to get permission for the flight from the Taliban.

Just as we were about to write off another day, one of the

guards sauntered over to us. 'We have received word from our commander. You may go to Konarlan.'

In case they changed their minds again, we scrambled aboard and I fired up the engine. I glanced across at Jeff as the others settled themselves in the back. His face was even more pale than usual and his hand was already clamped around the flare release. 'All right?' I said.

'Sure, let's get to it.'

I was already more confident of the handling of the Hydra, and our ascent, if a little ragged, was much less turbulent than the day before. This time there were no raised rifles or shots from the Taliban guards.

I held the heli in a tight spiralling climb over the compound, and Jeff kept his grip on the flare release, his knuckles white as he punched out clusters of flares, counting down the intervals between launches, the five seconds it took for each white hot flare to burn itself out.

For the 300-mile journey to Konarlan, we had to fly at over 6,000 feet to keep clear of the ground. In order to stay out of AK47 firing range from the heights, we would have had to fly at above 9,000 feet, close to the Hydra's flight ceiling.

The altimeter crawled upwards as the rotors flailed through the thin air. At last we reached the safe height and I levelled, lowering the collective a couple of notches to ease the burden on the labouring engines and to conserve fuel.

We headed north-east towards the range of mountains soaring into the sky, their snow-capped peaks gleaming gold in the afternoon sun. I dropped my gaze to focus on the terrain below and ahead of us, keeping myself at maximum alert, my eyes never still, ranging over the bare hillsides.

'Beats flying fast-jets, doesn't it?' I said.

I saw the sun glint off Jeff's visor as he turned to look at me. 'Does it? You could have fooled me.'

'Then why are you doing it?'

Before he could reply I saw light flash from the windscreens of a line of vehicles moving along a dirt road towards a small town. The dark, rectilinear shapes of other vehicles, possibly tanks, were drawn up in the cover of a belt of trees overlooking the valley floor.

I pressed the right rudder, giving us a little extra distance on them, then glanced away, checking the fuel levels and oil and engine temperatures.

There was a shout from Amica over the intercom. 'Look out! Missile!'

I felt cold sweat on my brow. Before she had finished speaking I had thrown the heli into a hard left-hand break and hauled the collective up to the stops. 'Flares! Flares!' I yelled.

Jeff froze.

'Flares! Now!'

His hand jerked once, twice, and a shower of flares spilled out behind us. 'Flares gone.'

I craned my neck around, trying to get my eyes on the missile. As I held the heli in its corkscrew dive, I glimpsed a burst of smoke and flame on the ground below and to our right. I scanned the sky around us, then pulled the cyclic back to end our dive and regain our lost height. I lowered the collective, allowing some of our speed to wash off.

I flicked the intercom switch. 'It's okay. It was ground fire – artillery or a mortar or something – there's some sort of skirmish going on down there.'

'I'm sorry. I saw a flash, flame and smoke. I thought—'

'You did the right thing. We'll give them a wide berth, they just may not be happy to be overflown.'

There were a few more bursts from assault rifles as we flew on. I saw the muzzle-flashes in the shadows among the trees, but if they were aimed at us, we were well out of range.

I adjusted the controls again, then glanced across at Jeff. 'What happened back there?'

'We both know what happened. I bottled it.'

'You're all right now, though?'

'Yes, I'm all right.'

He didn't sound it.

As we approached Konarlan, Dexy's voice came over the intercom: 'Take a sweep north and east of the village as you come in. Take it down to a thousand feet and navigate for a fork in the river about ten miles north. Come around forty degrees from there to overfly the track where it crosses the ridge, then swing south again back to Konarlan. Okay?'

I glanced at the map on my knee. 'It's marked as a restricted area.'

'I know.'

'So why are we flying into it? We already know that the Taliban tend to shoot first and ask questions afterwards.'

'Because there's a minefield that we want to take a look at from the air,' Amica said.

'Are we doing it with their permission?'

Dexy cut in. 'Just do it, will you?'

I glanced at Jeff. He shrugged. 'They're the bosses.'

As I began the sweep I heard the loading door in the cab slide open. I glanced behind me. Dexy was lying flat on the floor, steadying a camera against the door-frame. I concentrated on flying. We passed low over the fork in the river and skimmed over the track, provoking a flurry of activity from a guard post on the ridge.

I held my breath, barely daring to turn my head, but there

were no shots. Then we were safe, speeding back down the valley towards Konarlan.

Amica talked me in to the compound, on the hillside just above the village. The groundwash whipped up a dust-storm that shrouded everything from view, making the final few metres of our descent as much a matter of guesswork as teamwork. I shut down the engines and climbed out of the cockpit.

The compound was much smaller than the one in Kabul. The only building had once been a girls' school, redundant since the Taliban came to power. Dexy disappeared inside with his cameras and Jeff followed him in search of food. I took the chance to explore the village with Amica.

Konarlan was a cluster of mud-brick houses at the foot of a thickly forested hillside. Above us the river tumbled over rocky rapids in a thunderous cascade of foaming green water, then flowed fast but silent along the edge of the village before disappearing from sight.

The dome of the mosque had once been covered in dazzling sky-blue tiles, but centuries of wind had eroded its western face, stripping the tiles and eating into the mud-bricks beneath. A piebald patchwork of tiles still covered the leeward side, and at the foot of the walls glazed fragments glittered like gemstones in the dust.

At the front of the mosque was a pool for ritual ablutions, shaded by an ancient walnut and a clump of mulberry trees from which clusters of white, pink and purple fruit shone against the dark green of the leaves. Banks of dog roses, wild lavender, juniper and thyme grew alongside the lanes, filling the cold, clear air with perfume.

Above them the tree-clad slopes gave way to stark, rocky peaks, piercing the deep, almost violet blue sky to the north and east. High above me I could make out eagles circling on the thermals.

I breathed in deeply. 'It's hard to imagine a more peaceful or idyllic place.'

Amica nodded. 'Yet every family here is touched by war.'

We walked back to the compound. Jeff was nowhere to be seen, but I found the cramped room we were to share easily enough. I left most of my gear in my bergen — there was nowhere else to store it anyway — but I put my clock, and a photograph in a battered pewter frame, on the window ledge.

I was still staring at the photograph when Jeff came back in. 'You should check out the latrine, it's the usual shit-pit with straining bar, but it's got the longest drop I've ever—' He paused. 'Sorry, am I interrupting?'

I laid down the photograph. 'No. I was just thinking.'

'Sean, tell me to mind my own business if you like, but you can't keep toting that picture round with you. All it's doing is dredging up the past. I know you loved her and what a tragedy it was that she drowned, but you've got to let her go. How the hell are you ever going to escape the past with Jane looking over your shoulder all the time?'

'I'm not sure I want to,' I said.

Jeff took a deep breath. 'Mate, you're plug ugly, but you've got everything going for you. Don't waste the rest of your life grieving for what you've lost.' He checked my expression. 'Jane wouldn't have wanted you to be like this.'

'You didn't know her.' There was an edge to my voice.

'I only met her a couple of times, but I could see how full of life she was.' He flushed. 'Sorry, that was a dumb thing to say, wasn't it? I only meant— I'm not saying anyone will ever replace her, but you've got to be open to the possibility of other relationships, other friendships at least. Keep her memory in your heart, but don't keep sticking a knife in yourself by having her picture where you can see it every time you look up.'

I felt a hot surge of anger. 'Don't lecture me. You don't understand. You've no idea what it's like to watch people die – your mates and the person you love. We were cheated of our time together. We fell in love in the middle of a war and by the time it was over she was dead. You don't know what that feels like, do you? Well, do you?' I heard my raised voice echoing from the bare walls and bit my tongue to stop myself from snapping at him again. 'I'm sorry,' I said at last. 'I know you're right, Jeff, but if I put it away, the last trace of her will vanish. While I keep it near me, it's as if she's still with me.'

Before he could reply, I heard the roar of an engine and a screech of tyres. I ran outside. A black pick-up had swept through the gates and pulled up in a flurry of dust. Dexy had taken one look at it and was disappearing back to the building. 'I'm not here, okay?' he said. 'I don't exist.'

Amica ignored my questioning look.

A powerful, black-clad figure got out of the vehicle. He was accompanied by a boy of twelve or thirteen. 'Taliban?' I said.

She shook her head. 'The next best thing – Agha Shah Azuin. He's a local warlord. Come with me, you'll have to speak for us.'

I walked over to the vehicle with her. The soldiers clustered in the back of the pick-up eyed us narrowly as we approached, but their weapons remained slung over their shoulders.

Azuin was an even more impressive figure at close range. Everything about him was slightly larger than life, from his barrel chest to his broad, flattened nose, broken in some past conflict. He wore his hair long in defiance of the Taliban code, and he had a full black beard and a piratical smile.

'*Manda nabashen* – may you keep your strength.' To my relief, he greeted me in Farsi, not the Pushtu of the Taliban, touching his hand to his heart in the gesture I was beginning to recognise as an Afghan trademark.

'*Zenda bashen* – long life to you,' I said.

He introduced the tousle-haired boy as his son, Daru. After the brief ritual of greeting, the warlord came to the point. 'I am told that your helicopter flew in a forbidden area.'

I hesitated, then nodded.

'Tell him that you have just arrived here and made a navigational error,' Amica said, in English.

His eyes flickered towards her, then back to me as I repeated the explanation in Farsi. There was a long silence. 'Since you now know that you were in error, it is not a mistake you will be repeating, I think,' he said at last. 'It would be most unwise. You are lucky it was my men that you overflew. They are good soldiers and well disciplined. The Taliban also patrol this area. They would be quicker to shoot and would no doubt require rather more of an explanation from you.'

There was a noticeable easing of tension and his men turned away and began talking quietly among themselves.

'Offer hospitality,' Amica said, again in English. 'Our custom requires it.'

'Thank you,' Azuin said before I could speak. 'We will take tea with you.'

'You speak English.'

'A little. I fought with some of your countrymen during the war against the Soviets.' He gave a broad smile. 'We killed many Russians together and shot down several of these.' He jerked his thumb towards the Hydra.

As Amica hurried away to bring tea, the warlord strolled over to the helicopter and walked around it, peering inside. Daru shot a quick glance in his father's direction, then held out his left arm towards me. 'You want to buy watch, Inglisi? I'll make you good price.' He pulled back his sleeve to reveal a row of six Russian watches strapped to his forearm.

I smiled, but shook my head. 'I already have one.'

'Then as a present for your woman.' He rolled his eyes and drew a double curve in the air with his hands.

'Thanks, but no.'

'Cigarettes then. American.' He pulled the sleeve of his jacket down over his arm and produced a pack of cigarettes from an inside pocket.

'No, thanks, I don't smoke.'

He pointed along the track up the hillside. 'Our village is thirty kilometres from here. Anything you need, I can get for you. Ask for Daru, son of Agha Shah Azuin, everyone knows me.'

I smiled. 'I can well believe that. I'm Sean, son of Donal, and I'll keep it in mind, thanks.'

Amica returned with the tea, then withdrew a few yards. As we drank it, the boy pestered me with questions about the West 'I shall go there one day,' he said in a conspiratorial whisper.

His father overheard and silenced him at once with a curt command. Daru glowered but fell silent.

The warlord drained his cup and held it upside down, shaking it in a gesture that showed he wanted no more. He again touched his hand to his heart. 'We may meet again. May you travel safely.' There was a glint in his eyes.

I bowed my head. 'And may you not be weary on your journey.'

Azuin strode back to the pick-up.

Daru winked at me. 'Remember, Inglisi, anything you want, I get.'

As I walked back towards the building, I saw Dexy watching from the shadows inside the door. 'Are you always this shy with strangers?' I said.

'Only with the ones I know.' He walked over to Amica. I watched them talk, their heads close together, their voices low and urgent, and suddenly envied their intimacy.

Chapter 4

For the next few weeks I ferried the mine-clearing team and their equipment to and from the minefields around the village. To my relief we overflew no more guard posts, but at Dexy's insistence we took a slightly different route each time and a wider arc to the north and east, while he lay on the floor in the cab taking photographs and calling out reference points from his map to guide us.

The terrain grew ever more brutal the further north-east we flew: rank upon rank of jagged peaks, some towering far above us, thrown into sharp relief by the low sun. Between them were narrow valleys, with near-vertical slopes of broken rock and scree, down which ferocious mountain torrents plunged.

There seemed no level ground to be seen, no trace of man's presence other than a handful of thin, wavering tracks disappearing into the shadowed darkness of ravines. One, far to the east, seemed to end in a huge waterfall that arched outwards over a sheer cliff face. The wind blew the spray high into the sunlit air, creating a shimmering rainbow mist.

When not flying, Jeff and I watched the clearance teams inching their way across the minefields. Amica was usually with us, on standby in case of an accident. A few times, I noticed Dexy drift away from the group into the cover of the woods. On each occasion he was gone for several hours, returning without explanation just before we returned to base for the day.

At other times he led the clearance teams. Men armoured like Kevlar knights used their steel lances to probe the stony soil for its deadly crop. At each find they retreated while a charge was detonated, then resumed their ponderous progress, the area they had cleared marked by fresh craters in the red earth.

The team was a polyglot collection: ex-soldiers from black Africa and the Muslim republics of the former Soviet Union, Arabs and a few Afghans, all drawn to one of the most dangerous jobs on earth by the chance to earn what by Western standards was still a pittance. My wages were paid by the RAF, but I could not help wondering how many extra mine-clearers could have been employed with the £100,000 a year that Jeff was drawing from AMCO's limited funds.

I felt such guilt sitting in relative safety while they risked their lives that the next day I asked Dexy if he would train me to work as part of a clearance team.

He laughed. 'You're here to fly helicopters, Sean.'

'I could do both.'

'You could, until the point where a mine blows your leg or your fool head off. If you're lying there in a pool of blood, who's going to fly the chopper to get you and any other casualties to safety?'

Even as I bridled at his brusque dismissal, I saw the logic in what he said. He slapped me on the back. 'Come on, let's take five.'

We walked down the hill into the village. The streets leading to the central square were thronged with traffic. Mules and horses, trucks, and men pushing bicycles passed us, each of them weighed down by swaying sacks of wheat. A mill had been set up in the square, driven by a clanking, ancient, wood-fired steam engine. An old man sat cross-legged on the ground, waiting as his wheat was ground. Others were winnowing, tossing grain high into the air with wooden shovels. The chaff drifted down like snow, covering everything with fine yellow dust.

The village bazaar consisted of a handful of stalls, a few awnings pinned to the mud walls of the houses, and cardboard boxes and wooden cases spread in the open.

I saw Daru selling single cigarettes at a price that would have bought a pack in Kabul. He smiled and waved as he saw me. 'Remember, Inglisi — anything you want I get.'

The blacksmith's forge was surrounded by piles of rusty metal. Pieces of armour plating and truck body panels, the turret of a tank, a length of one of its tracks and a broken rotor blade from a helicopter lay among a mound of unidentifiable metal fragments awaiting their transformation into scythes, axes, shovels, buckets and cooking pots. A circular bomb crater nearby had been turned into a fish pond. It was fringed by spent bomb and shell casings filled with soil and planted with flowers.

Four Taliban soldiers kept an indolent eye on the proceedings, lounging against their pick-up in the shade of the giant walnut tree. They looked at us with some curiosity and muttered to each other, their eyes following us as we walked down the street.

In the corner of my eye I caught a sudden flash among the

trees on the hillside above the village. Dexy reacted immediately. 'Incoming! Get down. Get down.' He pushed me forward, sending me sprawling in the dirt, and dropped alongside me.

There was a roar, a huge explosion and debris thudded and spattered on the ground around us. Then there was a soft rain of finer fragments. I heard a piercing scream and the crackle of flames.

An RPG, fired from the hillside, had missed its intended target – the Talibans' pick-up – and had blasted apart a market stall and the house behind it instead. The contorted body of a young boy lay on the ground a few yards away. He lay unmoving, his face a mask of blood, one leg torn off.

I thought of Daru and leapt to my feet, then saw him untouched a few yards away. The dead boy's mother ran screaming to her child, her arm bloodied, the skirt of her burka shredded by shrapnel. A man rushed to cover her with a blanket, more concerned by her indecency than her wounds or her loss. She cradled the dead child to her, rocking him as she howled her grief.

The Taliban vehicle stormed away from the village, up the hillside, the soldiers in the back firing wild bursts into the trees, while the mother was led away, still clutching her child. A blood-stained sandal lay in the dirt. A villager picked it up, threaded a single rose through it, then laid it in the centre of the pool of blood.

A group of men shoved the still-smoking debris of the market stall to one side, the owner scrabbling in the dust on his hands and knees, searching for fragments of his stock that he could salvage. The others, including Daru, resumed trading as if nothing had happened. Behind me I heard the wheezing clank of the threshing machine as it was restarted.

Dexy glanced at me as he dusted himself down. 'Just another perfect day in paradise.'

There was scattered firing from inside the forest for several hours, but the Taliban returned empty-handed. Their vehicle pulled up outside the gates in a cloud of dust. Shouts were exchanged, and then it drove away.

Amica went to investigate and hurried back a few moments later. 'A Taliban commander from Kabul is arriving later today. It can only be Salan.'

'What does he want?' I asked.

'I don't know, but he is a powerful man. It would be wise to offer the best hospitality we can give.'

'I know the hospitality I'd like to give him.'

Amica put a hand on my arm. 'Perhaps you will have a chance one day.'

One of the village boys was dispatched to the bazaar to buy a sheep, while others cleared the debris from the cooking pit and began lighting a fire. A scrawny sheep was dragged up the hill, bleating as if it already knew its fate. It was ritually killed and drawn, then impaled on a spit over the fire, still with the stubble of its fleece attached. The stench of burning wool filled the air for some time.

We heard Salan's convoy approaching long before it arrived, horns blaring, rifles firing endless volleys into the air.

'We should get under cover,' Dexy said. 'It'll be raining lead when that lot comes down again.'

We watched from the wall of the compound as the convoy paused in the village square and Salan descended from his Toyota like a potentate to greet the village elders.

I caught the glint of the bullet hanging around his neck on a thong. 'What's with his personal jewellery?' I said.

'A bullet retrieved from the body of a wounded man is a very powerful talisman,' Amica said.

'What about from a dead man?'

'Just the opposite.'

As if his arrival was the signal that she had been awaiting, the mother of the dead boy appeared from her hut on the edge of the village, surrounded by other women competing in volume with her own lamentations.

Amica followed my gaze. 'No death is more noble than to die fighting in the jihad,' she said. 'Or so the mullahs tell us.'

'Then the mullahs are talking shit,' I said. 'There's no nobility in the death of someone years before their time, only heartbreak for those they leave behind.'

She studied me in silence for a moment. 'Who did you lose?'

I didn't reply.

'Was it your wife?'

I hesitated under the scrutiny of those dark eyes, but suddenly felt the need to tell her. 'She died before she could become my wife,' I hurried on, glad of the chance to explain to someone who had lost her own love and might understand something of what I felt. 'She was my navigator when I flew fast-jets. She drowned almost three years ago. We had to bale out of our aircraft into the sea.' I swallowed, trying to clear the lump from my throat. 'I was there. Her hand was in mine, but I still couldn't save her.'

Amica touched my arm for a moment, her fingers cool against my skin. Then she was silent for a long time, staring past me into the gathering darkness. 'I am sorry for you. The hardest thing is to be the one who survived. There is not a day that I do not ask myself if there was some way I could have saved my husband – distracted the Taliban, attacked them – anything so that they would have taken me and spared him.'

She shrugged. 'I keep forcing myself to remember that day. I tell myself that I do it in the hope that the repetition will eventually make the horror fade, but I sometimes wonder if it is just to keep some memory of him alive. So much has gone. My memories almost seem as if they belong to someone else. Sometimes I cannot even remember his face. All I have are fragments, the feel of his hand in mine, the sound of his laughter, and even that seems to grow fainter the more I strain to hear it.'

She fell silent again, her head tilted to one side as if listening for a voice in the night breeze, and I did not break that silence. In fact I found it strangely comforting to have found someone who apparently understood the grief I felt. Amica put her hand on my arm and let it rest there for a moment. 'I hope you find happiness one day.'

'You too.'

Neither of us stirred, or met the other's eye. Then she moved away across the compound, the rustle of her clothing like a whisper in the dark.

An hour passed before the convoy returned. As the vehicles stopped inside the compound Amica emerged from her hut, once more shrouded in the mauve burka.

I greeted Salan in halting Farsi, feeding him a mixture of obsequious politeness and blatant flattery. My mouth was dry, but his face betrayed no sign of recognition. My few days' growth of beard might have fooled him, or perhaps he saw so many frightened faces that one looked much like another to him. His one keen eye roved the compound as he made the formal replies required by custom.

One of the Taliban soldiers was helped down from a pick-up, his leg dark with blood. While searching in the forest for the man who had attacked the village, he had been mistaken for an enemy and shot by one of his companions. Amica volunteered to look at the wound.

Salan turned his gaze towards her. 'It is not fit work for women.'

'Then let me have a look,' I said, anxious to divert his attention.

He swung round and stared at me. 'You are a doctor?'

'I trained as a medic.'

The Taliban soldier was laid on a low table and I crouched alongside him. 'The shinbone's broken,' I said. 'I'll have to set it.' I reached into the medical kit for some morphine.

Salan held up his hand. 'What is that?'

'A drug to ease the pain.'

'No drugs.'

'They are used when cutting the hands off thieves.'

His fierce gaze held mine. 'They would not if I was ruler of Afghanistan.'

'It will hurt.'

'No drugs.'

The soldier took the loose end of his turban between his teeth as I began cleaning the wound. Then with the point of a knife I dug out the bullet lodged against the bone. The soldier lay still, apparently impervious to the pain. I could hear the broken bones grating against each other as I set the leg, but he made no sound. Only the sheen of sweat on his forehead and the set of his jaw as he clamped his teeth into the filthy cloth showed the agony he was suffering.

There was a murmur of excitement from the other soldiers as the bullet was passed round. I finished bandaging and splinting his leg, then two of Salan's men carried him to the pick-up and laid him on the bare metal floor.

A moment later there was a thunderous explosion. Shrapnel was rocketed overhead, and rocks and clods of earth the size of footballs thudded down around us.

A Palestinian AMCO volunteer walking to the shit-pit up the hill had triggered a booby-trap.

The earth and debris were still spattering down around us as Amica sprinted towards the gates. Before I knew what I was doing, I was running after her.

A knot of AMCO mine-clearers and Taliban soldiers stood around the wounded man, who lay on his back screaming. Gouts of arterial blood spurted from his leg, and his face was a mass of bloodied lacerations.

Amica dropped to her knees alongside him and began to cut away what was left of his trousers to expose the wound. I heard an angry shout from behind me and recognised Salan's voice.

I turned to a Taliban soldier. 'Please tell your leader that only the woman has the skill to treat this man's wound. If she does not, he will die.'

The wounded Palestinian was yelling over and over again in Arabic, 'My eyes! I can't see. My eyes, I can't see!'

Amica shot a glance at me. 'You speak Arabic, don't you? Talk to him. Tell him it's flash-blindness, it's only temporary.'

'Is it?'

'Sometimes.'

I began to talk to him, mumbling reassurances, as Amica jerked a tourniquet tight around his thigh and put on a shell dressing, then scanned his pupils, her long slim fingers gently probing his skull for fractures and testing his stomach for internal injuries.

She placed another dressing over his damaged eyes, took his pulse and blood pressure, and scribbled a few notes in her pad. Then she pulled a syrette of morphine from her pack and injected him. 'Keep talking to him until that takes effect,' she said. 'Then get a couple of the others to help you carry him.'

She hurried away. By the time the man's cries and groans had subsided into morphine-fuelled babbling, she had cleared the floor of one of the rooms at the compound, spread a sterile sheet, laid out her suturing kit and fixed up a saline drip.

'Shouldn't we get him to a hospital?' I asked as Dexy and I laid him down.

She gave me an amused look. 'This is Afghanistan,' she said. 'There's more kit in this medical pack than in most of the hospitals.'

She checked his pulse and blood pressure again, frowning as she glanced at her watch.

'Need any help?' I asked.

'If you know what you're doing.'

'I've done the basic medic's course.'

'Then yes, thanks. You can put in the drip while I start tying off the bleeders. We'll have to release the tourniquet in a few minutes.'

She kept half an eye on me as I fixed the drip, then swabbed the wounds while she sutured the arteries, veins and torn muscles. Once again her work was calm and methodical, but very fast.

At length she tied off the last suture and released the tourniquet. A couple of bright drops of fresh blood oozed from the wound, but there was no sudden spurt.

Satisfied, she packed the wound and applied a dressing, then stepped back and stripped off her surgical gloves.

'Great work,' I said, 'you saved his life.'

Her face was hidden by the burka, but the elation showed in her eyes. 'Thanks for the help.'

'What now? Do we fly him out?'

'Once we get permission from the Taliban. From previous experience, that may take anything up to a week.'

As I walked back down the corridor I heard a low, urgent voice. Dexy was standing in the shadows of his room, talking into a sat-phone. As soon as he saw me, he broke the connection.

'A sat-phone, a hundred grand for a helicopter pilot – how much money do AMCO have?' I said.

'Enough to do the job,' he replied. He pushed past me, his expression grim.

'Bad news?'

He didn't reply. A few moments later I heard him call to Amica and saw the two of them pacing across the compound, deep in conversation.

Chapter 5

I got up at dawn the next morning, but Amica and Dexy were way ahead of me. When I walked out into the compound I found them already loading the cameras and other equipment into the heli. 'Either you guys are prodigiously early risers,' I said, 'or you haven't been to bed at all.'

Dexy just smiled and carried on loading.

'So what's up? Are we back at work or are we cleared to fly the injured guy out?'

'Clearance is being obtained,' Amica said. 'We need you to work out a route through Pakistan and Oman to Jordan.'

I looked from her to Dexy. 'In the heli?'

'In the heli. Dexy and I will also be flying with you.'

'We'll need to refuel at least twice.'

'Arrangements are already being made. Fuel will be available at Bangur in Pakistan and Masirah in Oman.'

'But why take him all that way? What's wrong with a hospital in Pakistan?'

'He's Palestinian.'

'So get him treated in Pakistan and then send him home.'

Amica gave Dexy a glance. He hesitated, then nodded. 'Get Jeff out here, will you?'

I had to drag him out of bed, but returned with him a couple of minutes later.

Dexy glanced around the compound. There was no one in sight apart from the Taliban guard on the gate. 'You're both being recalled,' he told us.

'What? Why?'

'I can't tell you that.'

'They can't recall me,' Jeff said. 'I left the Air Force. I'm a free agent.'

'You're still on the reserve list, aren't you?' Dexy said. 'They can recall you any damn time they please.'

'But why us? If they want a heli crew there must be at least a hundred others as good or better than us. Why bring us all the way back from Afghanistan?'

'I can't tell you any more than I already have. You've got sixty minutes to pack your bags and work out a route. I suggest you get to it.' He turned away, ending the discussion.

'What the hell is going on?' Jeff said as we threw our few possessions into our bergens and began sorting out a route for the journey.

I glanced around and lowered my voice. 'Work it out for yourself,' I said. 'It makes sense of a lot of stuff. We're working with a guy who's got Special Forces written all over him, and who keeps going walkabout in the valleys north-east of here. My bet is we're going to be tasked with flying Dexy and some more of his pals into Afghanistan. We'll find out what the mission is when we get to Jordan – if that really is our destination.'

'But the SAS have got their own heli flight; why the hell would they want to use us?'

I shrugged. 'I'm not sure I want to be used; but we know the terrain and can fly the Hydra, and we speak Farsi – at least I do; you can't even speak English.' I paused. 'What I really want to know is where Amica fits into this.'

'I can't tell you that yet.' Amica was standing in the doorway. She gave an apologetic smile. 'I didn't mean to eavesdrop.' She paused, holding my gaze. 'But I heard what you said about not wanting to do the mission. I'm sure you'll reconsider when you understand its importance.'

'Amica,' I said quietly, 'you know I don't want to be responsible for any more people dying. I want to save lives, not take them.'

She studied me for a moment, measuring her words. 'And if I told you that what we are about to do will save more lives than a lifetime's work for AMCO . . . ?'

'I—' I hesitated. 'I don't know.'

She laid her hand on my arm. 'I think you do.'

She turned and walked back down the corridor.

We took off an hour later. Dexy and Amica sat in the cab alongside the prone figure of the Palestinian. He lay on the floor, a saline drip hooked on to one of the bare steel cross-members of the cab roof.

We made the usual steep, spiralling ascent, scattering flares in our wake, then turned south-west, following the line of the river down towards Kabul. I kept clear of the scene of the fighting we had overflown on our way to Konarlan. Though the dark shapes of tanks were still visible in the distance, their guns were silent.

We passed well to the south of Kabul and flew on over the

barren, treeless mountains, their slopes burned by the sun to muted shades of ochre, brown, khaki and grey.

At their foot was a dark smudge — the city of Qandahar. As we drew closer, the glint of sunlight from the minarets and domes of the mosques pierced the dust-laden haze ahead of us.

I swung the heli due south, over the desert towards the frontier with Baluchistan. As we cleared the next summit I saw Jeff's white knuckles relax on the flare lever for the first time since we had taken off.

As soon as we landed at Bangur to refuel, Amica walked over to the shack. She took a look inside, shook her head, and began to shrug her burka over her shoulders where she stood, keeping her back to us. Her black hair cascaded around her shoulders and the olive skin of her back glowed in the sunlight as she wriggled into a pair of jeans. She pulled on a white T-shirt, then turned and saw me watching her. 'If you knew how I hate this burka,' she said. 'I wish I could burn it.'

'So do I. This is much better.'

She flushed, then stooped to pick up the burka from the dust where she had thrown it.

As we waited for the tanks to fill, a brown van with a red crescent on its side pulled up by us. I glanced at Amica. 'So your patient gets off here?'

She nodded.

'And our destination?'

'You'll find out soon enough,' Dexy said.

We carried the Palestinian to the ambulance and, oblivious to his change of transport, he was driven away.

We took off again and flew on to the south, parallel with the Iranian border and out over the Arabian Sea. Once beyond the limit of Iran's territorial waters, we turned towards the distant coastline of Oman.

The long flight stretched the day and we landed at the giant airbase on the island of Masirah in the fading light of late afternoon. I shut down the engines and glanced back at Dexy. 'What now? Another refuel?'

He shook his head. 'Journey's end.'

'And the flight plan on to Jordan?'

'Just cover.'

I took off my helmet and wiped the sweat from my eyes. After the thin, arid mountain air of Afghanistan, it felt as if I could have squeezed handfuls of water from this hot, humid atmosphere.

Troops in unbadged combat fatigues surrounded us as we clambered from the heli. We were hustled into an olive drab bus and driven across the field to a separate compound, ringed by a triple fence of razor wire. Armed guards boarded the bus and scrutinised our faces and ID before waving us through.

We passed through three further security checks as we made our way into a squat, reinforced concrete building. The entrance was a narrow passageway, screened by huge concrete blast shields. I walked inside, shielding my eyes for a moment as they adjusted to the harsh neon light.

The only way in to the building was through an airlock. Behind its smoked glass I could see the dim outline of figures.

An unseen watcher interrogated me in Dalek-speak through the entry phone, I dropped my ID into a steel box that slid out of sight with a pneumatic hiss, then I stepped into the airlock.

I heard the outer door click shut behind me and felt a tremor of claustrophobia in the few seconds' pause before I felt the outrush of pressurised air as the inner door swung open.

The lobby beyond the airlock was guarded by half a dozen armed men. A lean, wind-burned American walked towards us, his boot-heels ringing on the concrete. He had the clean-cut looks and hard-eyed certainty of a Mormon missionary selling Jesus door to door. His eyes flicked to the name badges on our flying suits as he shook our hands.

'Sean Riever, Jeff Parsons?' Though his speech was clipped, there was a trace of a southern drawl. His olive drab fatigues were unbadged, but he had the air of a man who was used to having his orders obeyed.

'That's us.' I stretched, easing the stiffness from my limbs.

'I'm Dave Regan. Welcome to Masirah.'

Dave led us through a decontamination room, filled with racks of charcoal-lined NBC suits, and through another open airlock into a smaller lobby. Two more armed guards stood at either side of the grey steel doors of a lift, which we entered. My knees buckled at the rate of descent.

The doors slid back to reveal a larger lobby, from which radiated four identical, featureless corridors. The floors were angled so steeply that I had to stoop to see more than a few yards up each one. When I did so, they seemed to stretch away for ever.

We walked along one of them, its harsh fluorescent lighting softened by the dove-grey paintwork and carpet. I could hear the faint whirr of air-conditioning and the sound of muffled voices from behind closed doors.

We were shown into a tomb-like, subterranean briefing room. Four floors below ground level and shielded by a massive concrete carapace, it was protected – in theory at least – even from a direct hit by a nuclear weapon. The featureless walls were broken by only two doors and a projection window at the back. Ranks of steeply tiered seating were arranged in an arc facing a screen that covered the entire front wall.

About fifty men were already waiting in the room. We were obviously the last arrivals, for I heard the doors locked behind us as we moved towards some empty seats.

Dave walked to the raised platform at the centre of the stage. 'The film you are about to see was compiled from amateur footage – mostly plane spotters and holiday makers with VCRs. Technicians at Langley have edited it so that you will also hear the cockpit flight data tapes in real time. They record the last flight of British passenger jet, flight number BZ169, outward bound from New York to London three days ago.'

The blank screen filled with a grainy colour image of a 747 rolling along a taxiway, through a haze of heat rising from the tarmac. A nasal, slightly bored Brooklyn voice crackled from the loudspeakers. 'BZ169 heavy, this is New York Center. You have traffic at one o'clock and seven miles southward, one thousand feet below you.'

'BZ169 heavy, no contact.' There was a pause. 'Center, BZ169 heavy, requesting clearance to climb to one five thousand feet.'

'Roger that, BZ169. Climb and maintain one five thousand feet.'

'Roger, New York. Leaving one three thousand. Transferring control to Boston Center. Thanks, see you next time.'

I imagined the pilot, gaze never still, moving restlessly from the instruments to the sky around and ahead. Once at cruising height he could set the autopilot and sit back for a few hours, but here, in one of the busiest air traffic corridors in the world, he would be on full alert.

The viewpoint abruptly changed again to a camera somewhere on the Long Island shore. The CIA technicians had highlighted the jet with an arrow. There was a sudden vivid flash from the ground and a trail of fire and smoke blazed up into the sky towards the jet.

I stiffened in my seat and imagined for an instant that the pilot was talking to me, not to his co-pilot 'Relax,' he said. 'It's the Fourth of July.' As he spoke the firework exploded in a starburst of gold and silver. 'They're putting on a good show for us tonight.'

'They can afford it.'

'One four thousand.'

There was a flash much bigger than the others and a white streak sped upwards towards them, bridging the distance to the jet in a heartbeat before exploding in a vivid ball of orange flame. The crew in the severed cockpit survived the initial blast and remained alive throughout the three and a half minutes it took to fall the 14,000 feet to the sea. Their terrified voices, almost drowned by the clamour of the cockpit emergency warning sirens, underscored the horror unfolding on the screen, which went blank as the final, thunderous concussion faded into the sibilant white noise of static, and I dragged my eyes away from the speakers relaying that cold, dead sound.

I knew one of those voices. He had been among the veterans on my squadron in the days when I flew fast-jets. He had served three frontline tours on Tempests before retiring to the quieter life of commercial aviation. Now he was dead.

The other figures lining the benches also sat motionless. I shuddered, trying to clear from my ears the lingering echo of that doomed voice.

Dave broke the silence. 'Over 400 people died, including 84 children. Not a single person survived. Those not already dead hit the sea with such force that it fractured every bone in their bodies. One six-foot man hit the water upright. His corpse was identified only by a wedding ring; the body's height was four feet two.' He paused, scanning the rows of faces in front of him.

'Apart from the President and the Prime Minister, the people in this room are the only ones in the world to have seen that film or heard those recordings. As far as the rest of the world is concerned, the black box flight data recorders have still to be recovered from the sea off Long Island.

'The seabed is so littered with debris that the divers can't even walk on it. It'll take months to bring it all to the surface. When the black boxes are officially recovered, they'll show only routine exchanges between the cabin crew and New York Center, followed by an abrupt and inexplicable silence.

'As usual, the National Transportation Safety Board and the FBI are conducting their own rival investigations and jealously guarding their information from each other, and anybody else. Conspiracy theories are filling the void, particularly on the Internet, but we're holding the speculation in check and redirecting anything that gets too close to home by holding off-the-record press briefings. While not ruling out a bomb or missile as a potential cause, these briefings are pointing the finger of suspicion at a mechanical fault.' He paused. 'This is a US election year after all, and terrorist acts do not play well in presidential politics – they make the President look powerless. If a mechanical fault appears to be the cause, the blame is diverted to the airline companies.'

'And the reality?' A rangy, grizzled looking US soldier wearing sergeant's stripes stood up. 'Film evidence, particularly of that poor quality, can be misleading. Is there any doubt this was a missile attack?'

Dave smiled. 'Glad to see they managed to drag you away from the golf course for this op, Boon. The answer is no, though it may be some time before forensics can actually prove that. It took long enough to prove that Lockerbie was caused by a bomb, and that happened over land, not the sea.'

'What makes you so sure that it couldn't have been a bomb?' Boon said. 'An explosive device fitted with a timer or a barometric pressure trigger could have done it.'

'In theory, yes, and the fact that the jet's previous call was Athens, the airport of choice for all Middle Eastern terrorists, gave us pause for thought, but radar screens showed a smaller second blip closing with the plane just before it exploded, and the other evidence pointing to a missile – including the film you've just seen – is too strong to ignore.' He paused. 'The altimeter of the jet stopped at 13,740 feet, comfortably below a Stinger missile's operational ceiling. We believe that BZ flight 169 was brought down by a US-made Stinger.'

'But you're not suggesting it was friendly fire?' Boon said.

Dave shook his head. 'No organisation has claimed direct responsibility for the attack but we have little doubt that it was the work of the Movement for Islamic Jihad. It's a store-front organisation with no base and no permanent members – a flag of convenience for a shifting alliance of Muslim extremists.

'Cadres from the Middle East, Sudan, Pakistan, Kashmir, Afghanistan, the Muslim republics of the former Soviet Union and the western provinces of China, are assembled and trained for specific terrorist attacks – like the bombs used against our bases in Saudi Arabia – and then dispersed. However, virtually all the MIJ's recruits fought with the Mujahedeen against the Soviet Union in Afghanistan and the organisation is funded by a Saudi exile sheltered there by the Taliban.

'A London-based Arab newspaper received a fax from the MIJ on the thirtieth of June. It read: "The forces of the infidels contaminate the soil of the holy places. They must leave at once or we shall turn the weapons of the Americans against them."

'On the fifth of July, the paper received another fax: "The sentence of death has been carried out. We shall strike every month from now until the time when the guardians of the holy places expel the infidels."

'That fax was received just after 01.30 London time, one hour before the shooting down of the jet, but no other terrorist incidents were reported that day and it's probable that the sender had miscalculated the time difference between the point of origin of the fax – a hotel in Athens – and New York.

'As soon as the cause of the disaster was suspected, all field agents were alerted and the NSA and GCHQ began running checks on all intercepted communications over the previous four weeks. We have established that six terrorist suspects were in New York on the day of the missile attack.

'Two Arabs travelling on Jordanian passports checked out of their hotel at noon that day. At eleven that night – ninety minutes after the jet went down – they caught a train to Baltimore, then took a cab to Washington International and boarded a flight for Paris. They flew on from there to Islamabad in Pakistan and then disappeared.

'Two other men of Middle Eastern appearance, using Saudi Arabian passports and staying at a different hotel, also checked out that day. They drove to Niagara, crossed into Canada and caught a flight to London from Toronto the next morning. There is no record of their onward movements, but two men of similar appearance, by now travelling on Egyptian passports, flew to Cairo from London later that day.

'A third pair, apparently Indonesian businessmen, caught a shuttle to Boston and then flew on via Tokyo to Jakarta. Once more, they disappeared without trace, but we are certain that some, if not all of them, have made their way to Afghanistan.' He paused and sipped a glass of water.

'Where the hell did the Stinger come from?' Jeff said.

Dave shrugged. 'We supplied them to the Mujahedeen during the war with the Soviet Union.'

'How many were they given?'

'A thousand.'

I waited, but nobody else seemed to want to ask the obvious question. 'And how many have they got left?'

He took another sip of water before replying. 'The Taliban and their Fundamentalist allies could hold as many as 200 Stingers, giving them the capability to shoot down a jumbo jet every day for the next six months if they so choose. We have to find and destroy those Stingers. That is the mission for which you have been chosen.'

He signalled for the lights to be dimmed and a 1:1,000,000 air-navigation map of Afghanistan was projected on to the wall.

'As you can imagine, intelligence from inside Afghanistan has been a little thin on the ground since the Taliban took over, although we do have a couple of active agents there, one of whom has been brought out to brief you. She'll be doing so in a moment.'

Jeff cocked an eyebrow at me. 'She?'

I nodded.

Dave's gaze picked us out. 'Did you have a question?'

Jeff flushed and shook his head.

Dave touched the pointer to three marks on the map, forming a crescent almost 200 miles in length, with its centre in the heart of the mountains of the Hindu Kush and its arms extending in an arc north and east of Konarlan. 'Despite the difficulties, we have been able to form a strong opinion that Stingers are being stored at these three sites.

'We will be providing you with detailed intelligence on your respective targets after you have separated into your assault teams, but for obvious reasons, all three must be attacked simultaneously. We believe that, although well protected, sites A and B are both vulnerable to attack by raiding parties inserted by heli at low level. They can make the assaults and be on the helis out of there before the Taliban know what has hit them.

'Target C poses different problems, however. There is no safe approach route by helicopter, even at low level, and the nature of the terrain also rules out the possibility of a freefall insertion.'

One of the SAS men cleared his throat. 'So how will we be inserting?'

'We'll be discussing that once you've separated into your attack groups. Need to know applies; if you don't, you won't get told.'

'How long have we got?'

'The warning phoned to the Arab newspaper threatened "to strike every month". We must assume that another attack is planned on or soon after the first of August. For an operation of this complexity, that leaves us with precious little planning and training time, but realistically, that's all we've got.

'Right – intelligence brief.'

Amica stood up and walked to the podium, drawing appreciative looks from most of the guys.

Boon was an exception. 'Just a minute,' he said. 'We're talking about an operation in a country where women aren't even allowed out of the house—'

Amica silenced him with a look. 'A clean-shaven Anglo-Saxon man like you would be stopped before you'd gone twenty yards, a woman in a burka is just a woman in a burka, and since women are practically non-beings in Afghanistan you would be amazed how much we learn by eavesdropping as we turn our faces respectfully to the wall, or wait submissively near the table for the scraps left over from the men's meal.

'I haven't found my gender too much of an obstacle to my work there, but in any case, since I'm the only active agent in that area, it's me or nothing, I'm afraid. Now, unless there are any more questions . . . ?' She glanced around the room, daring anyone else to challenge her expertise. 'No? Then perhaps I can get on with my briefing.'

She gestured towards Dexy, Jeff and me. 'Some of us have already been working inside Afghanistan and speak enough of the language to get by. Our cover is our work for the Afghan Mine Clearance Organisation. AMCO will also provide cover for the rest of you. The AMCO headquarters is in Geneva, and its staff there and in Afghanistan are of course unaware of my – or your – double role. They would be most unlikely to countenance the employment of a dozen additional people on my recommendation, and your insertion into Afghanistan will therefore be covert. You will arrive at our base in Konarlan as official members of the AMCO team, however – at least as far as the Taliban are concerned.'

My mind wandered a little as she briefed the new guys on conditions inside Afghanistan, but I was jerked back to attention by her closing words.

'Captured Soviet troops were routinely castrated and then the skin was flayed from their bodies while they were still alive.' She gave a sardonic smile. 'Welcome to Afghanistan. I look forward to working with you.'

I stared after her as she returned to her seat.

Dave walked back to centre stage. 'Just two more points. First, it is vitally important that the Movement for Islamic Jihad and its Taliban backers are given no inkling that attention is focusing on them or that military action is planned.

'The mountains of Afghanistan are riddled with tens of thousands of caves, some natural, some drilled out of the rock by the Mujahedeen during the war against the Soviet Union. If they see the slightest indication of a threat, those Stingers will be dispersed to a hundred different caves and store places, and your already difficult task will be rendered impossible.

'In a moment you will be separating into your attack groupings, Raiders One, Two and Three, but first I want to say one more thing. A British jet was shot down over US territorial waters, which makes it appropriate that this is a joint US–British operation. There is also another very valid reason for British participation.

'Six of the SAS men in this room have already operated inside Afghanistan. They went there to train the Mujahedeen and fight alongside them during the war against the Soviet Union. Their knowledge of conditions in Afghanistan and their experience there are crucial.

'We've worked together on plenty of exchanges and joint exercises before, and there is no room for any petty national rivalries or cliques within each team. You are not American or British forces. You are one unit, with one common purpose: to destroy those Stingers before more innocent people are shot from the sky. Good luck. That is all.'

Chapter 6

As Dave stepped away from the podium, a grey-haired, crew-cutted warrant officer stood up and began reading names from a sheet. Jeff and I were assigned to Raider Three. I had an uneasy feeling that our objective would prove to be Target C, so I was relieved to see Dexy among our group.

The other SAS men stood up. There were no jokes or wisecracks. They were grim-faced and silent. The look on his face suggested that Jeff felt the same way.

'What do you reckon?' I said.

'The same as you — not much.' He studied me in silence for a moment. 'But you're going to do it, aren't you? Is it because of what Amica said to you?'

I felt uncomfortable. 'No, but she was right.'

He gave a slow shake of his head. 'A few hours ago I was celebrating getting out of Afghanistan in one piece and dreaming about getting home for a few days, eating beans on toast and wondering how many pints I could get down my neck before watching the United match on TV. Now I'm stuck in the middle of Nowheresville, Arabia, being invited to volunteer to go back and get my balls cut off in one of the most lawless and God-forsaken countries on the face of the planet.'

He didn't get any further because Dave appeared and led us outside. We strolled across the deserted tarmac towards a huge hangar.

'Are you on the mission?' I said.

'I hope so. But at the moment I'm just here to co-ordinate the training. Dexy and Rami will be co-leaders on the ground.'

'Rami?'

A figure materialised out of the darkness. He was black-haired and so swarthy that it was difficult to make out his features in the moonlight. 'I'm Rami. I look forward to working with you.' His English was faintly accented.

'An unusual name.'

'I'm Iranian by birth.'

He left the sentence hanging in the air and Dave supplied the rest of the explanation. 'We have three native Farsi speakers on the team, all Iranian. Rami's father was head of Savak under the Shah. He still works for us too.'

'Who's us?'

Dave smiled, but didn't answer. He opened a door in the side of the hangar and led us inside. 'This is it.'

The helicopter had already been winched off the low-loader. The ground crewmen had removed the tarpaulin and were masking off sections of the fuselage, ready to respray it. The rotors were folded back, like an insect's closed wings, but I recognised it even before Dave spoke. 'The Soviet Hydra, Mark V. A combined attack helicopter and troop carri—'

Jeff interrupted him. 'We know what a Hydra is, for God's
sake. We've been flying the Mark I for four weeks. Why all the
secrecy? The Cold War's over, in case you hadn't noticed.'

Dave glanced at me. 'Is he always like this?'

'Only when he isn't getting his beauty sleep.'

'I would have thought the reasons were obvious,' he said.
'You'll be flying this aircraft, suitably repainted, back into
Afghanistan.'

'What was wrong with the other one?'

'Apart from being too old, too slow, too unreliable and only
having one engine, you mean? With the assault team and all their
equipment on board, you'd never get it airborne. This one will
get you there and – God willing – back again once the job is
done.

'The Taliban will undoubtedly suspect US and British
involvement in the attack, but they won't be able to prove it.
Should anything go wrong, they will find only a former Soviet
helicopter and a lot of ex-Warsaw Pact equipment. You and the
assault team won't be wearing dog-tags, and even your underwear
will be untraceable to the West. There will be nothing to link the
attack to the US and Britain.'

I was staring at the helicopter. 'This still has Soviet markings.
Where did it come from?'

'We got it during the Afghan war. Mark Vs were brand new
then and they were having a big impact on the fighting – the
Mujahedeen were shit-scared of them, with good reason.' Dave
handed us both a thick file. 'There's no crew-manual but this is a
total spec of the chopper's capabilities and limitations – maximum load, range, speed, angle of bank, flight envelope, and so
on – plus the technical stuff and some briefing notes on its
handling characteristics.'

'Who wrote this?' Jeff said.

'One of our guys who test-flew it soon after we acquired it.'

'Maybe you should have let him fly the mission.'

'We would but for two small problems: he's now forty-nine years old and recognisably Jewish, which might have made life a little hot for him in Afghanistan.'

'Hotter than Sean's blond beard and locks?'

'You can dye hair. You can't sew a foreskin back on. Not if it was chopped off forty-nine years ago anyway. There's some hair-dye on the shelf by the tap, Sean. When you've used it, take the rest of the bottle with you in your kit; you'll need to do the roots every few days.'

'Were you a hairdresser in a former life, by any chance?'

'Just do it.'

I shrugged, walked back over to the tap and stripped off my T-shirt. Peering into the cracked mirror, I began to smear the oily brown liquid on to my hair.

'Don't get any on your forehead, it'll stain that too.'

'Now you tell me.'

'Here.' He picked up a grease gun and squeezed some into his palm, then rubbed it across my forehead.

'Thanks,' I said. 'It's so good for the complexion. Any ideas about what to do about my baby blue eyes? Coloured contacts perhaps?'

'We're trying to get you to pass in a crowd, not stand up to close scrutiny, and anyway, contacts would be no use in Afghanistan – too much sand and dust and too little clean water.' He paused. 'Now, if we've finished the beauty consultation, perhaps we could get to work.'

I studied the file for over an hour, skimming some of the technical data but memorising the key sections covering its handling characteristics, climb rates and the other information that might keep us alive in a crisis.

Finally I closed the file with a snap and walked over to the Hydra. I checked it externally, then clambered into the cockpit and settled myself in the seat. I spent some time studying the layout of the instruments and dry-flying it on the ground. I tested the movement of the controls and rehearsed the checks on fuel levels, oil and hydraulics pressures, and the thousand and one other things every pilot of every aircraft has to cover, in the knowledge that one missed, one day, might cost you your life.

I connected the oxygen, intercom and radio cables to my helmet, then reached for the starting switch on the left engine. There was a high-pitched whine as the turbine began to rotate and a crackling noise like distant small-arms fire as the igniters fired to burn the fuel.

Jeff kept checking the instruments as the revs built up, then I slid the lever from stop to ground idle and he released the rotor brake. I felt the heli begin to move and paddled the right rudder gently, easing clear of the tail of a parked Jaguar. We rolled out of the shade of the hangar and into the fierce heat.

I checked in with the tower and was cleared for take-off. We made the final set of pre-flight checks. 'This should be a piece of piss,' Jeff said.

'Oh, sure. Apart from twin engines, an airframe that's twice the size, a completely remodelled interior and half a ton of additional kit, it couldn't be more similar to the Mark I.'

'Stop moaning and let's get airborne.'

We taxied around the tarmac for several minutes, while I accustomed myself to the play of the controls. The movement was far more positive than the Mark I; the least touch on the cyclic or collective produced an instant response. 'It's going to be a bumpy ride,' I said. 'I'll be oversteering and overcompensating like crazy until I get used to this. Anyway, here goes.'

I checked the sky above us, then pulled the collective lever slowly upwards, using the cyclic to adjust the trim. The engines bellowed as we rose into the air, but within seconds I had overcooked the cyclic and we crashed down again, rocking on the springs, then bouncing back into the air. I did it again and again. We progressed around the airfield in a series of kangaroo hops, testing the resilience of the springs and Jeff's patience to the limits as his helmet repeatedly banged against the roof of the cockpit.

I was oozing with sweat and alternately cursing and praying as I tried to get the Hydra into a stable hover. Even a straight and level flight proved beyond me at first, but as I eventually began to get a feel for the controls, the bounces off the tarmac and the drunkard's lurches from side to side became less and less frequent.

Finally I was able to settle it into the hover slightly nose-up. I held it close to the ground, while I checked the instruments and tested the attitude and stability, then I raised the collective, holding us level with the cyclic as the extra power sent us soaring skywards. The vibrations through the airframe diminished as we rose out of the ground effect from the downwash.

'Not bad for Warsaw Pact shite,' Jeff said.

We flew for two hours, testing the Hydra's performance at different heights and angles of climb and descent, soaring up into the clouds and then dropping to skim the waves off shore.

Finally, low on fuel, we turned back towards the airfield. I brought the Hydra in close to the hangar and put it into the hover. Jeff checked below and then talked me down, metre by metre, as I slowly lowered the collective, adjusting the cyclic to trim the heli as it descended. The rear wheels touched down first, the front a moment later. I taxied back into the darkness of the hangar and shut down the engines. For the first time in an hour, I became aware of the heat. My flying suit was soaked with sweat but I had been concentrating so hard that I had barely registered it.

As soon as we had clambered down and taken off our helmets and flying suits, Dave led us back to the briefing room. The doors were closed and locked behind us. We sat down on the battered canvas chairs. Dexy joined Dave, Rami and Amica on the platform. 'Before we start,' Dave said, 'a message came in from Washington earlier this morning. A fragment of titanium found embedded in a bulkhead from BZ169 has been identified as part of a Stinger missile. If there was even the slightest trace of doubt before, there is none now.'

He signalled to the back of the room, and as the lights dimmed an air-navigation map was replaced by a series of satellite images flashing up on the screen. They revealed the familiar, harsh and unyielding landscape of north-eastern Afghanistan.

The images became tighter and tighter, zeroing in on one area, the mid-section of a single valley. Its corkscrewing, precipitous walls made it inaccessible even by the standards of those that surrounded it. In the centre of the image the rock walls of the valley pressed together so close that they formed a black gorge running roughly east to west and so narrow that it was hard to imagine any light had entered since its creation.

Around the cliffs at either end of the gorge was a series of rough curves and geometric lines. Dave tapped the screen with a pointer. 'There are sangars on the cliffs above the gorge. Supplies are raised and lowered from the floor of the valley, using a basket and rope. The only other access is up a track that a goat would look twice at.

'There are two other store caves where we believe Stingers are held which we hope Raiders One and Two will be taking out, but we think this is the principal store used by the Taliban, selected precisely because of its inaccessibility. We have no reliable intelligence on the internal layout, but we believe it is a natural cave which was extended and fortified by the Mujahedeen during the war with the Soviets.

'That, gentlemen, is your target. All you have to do is decide how to attack it, but here are some of the ways you can't.

'First of all, just to get it out of the way, an air or cruise missile attack is not a viable option. When President Clinton wanted to target Osama bin Laden's training camps it took fifty cruise missiles to destroy an encampment of tents in open desert. Quite apart from the unacceptable political consequences, in this case the nature of the terrain makes it impossible.'

Tank, another soldier assigned to Raider Three, glanced up. 'Even using laser target designators?'

'Even using LTDs.'

'What about using the Hydra as an attack-heli?' Dexy said. 'We could fake it up in Afghan markings, fly in from Russia or Pakistan, and rocket the caves.' He clocked Dave's sceptical expression. 'It worked in the Gulf War. We borrowed a Russian helicopter from the Egyptians, painted it in Iraqi colours and flew it most of the way to Baghdad.'

'But it wouldn't work here,' I said. 'The height of the passes surrounding it to the north, south and east is over 16,000 feet. Even an empty helicopter can't fly that high, let alone one carrying a full weapons load or an attack force.'

Dexy was checking a map on his knee. 'There's an airport marked on the map just over the border to the south-east. If the Pakistanis can fly into it, surely we can.'

Dave shook his head. 'They don't fly into Afghanistan from there. There are no scheduled services from it. It's used for freight and charter traffic mainly – pilgrimages to Mecca and that sort of thing. Jets take off from there, but they just bank around and follow the southern slopes of the mountains all the way west. You could wave to the Taliban from the windows — they'd be on the mountain tops looking down on you, but you couldn't fly over them.

'The only viable approach to the target by helicopter is from the south-west, following the course of the river, but that would almost certainly result in the shooting down of the helicopter by people armed with the very Stingers we're charged with destroying.

'The Taliban are also armed with heavy machine guns and rocket-propelled grenades. They have been trained' — he smiled at Dexy — 'by the best in the business, to shoot down helis and aircraft by catching them in a crossfire from the walls of these narrow-sided valleys.

'Even if, by a miracle, you weren't shot down on the approach, the gorge is too narrow and serpentine to fly through. You can't even sight the caves until you've entered the ravine.

'We believe that the only possible approach is on foot. You will be inserted by helicopter, but your drop-off point will be well to the east of your target, and you will make your way there overland.'

Chapter 7

'Survival brief.'

Dexy stepped up to the platform. He sat on the edge of the desk and spoke without glancing at his notes. 'If Escape and Evasion becomes necessary, drinking water is plentiful everywhere except the south-western deserts, but even in the mountains it is likely to be contaminated and Puritabs must be used. In the foothills and plains, food should be no problem: there are rice paddies, wheatfields, nuts and fruit. Afghanistan is famed for its grapes; there are – or were before the fighting started – seventeen different varieties, plus pomegranates, mulberries, stone fruit like apricots, and walnuts and almonds.

'If everything goes to rat shit and we have to E & E overland, however, Afghanistan is probably the worst country in the world to leave. There is desert in the south and west, and every other frontier is mountainous. All the surrounding countries are

Muslim, and most have at least some sympathy for the Taliban. In Pakistan's case, there is overt support.

'Iran is hostile to the Taliban – no surprises there, it's the old Shia versus Sunni hatred – but the degree of warmth towards British and American special forces in Iran should not be overestimated.' He paused. 'The Muslim former Soviet republics are equally tricky, and the Chinese frontier is not only beyond the highest and most difficult mountain ranges, but the western border areas are also populated by Muslims with strong sympathy for the Taliban – and questionable loyalty to the government in Beijing.

'Pakistan is probably the best of a bad bunch; the government supports the Taliban, but can't afford to antagonise Washington too openly, and the border guards and police may well be – how can I put it tactfully? – pragmatic individuals with capacious pockets.'

Dave took Dexy's place. 'We've given you the broad outlines, but the detailed planning is down to you.' He looked slowly round the room. 'You have already heard what happens to prisoners. It's an individual decision obviously, but I wouldn't want to wait until I had been captured.' He turned and strode out of the door.

Dexy was already on his feet. 'Right. I want every map and satellite image we've got of the area from the proposed drop-off to the target. Have proposals ready to put before a Chinese parliament twelve noon tomorrow. Anybody with nothing useful to contribute, fuck off out of the way. That's it.' He checked and turned to Rami. 'Unless you've got anything to add?'

Rami shook his head, but a fleeting look of irritation showed on his face.

'Our man doesn't seem to realise there are co-leaders, does

he?' Jeff said as we walked out of the room. 'And Rami doesn't look too thrilled about it.'

I nodded, distracted, my eyes following Amica as she walked slowly down the corridor ahead of us, deep in conversation with Dexy.

Dave had come up behind us. 'There's no such thing as a co-leader,' he said. 'I'm trying to do a political balancing act, but it doesn't matter whether the leader is American or British—'

Jeff interrupted him. 'Or Iranian.'

'Or Iranian. Whoever's got the skills, the personality and the respect of the rest of the group, will lead.'

'Looks like Rami's out of a job then.'

'One team, remember, Jeff? One team.'

'Sure. I'm just hoping we get the right captain, that's all.'

'And if that turns out to be Rami?'

'It won't,' Jeff said, 'but if it did, I wouldn't have a problem with that.'

While the rest of the guys began the detailed planning of the assault on the target, Jeff and I worked on the routeing for the mission.

'How do we know the Taliban won't want to inspect the heli when we're bringing in the assault team's kit?' Jeff said. 'Surely we're better trying a low-level covert entry than landing openly outside their front door carrying enough explosives and arms to wipe out half of Kabul?'

Dave shook his head. 'Even if they do inspect it, they won't find anything.' He acknowledged my unspoken question. 'Sorry, that's all I can tell you for the moment. You'll be given more information when there's a need for you to know.'

'But we're already in quarantine now,' Jeff said. 'Who are we going to tell?'

Dave's expression didn't change, but his eyes had a hardness I hadn't seen before. 'The Taliban, if they break your cover and start torturing you.' He glanced at his watch. 'Now, unless there's anything more I can tell you, I suggest you spend the rest of the day on the detailed route-planning to Kabul and the landing zone for the operation. Once that's complete, any spare time you have left can be spent in the language labs. Any questions? Then I'll see you for the briefing at noon tomorrow.'

Jeff waited until the door closed behind him. 'I'd like to punch that smug bastard's lights out. He's treating us like a pair of new recruits.'

'Easy, Champ,' I said. 'Dave's all right. He's just trying to keep us up to the mark.'

'Bollocks. He's just playing power games with us. "You'll be given more information when there's a need for you to know," for Christ's sake! If they don't trust us, why choose us?'

'If they didn't, they wouldn't have.' I took a deep breath. 'Listen, Jeff, try not to take everything so personally. Dave and Rami and everyone else are trying to do their part of the job the best way they know – just like us. Like the man said, it's a team job.'

'And when this part of the team's risking our arse in Afghanistan, Dave'll be sitting back here safe and sound.'

'That's below the belt. I don't know the guy, but the respect he gets from the others shows he's not just a backroom hero. He's been there and done it himself.'

I got up before dawn, but found the ground crew already tinkering with the heli's engines. The crew-boss, Janks, a dour mid-westerner with an oil-stained baseball hat pulled down so tight on his bald head that it looked as if it was stitched to his scalp, nodded to us as we walked over.

'How's it look?' I asked.

He shrugged. 'It's Russian and it's fifteen years old. How good could it be? Still, we've done the best we can with it. It should get you where you're going.'

'It would be nice if it got us back as well.'

He cracked a smile, showing a mouthful of tobacco-stained teeth. 'So long as you treat it right, it'll do that too.'

'We're close to maximum range for it, even with the extra fuel tanks, and we're going to have to fit some rollers to shift cargo, so we need to get the rest of the weight down as low as possible. I want everything stripped out of there that doesn't have a reason to be there.'

Janks glanced at Jeff. 'A few pounds off your co-pilot might help.'

'We've already got that in hand, you can concentrate on the heli. Lose the insulation, strip out any panels and struts that aren't load-bearing, and take out the guns and the spent cartridge buckets.'

Jeff stared at me. 'You're kidding, aren't you?'

I took him to one side, out of earshot of the ground crew. 'There's no point in carrying guns unless we have the ammo to fire them. If the Taliban see loaded guns on a supposedly civilian aircraft, they're going to be mighty suspicious. If the guns have been removed, it'll support our cover story that we're just harmless friendly folks helping them clean up their minefields.'

'And if we get shot at?'

'If it's on the way in, we'll just have to evade.'

'And on the way out?'

'We'll probably be at minimum low level and too busy avoiding the ground to worry about firing the guns. Anyway, we'll have a cab-load of Special Forces in the back, blasting off through the doorway at anything that moves.'

'Okay.' He looked unconvinced.

I walked back over to where Janks was standing and pointed to the Herc drawn up at the end of the dirt airstrip. 'Could we cannibalise the roller-conveyor out of that?'

'We could, if we were authorised to.'

'There's no problem about authorisation. See Dave Regan if you like, but on this operation, anything we want, we get.'

'My Lord, that makes a change,' he said. 'In that case, put me down for a widescreen TV and a case of Jack Daniels.'

I left Jeff and the rest of the ground crew ripping out the insulation from the heli, while Janks and I walked over to the Herc. He took a look inside. 'It's too big as it is. We'll have to cut a length off it with an oxy-arc. You want it welded into the Hydra?'

'No. We need to be able to dump it when the job's done. Can you fix it so it can be swung up out of the way and secured against the far side of the cab when it's not in use?'

'Sure, though we may have to lash it with wire.'

'Let's hope it doesn't break during the landing then.'

'It won't, if you don't make a horse's ass of the landing.' He paused to wipe the sweat from his brow. 'We'll use bolts to secure the back end of it. When you want to ditch it, all you've got to do is pull the bolts and kick it out the door.'

'No problem. Let's do it.'

He gave the standard ground crewman's salute, just this side of an insult, and strode away yelling orders to his men.

Jeff was standing by the heli, swatting irritably at the cloud of flies around his head. 'All right with you if we break for breakfast now?'

I gave him my best smile. 'Sure. Want to bring your friends?'

Dexy briefed the mission later that morning, laying down the infiltration route, the detailed attack plan and the timings and

RV points for getting out again. He might have been discussing a walk in the park for all the emotion he showed. 'There's no casevac on this operation, no air support, nothing but one heli and your mates to rely on. We trained the Muj, we know what they can do. They're good long-range shots and they're brave as hell, but they're not that well organised. We're no braver than them, but we are more professional. That's what will get us through.' His expression darkened. 'This is a covert cross-border op. You all know what that means: we cannot take bodies out with us; they will be left behind and can never be claimed. The families will never know exactly where they died.' There was complete stillness in the room. 'If we take casualties, the only promise we can make to each other is that – one way or the other – they will not be left for the Taliban to capture. That's all.'

I was the first to break the oppressive silence that followed. I stood up and made for the door.

Jeff followed me outside into the burning midday heat. His hand gripped my arm. 'Did you see their faces?'

'What do you mean?' Although I already knew what he was going to say, I kept my tone even.

'They know they're not coming back from this.'

I looked behind me, then led him further away from the building, out of earshot.

'No one's going to die, Jeff. The guys are going to do the mission, just like all the others they've carried out, and we're going to be the taxi service that drops them off and picks them up again afterwards.'

I saw anger in his eyes. 'Don't lie to me and don't patronise me. You know it as well as I do.' He stared at me. 'What is it with you? You nearly get yourself killed half a dozen times in the Falklands, but that still isn't enough?'

'You know that's not why—' I began.

'What is it?' He came close to shouting. 'Do you want to die?'

I shrugged. 'There are people who are dead who had a lot more right to life – but I'm not looking to die. All this is just part of the job, Jeff, it goes with the turf. If you don't want it any more, give it away. You told me you were only in it for the money. You've got nothing to prove. You've done the flying hours and the operational missions, you've got the campaign medals. Let someone else take the risks.

'I'm serious, Jeff. If you don't feel right about this, pull out of it now. You won't be letting me or the side down. They can have another co-pilot here inside twenty-four hours. No one will think any the worse of you.'

'We both know that's not true.' He jerked his head towards the building. 'I've got to do it, or every one of those guys in there would know I'd bottled it.' He seemed close to tears. 'And I'd know too.'

As I watched him walk off across the parade ground, I tried to remember the faces of his wife and children. I'd flown with him for the best part of three years, but I doubted if I'd met them more than twice in that time. All I could recall were three shy girls at the open day at our base in the UK, and Jeff's wife, an adult version of her children. He'd introduced us, but she'd hung back behind him, tongue-tied, and after a minute he had taken her arm and led her away. The children trooped along behind them and they all sat down on the grass together, some distance from everybody else, quiet and self-contained.

I turned and headed back into the building. I found Dave in the office at the back. He glanced up as I walked in and turned the papers he had been reading face-down on his desk. 'What can I do for you, Sean?'

'I—' I broke off as I caught sight of Amica sitting at a table at the back of the room. 'I wanted a private word.'

'This is as private as it gets around here. Fire away.'

I glanced back towards Amica. She had not looked up and was making notes from a file in front of her. I took a deep breath. 'I want you to take Jeff off the job.'

Dave studied me for a moment. 'Why?'

'He's lost it. He thinks it's suicide.'

'But he won't refuse to fly?'

'Of course not, but in his present state I'm afraid he'll jeopardise the mission.'

Dave remained silent, staring at me, and I grew uncomfortable under his prolonged scrutiny. 'I'm sorry, Sean. I appreciate that you're trying to help a friend, but I can't do what you want. You heard yourself that there's a good chance of an Immediate Action being called at any moment. Jeff's familiarised himself with the Hydra; he knows the routes and the operational plan. I can't take him off and throw someone else in at the deep end.'

'If he cracks up you'll have to.'

He shook his head. 'But we both know he's not going to do that, don't we?' He picked up his papers again, ending the conversation.

Chapter 8

I had ferried soldiers on several training missions before, but in every case I had been nothing more than a glorified chauffeur, dropping them off at their destination and picking them up again when the job was done.

If all went according to plan, that was all I would have to do this time, but I couldn't shake the feeling that once inside Afghanistan this operation would prove very different. I had not been directly involved in combat since the Falklands, but while I stayed in the forces the risk was there. I accepted it with some sort of fatalism, but I tried never to think about it. The thoughts evoked memories I preferred to leave buried.

I looked up and saw Amica come out of her hut and walk towards me. Her face was in shadow, but I saw the glitter of her eyes. She stared at me in silence for a moment. 'You look so different with dark hair. It seems to change your face.' She gave a distracted smile. 'I've been waiting for a chance to speak to you alone. I just wanted to say' – she paused – 'that I'm sorry I couldn't tell you before about my real role in Afghanistan.'

I held up a hand. 'Forget it. You wouldn't last long if you told every stranger you met.'

'Nonetheless, I was not happy about deceiving you.' She held my gaze until I looked away. I was unsure whether I was reading more into her words than she intended.

'We'll be back there soon,' I said, to break the silence. 'Are you worried?'

'Not about returning to Afghanistan. I worry more about what may happen to you – all of you. It's foolish, I know, but I cannot shake off a feeling of personal responsibility, as if you were guests in my house, not soldiers fighting in my country.'

'We all have a responsibility to each other.'

She nodded, a little impatient. 'That's not what I mean. You'll go into the mountains, you will fight there, perhaps you will die – like my husband – with no-one to know where you fell or where your broken bodies lie.'

'Do you know what happened to him?'

She was silent for so long I thought she had not heard me. When she spoke, her voice was very low and I had to strain to hear her words. 'The day the Taliban took Kabul they began beating any women they found not wearing the burka. Several were beaten so savagely that they died of their wounds. Anyone who tried to intervene was also beaten. A woman bled to death on the street outside our building as a group of Taliban stood by and watched.

'They came into the university that afternoon. I was wearing no make-up, but my clothes were 'un-Islamic'. They hacked off my hair with a knife and tore the gold earrings from my ears.' Her voice was flat. 'When my husband tried to protect me, he was hit in the face with a rifle butt. They lined us all up in the courtyard and began piling up books in the middle. Then they set fire to them – like the Nazis burned books. In the long years of fighting we had already lost many students and teachers. Buildings, laboratories and lecture rooms had been destroyed – but we had kept the spirit of the university alive. Now the Taliban were destroying even that. They burned everything but the Holy Koran – books, manuscripts, research notes – everything.

'My husband pleaded with them, begged them, then tried to stop them by blocking the way with his body. One of them – he was so young he did not even have a beard, just black down on his lip – shot my husband as if he were a dog.

'They would not even let me hold and comfort him as he lay dying. I was kicked, punched and dragged away to be raped. The commander forced the barrel of a Kalashnikov inside me. He even pulled the trigger. It was his idea of a joke – the magazine was empty. Sometimes I wish it had been loaded. The injuries they gave me that day mean I can never have children.'

I hesitated, then put my arms around her. She let her head rest against my chest for a few moments and I felt the wetness of her tears on my shirt. Then she pulled away a little and her expression hardened again.

'Don't tell me,' I said. 'It was Salan.'

'When he had finished with me, I was thrown into the street with the other women. We were told to go home and put on the burka. There was to be no more university, no more education for women – not even for girls.

'Our house had been ransacked, but we had a little money hidden. I bribed a merchant to smuggle me out of the city and joined the refugees fleeing the fighting by crossing the mountains to Peshawar in Pakistan. The Taliban are very powerful there too – it was where they were formed – but I made my way to Islamabad and sought refuge in the American Embassy.

'They took me to the US, trained me and provided me with a new identity, then I was sent back into Afghanistan with AMCO, travelling on an Egyptian passport. My friends and contemporaries are either dead or in exile and there are no records to contradict me; the Taliban have destroyed everything.' Her eyes were again wet with tears. 'I hoped to at least find my husband's grave, but it is impossible. I cannot ask questions without arousing suspicion, and in any case so many people were killed in the fighting and its aftermath that there are thousands of unmarked graves.

'What will you do after the operation?' I asked.

'My cover will be blown. I'll have to get out.'

'And where will you go?'

She searched my face before replying. 'To America, or perhaps to Europe.' She touched my face with her hand, then I felt her breath like a silent whisper against my cheek, and she kissed me. Her lips were warm and soft on mine, but as I began to respond, I froze for a fraction of a second, remembering the last kiss I had shared.

She sensed my hesitancy and pulled away from me at once. 'I'm sorry. I thought –' She began to walk away across the parade ground.

'No, wait. Amica, please. You surprised me, that's all.'

She turned and searched my expression again, then shook her head. 'No. It's too soon for you. I'm sorry. I should have realised.'

I saw little of her over the next couple of days. We trained at maximum intensity for the mission, testing the limits of the flight envelope and absorbing every facet of the heli's flight characteristics, loading and unloading pallets bearing dummy fuel bladders, and practising rolling drops and fast-rope insertions until we could do it in our sleep. Each night I fell into bed exhausted, but dreams and the heat still troubled me and I woke each day feeling little rested.

As we walked outside I saw Dave waiting for us by a Herc drawn up alongside the dirt strip.

'Looks like this is it,' I said.

Jeff followed my gaze. His pale face seemed lined, and far older than his thirty-five years.

'Tonight's the night,' Dave said. He jerked his thumb towards the Herc. 'Take a look at these before you go and get yourselves ready. They'll be shipped out tonight as well.'

I glanced in through the loading door of the Herc and saw two fuel bladders on pallets chained to the sides of the aircraft. 'Only one of them contains fuel,' Dave said.

I looked again. The grey rubber bladders looked indistinguishable from each other.

'How can we tell them apart?'

'Only by the serial number. The prefix is HE – that's a bit of a clue, in case you're the forgetful type.'

I shook my head. 'I'm not likely to forget this one.' I clambered in through the door and pushed my fist against the bladder. It gave slightly. 'It feels like liquid.'

'It is; well, semi-liquid anyway. It's actually an inert gel; high explosives surrounded by aviation fuel is a bit of a volatile combination. Inside there's another sealed bladder packed with the tools of the trade – Semtex demolition charges, fragmentation and white phosphorus grenades, rocket-propelled grenades, general purpose machine guns, Kalashnikovs, ammunition and anti-personnel mines.'

'What happens if the Taliban get suspicious and dip the fuel?'

'Try it.'

I unscrewed the cap and sniffed. A familiar odour filled my nostrils. I smiled. 'Another bladder within a bladder? What's it contain, about five gallons?'

'Not even that much.' He paused. 'You'll have two runs into Kabul from Bangur. You'll carry half the team and the fuel bladder on the first one. That way if any of the populace get trigger-happy, you've only got to worry about a few thousand gallons of fuel exploding instead of 500 pounds of Semtex.'

'Thanks,' I said. 'That's a great consolation.'

'It'll also give the Taliban the chance to have a snoop without finding anything to excite them. The rest of the assault team will go in with you on the next trip, with the bladder containing the surprise package. Obviously you're on minimum turnaround between those two trips. It means you'll be airborne from dawn to dusk, but until the kit is landed the assault force is virtually defenceless.'

'When does Amica go back in?' I said.

'On the first trip with you. If the Taliban make trouble or the other AMCO people have questions, she'll deal with them.' He paused. 'Right, you'd better go and pack your kit. We'll have it shipped back for you. You'll be taking nothing into Afghanistan that could betray your identity or origins – no clothes, jewellery, watches, dog-tags, no personal mementoes, and no money other than what we give you.

'You'll have gold and Afghan notes in your escape kit, not dollars, and everything you wear, right down to your underwear, is local, though it's fitted with the usual concealed equipment – button compass, customised belt buckle and so on. Your new clothes are laid out in your hut.' He glanced at his watch. 'And get some food and rest. We're briefing at 02.30, take-off at 04.00.'

I went straight back to the hut to pack my possessions as hurriedly and sparingly as I could. When my hand touched the shirt in which I'd wrapped Jane's picture, instead of taking a final look I closed my eyes and tried to conjure up her image. I could see the long, blonde hair framing her face, could almost hear her voice, but her features remained vague and blurred. I pulled out the photograph and stared at it. The familiar face looked back at me, but it seemed altered in some indefinable way. I traced the contours of her face with my finger as I willed the old feelings to return. Instead I felt a wave of desolation sweeping over me.

The fragile bridge linking me to the past was beginning to break.

Jeff had already finished his packing and sat on the edge of his bed, watching me. 'Sean? If – anything should—'

'You can bin that right there. The last person I heard make that speech died not long afterwards. It goes without saying; I'd do it for you, just like you'd do it for me.'

He nodded and lapsed into silence.

We went to the mess just after dusk, but for once even Jeff didn't fancy eating much. We sat in silence, each wrapped in his own thoughts, then went back to the hut and lay down on our beds to rest. Jeff pulled his Walkman out of his bag and tried to lose himself in some music. The tinny sounds leaking from the earphones and the flies buzzing around my head made it impossible for me to settle.

I walked out into the night, hoping to see Amica, but the parade ground was deserted and no light shone from the window of her quarters.

Chapter 9

I had slept for barely three hours when the alarm clock woke me. It was two in the morning. I washed and dressed in the gear laid out for me. The underwear was coarse and grey and the flying suit ill-fitting. I peered into the cracked and pitted mirror propped on the windowsill and smeared Vaseline on my forehead, cheeks and neck, then began staining the roots of my hair and beard where they showed blond. When I'd finished, I studied my reflection. The straggly growth of beard now covered my face, and my forehead and arms had been burned by the sun to a deep mahogany. Even my eyes seemed darker. I felt slightly reassured. If it came to it I might just pass muster – if not as a Pushtun at least as one of the other Afghan tribes.

The other guys were waiting with Amica in the briefing room. Rami sat a little apart.

'What's up with him?' I said.

Dexy shrugged. 'Dave's pulled a couple of strings to get on the operation. He's taken over as the leader. Rami isn't too thrilled about it.'

'Tough tit,' Tank said, loud enough for Rami to hear. 'Dave's earned the right to be there. And he's twice the soldier Rami is.'

Dave led the briefing. 'We have some new satellite imagery that you all need to see. You know why we're going and what we're going to do. You'll arrive at Bangur early tomorrow morning. You'll refuel, fit the AMCO panels to the chopper, load the fuel bladder and take off for Kabul at 10.00 hours.

'The Taliban authorities have been informed by AMCO that a helicopter will be crossing into their airspace at noon and will be transiting to Kabul via Qandahar and the Tarkan river valley. Despite that advance clearance, even in the areas where the Taliban writ runs unopposed, there's no guarantee that you will not be fired on. Any ground fire directed at you is most likely to be from AK47s. For that reason your safest course is to maintain a minimum height of 3,000 feet above ground level during the transit through Afghanistan. There have been several instances of aircraft on the approach to Kabul being fired on by anti-Taliban forces.'

'Tell us about it,' Jeff said

Dave inclined his head. 'When you get there, it may be wise to leave the helicopter unattended, with its loading doors open so that the Taliban can satisfy themselves that it is what AMCO have told them – another disarmed Hydra, usable only as a transport heli. If they're satisfied on that score, they may not pay as much attention to its subsequent flight – bringing in some rather more important cargo.

'Some contact with the other AMCO personnel is probably inevitable. They are bound to be curious about the simultaneous arrival of so many new volunteers and perhaps jealous of your access to a new helicopter. Amica will give them the cover story that you're a newly formed team willing to go into the most high-risk frontline areas to clear mines.'

While he was speaking, Dave had been pinning up some satellite photographs. 'This is the latest imagery we have of the target area, obtained at' – he consulted his notes – '18.20 hours yesterday. There are no signs of alterations or new defensive emplacements and no traffic has been noted, other than the usual mule trains bringing in supplies. There is one change to note, however.' He pointed to a circular shape perhaps six to eight feet in diameter, on the southern cliff-top, almost completely hidden by a clump of mountain cedars.

'A satellite dish,' Tank said.

'Right first time, and you can bet they haven't got it in to watch the news on CNN. It suggests to me that their communications are being beefed up, and the only reason I can see for that is if a leader of some importance is planning to base himself there, either temporarily or permanently. We'll keep a watching brief on that; if confirmed it may entail an increase in the mission tasks to include the elimination of all personnel at the site.'

Rami looked up. 'And then after lunch we'll go and overthrow the Taliban regime in Kabul.'

Dave turned to him. 'No one is underestimating the difficulty of the operation we're already undertaking, but if a terrorist figurehead were to put himself in the target area, we'd be insane to pass up the chance to take him out as well.'

'If they're in the caves when the charges go off,' Dexy said, 'you won't have to worry about it being in the mission plans. It'll take care of itself. But I'm sceptical about this being the right site. We trained them to route their communications through a remote site. They wouldn't stick a satellite dish on top of a place they're trying to keep secret.'

'One more thing,' Dave said. 'The potential cover offered by the sides and bed of the river as the water level continues to drop; we're well past the main snow melt and in the middle of the dry season now.' He tapped the images with his pointer. 'We're picking up detail down to four feet on these and you can see the size of these boulders. The banks of the river will give you some screening from the valley sides too. You'll need to recce it though. If the river bottom's covered in slime and weed, you'll be struggling to stay upright, never mind stay in cover.'

Dexy glanced from the satellite image to the map. 'With the gradient in that gorge and the force of the river, even those boulders must have trouble staying upright.'

'Intelligence brief.'

Rami stood up and began to speak in his soft, accented English. 'Nothing to add from Afghanistan, but we have an Intelligence report from the States. Two men and one woman of Arab appearance entered the United States by road from Canada eleven days ago. They were travelling in a Buick with New York plates, bought for cash at an auction in Buffalo three weeks before.

'The three were put under surveillance and tailed to a motel in Utica. There they abandoned the car and transferred to a Winnebago, purchased locally, once more for cash, by an as yet unidentified fourth party. A clandestine search of it revealed two Stinger missiles concealed in a compartment beneath the bunk seats.

'The three were arrested and interrogated. One is a Palestinian member of Hamas, one is Sudanese, the other of Saudi origin. He fought in Afghanistan during the war against the Soviet Union. All three have a record of terrorist activity, but a sustained and thorough interrogation has produced no stronger direct evidence of a link to the Movement for Islamic Jihad than that.

'Intelligence estimates that it will take the MIJ not less than ten days and not more than fourteen to select another target and carry out surveillance to find a launch site. It will take them four days to transport a further shipment of Stingers from the caves to the vicinity of the target. Since that may be done to coincide with the end of the surveillance phase, your own failsafe deadline to destroy the target is therefore six days.'

'Wasn't arresting them pretty short-sighted?' I asked. 'Throughout our training you've all been stressing how vital it is not to give the MIJ any indication that they are under suspicion, and now three of their operatives carrying Stingers have been rounded up.'

He favoured me with a patient smile, a teacher indulging a slow learner. 'The same day they were arrested, it was reported in the press that a Winnebago had suffered a brake failure on a mountain road in the Adirondacks. It had crashed through a barrier and plunged into a ravine, bursting into flames. Three bodies, two men and a woman, were found in the wreckage, too badly burned to be identifiable.'

'And the Stingers?'

'They were neutralised, but left inside the campervan before it took its fall. They're still there among the wreckage for anyone who cares to look.'

'And the three suspects?' Amica asked.

'Are still under interrogation.'

We walked out into the night. I paused, savouring the cool breeze on my face as I looked up at the sky, bright with stars. Then the thudding beat of the generator slowed and dropped an octave as the arc lights flared, throwing the shapes of the Hydra and the Herc into sharp relief.

Amica and the guys walked up the loading ramp of the Herc. She turned, saw me watching her, and raised her hand and gave a half-smile before disappearing inside. The door rumbled shut and a few moments later the Herc accelerated down the dirt runway and took off into the night.

We climbed into the cockpit of the Hydra. I pulled on the flying helmet and connected the cables. Jeff and I ran the checks, then I pushed the starting switch on the left engine. I heard the high-pitched whine of the turbine and the cracking of the igniters. Seconds later, as the heli began its ascent, I looked down to see a circle of faces staring up at us, pale in the reflected glare of the arc lights. I held up a gloved hand in farewell before the clouds of dust from the downwash obliterated them from sight.

I headed almost due east, passing high over the coast of Oman and out across the Arabian Sea, parallel to the coast of Iran, aiming into the red heart of the dawn.

We held that course, seeing nothing but the blue-green waters of the ocean and an occasional tanker or tramp steamer, until the beginnings of the Makran coastal range marked the frontier between Iran and western Pakistan.

The plains and deltas of the coast passed below us, vivid green against the turquoise waters of the sea. Then we were climbing over the forested foothills of the coastal ranges, towards Bangur in the parched interior of Baluchistan.

I descended steadily as we approached the rendezvous point. The Herc was drawn up alongside the dirt runway. I put the heli into the hover close to it and Jeff talked me down through a cloud of dust that rose to obscure everything from view. I lowered the collective inch by inch, sweating with the effort of holding the Hydra in the hover near the now invisible mass of the Herc. Then the wheels touched down.

I slowed the engines and waited, then taxied slowly towards the back of the Herc. The guys positioned and repositioned me until our loading door was directly behind the Herc's ramp.

I ran my gaze over the gauges and shut the engines down, drank greedily from my water bottle, then unstrapped and climbed out of the cockpit. I pulled off my helmet, and ran my hands through my hair. It was soaked with sweat.

Amica was sitting off to one side, and I walked over to her, easing the stiffness from my muscles. 'How was it in the Herc?'

She glanced round. 'About what I expected: uncomfortable, noisy, smelly and dirty.'

I smiled. 'It'll be all of those, only worse, on the next leg, I'm afraid. We'll be close to maximum load and the engine will be really labouring crossing the mountains.'

She nodded and turned away, her gaze travelling towards the mountains shimmering in the haze to the north of us.

The guys had already swung down the improvised roller track inside the Hydra and bolted it into position. The Herc's loading ramp began to drop, so close to the heli that its shadow darkened the roof. It stopped parallel to the ground and its crew began to extend the ramp, bridging the gap between the two aircraft.

They began manhandling the first pallet along the ramp. The Hydra settled low on its springs as the full weight of the ten-ton fuel bladder was transferred. The pallet and its load disappeared inside the heli and I heard the rattle of chains as it was secured.

We took off again at 13.00 local time. Amica, Dexy and seven of the other guys flew with us; Dave stayed with the rest of them, guarding the Herc and its precious cargo. They watched, impassive, as I hauled on the collective and we rose into the sky, the engines bellowing under the load we were carrying.

I swung away to the north, coaxing the Hydra up in a gradual, fuel-preserving ascent, and a desert vista opened ahead of us, stretching far to the north. We flew on for an hour, low over the desert floor. Then ahead of me I saw a dark line across the sands, the highway running west from Quetta to the Iranian border. It skirted the foot of the Chagai Hills; their summit marking the border with Afghanistan.

My skin prickled and my heart began to pound as I set the heli into a long climb towards the ridgeline shimmering in the heat haze. As we cleared the summit, I thumbed the intercom switch. 'We're crossing into hostile territory now. Any sight of ground fire, a missile launch or anything suspicious, call it at once, even if you're not sure. Better a few wasted flares than a Stinger knocking a hole in us.'

I saw Jeff's hand tighten on the grip that fired the flares. My finger had moved by instinct to touch the trigger of the Hydra's guns before I remembered the futility of the gesture.

To the north I could see the first wave of mountains rising above Qandahar. I checked our position, then paddled the right rudder, steering us wide of the outlying mud-brick suburbs, on a course bisecting the twin, steeply rising ridges of the mountains enclosing the Tarkan valley. We tracked the Tarkan river to the north-east, keeping the width of the valley between us and the Kabul–Qandahar highway. I saw lorries and a handful of tanks moving along it, but there was no fighting to be seen and no muzzle flashes from the wooded slopes.

As we approached Kabul, I reached for the radio. 'Kabul Centre, this is AMCO flight AM98.'

'Flight AM98 you are clear to land at Kabul airport. No other traffic.'

'Centre, our destination is the AMCO compound.'

'Negative AM98, you must first land at the airport to obtain clearance.'

'He must need the practice,' Jeff said, trying to bury his nerves under a layer of banter. 'He can't get too many opportunities here.'

'Let's hope that's all it is.' I called the tower again. 'Roger that, Centre. On finals now.'

I pushed the cyclic forward and trod on the left rudder, forcing the Hydra into a steep, spiralling dive towards the airfield below us. Only when we were below the minimum height for a successful Stinger launch did I slow the angle of turn and the rate of descent a fraction. I set down on the cracked and cratered concrete some distance from the terminal, and ran the final cross checks with Jeff. Then I shut down the engines.

The blur of the rotors slowed and stopped, and the dust cloud of the downwash blew away on the breeze.

A red Toyota pick-up truck sped away from the terminal building towards us, the back of it bristling with armed men. I glanced behind me. Amica had already shrouded herself in a pale blue burka. I saw only the glint of her dark eyes behind the lattice of her veil as she handed me a sheaf of papers. 'Our permits and safe-conducts.'

The Toyota screeched to a halt in a flurry of dust. The soldier monks jumped down from the back and formed a circle around the helicopter, the long black tails of their turbans fluttering in the wind. Most held Kalashnikovs; a couple had rocket-propelled grenade launchers across their shoulders.

The commander waved his hand, indicating we should get down from the heli. A crumpled bullet hung on a thong around his neck and the now-familiar scar showed white against his sunburned face. His men were all younger; some beardless boys. Their faces showed little interest, only a dull hostility as they stared at us.

Salan addressed me directly, but gave no sign that he recognised me. 'You have brought nothing into Afghanistan that is forbidden by our Islamic law?'

'We are carrying only fuel for the helicopter and equipment to help us with our work.' I pointed towards the open door of the cab. 'See for yourself.'

Three of his men walked towards the heli and climbed inside. Amica shrank back and averted her gaze, staring at the side of the helicopter as they passed her. One of them prodded the fuel bladder with the barrel of his Kalashnikov, then began fixing his bayonet.

Jeff let out a yell and was lunging for the helicopter when I held his arm. I turned to Salan. 'Please excuse my friend, he is afraid that your soldier may hurt himself and the rest of us. That container holds 25,000 litres of fuel.'

Salan's eyes widened. He took a step back, shouting furiously at the soldier, then swung round to face me. 'Show me.'

We climbed inside. I unscrewed the inspection cap, sniffed and then gestured for him to do the same. He did so, then glanced around the interior of the cab. He prodded a couple of our bags with his toe, then climbed out again. 'Is the helicopter armed?'

I shook my head and pointed to the black holes in the fuselage from which the guns would normally have protruded. 'They were removed as soon as we bought it. We are men of peace.'

'Men of peace?' He could not hide the contempt in his eyes. 'A man who does not fight to defend his home, his people and his religion, is not a man at all.'

He made a show of flicking through the papers, but either could not read or could not be bothered to do so. Then he handed them back and shouted to his men. Without another word, they got back into the Toyota and drove off across the airfield.

We clambered back inside and I cleared us for take-off with the tower. As we rose into the air I saw Salan's red Toyota bouncing its way along the rutted streets towards the centre of Kabul.

Leaving Amica and the guys at the compound in Kabul, we flew back to Bangur at dawn the following morning.

'No regrets that you're on the mission?' I asked Dave as his men transferred the fake fuel-bladder from the Herc to the heli.

He shook his head. 'It'll be my last one. I've had to smile and take the flak for a few screw-ups over the years – Eagle Claw, Grenada, Somalia – I've had Dexy rattling my chain about them ever since. This is the chance to do it right: show what my boys can do.'

We overflew the southern deserts and passed Qandahar without incident, but a full-scale battle had broken out further up the Tarkan valley towards Kabul. Tanks were rocking in their tracks among the trees, blasting salvos of shells into the valley. Several buildings were already in flames, but I could see the bright flashes of return fire from around them.

There was a sudden yell from the back. 'Incoming! Evade! Evade!'

'It's all right,' Jeff said. 'It's only ground fi— Shit! Look out!'

Ugly bursts of flak peppered the air around us as an anti-aircraft gun opened up from the ridge. I threw the Hydra from side to side, ramming the cyclic upwards for maximum power. There was a rattle and a screech of metal as shrapnel ripped into the fuselage.

I heard the side door slide open and we gave a torrent of return fire. Sweat pouring down my face, I kept up the gut-wrenching pattern of evasion, up and down, left and right, the engines screaming in protest.

Heart in mouth, I waited for Jeff's voice, calling an emergency. It never came. The shrapnel had missed the fuel and hydraulic lines and buried itself in the armour plating beneath us.

The black puffballs of smoke were no longer opening ahead of us. I maintained the evasion for another five seconds, then levelled and eased down on the cyclic.

'All right back there? Anyone hit?'

'No one's hit, we're just bruised to hell,' Dave said. 'Who taught you to drive?'

I laughed, high on adrenalin. 'The same wankers who taught you to shoot. You did know you were out of range there, didn't you?'

'There's no such thing when you've got gravity on your side.'

'You're right. Not if accuracy doesn't matter anyway.'

Boon interrupted. 'Listen, wise-ass. You stick to flying this heap of crap. We'll stick to shooting. That way we may all get out of this alive.'

'Not necessarily,' I said. 'I've got a bet on with Jeff that I can get down from 3,000 feet to the ground in less than twenty seconds.'

I lost the bet, but not by much – and for all their assumed nonchalance I could tell that a few of them were very glad to feel solid earth under their feet again.

Tank already had the fork-lift truck waiting by the time I'd wound down the engines. The fake fuel bladder was unloaded and stacked, still on its pallet, among the real ones.

We were sitting in the canteen, getting some food and a brew before the flight up to Konarlan, when we heard the sound of a revving engine and raised voices.

We ran outside. An ancient flatbed truck, decorated with vivid images of eagles dismembering their prey and warriors brandishing swords and guns, was parked in the middle of the compound. Salan and his group of Taliban soldiers stood next to it.

I hurried across the compound with Dexy. 'What's up?' I said.

Amica moved away from the soldiers before she answered. 'They're trying to take some of the fuel.'

Salan strode across to interrupt the conversation. 'Our people need fuel for their lamps and stoves. You have plenty. You will give some to us.'

'But this is aviation fuel,' Amica said. 'You can't burn it in lamps.'

He stared at her for a moment then back-handed her to the ground and turned on his heel, yelling orders to his men.

Dexy and I started after him, but Amica's warning shout stopped us. 'Wait! If you interfere you risk everything. I'm all right. Leave it.'

I helped her to her feet. A few spots of crimson now stained the mauve burka just below the mesh of the visor. 'Our time will come,' she said, her voice so low I had to strain to catch the words.

The roar of an engine broke the silence. One of the Taliban soldiers had started the fork-lift truck and was driving it across the compound. The others fanned out, covering us with their weapons. I checked the serial number on the bladder he was heading for, and relaxed for a moment . . . then let out a yell. The man had lowered the forks as he rumbled towards the pallet – but not enough.

The steel prongs caught on the lip of the pallet, which rose a couple of feet into the air before crashing down with a sharp, splintering crack. The extended forks pierced the skin of the bladder as it dropped, and a tide of pink fuel gushed out.

Everyone froze. I shouted at Salan in Farsi, 'The engine! Cut the engine!'

He gave me an uncomprehending stare, then his face drained of colour and he screamed an order. The soldier killed the engine just as the tide of fuel lapped around the fork-lift, hissing as it touched the hot metal of the exhaust. No one moved. We all stared, waiting for it to become a wall of flame. The spark never came. The fuel spread wider across the compound, staining the ground around my feet and sinking into the parched earth.

I strode over to Salan, ignoring the rifle barrels trained on me. 'That is our only spare fuel for the helicopter. It is useless for anything else, you cannot use it and you cannot sell it. We are here to clear minefields on the express authority of Mullah Muhammed Omar himself.'

The name of the Taliban leader had the desired effect.

'He will not be pleased that we are being hampered in our work by his own soldiers,' I added.

Salan's expression veered between anger and doubt. Finally he turned on his heel and barked an order at his men. They climbed back into the truck and drove off without another word.

Dexy watched them go. 'Nice going, Sean. You should have made him apologise.'

'Where the hell were your boys?'

'Look around you.'

I did as he said. In the shadows cast by the buildings and the stacks of equipment around the compound, I picked out the still darker shapes of prone figures with guns trained on the truck as it paused at the gates and then drove off.

'They'd only have sparked up if things had turned really ugly,' Dexy said. He frowned as he looked over my shoulder. The fake fuel-bladder was now in full view. The ruptured one that had been screening it lay deflated, the last of its fuel trickling into the earth. 'We can't risk unloading the gear in full view of those goons on the gate. We'll have to do it tonight and get the patrol up to Konarlan tomorrow. We can't afford any more delays.'

I glanced at my watch. 'We'd have been tight for time before sunset anyway.'

Later that afternoon, making enough noise to attract the attention of the Taliban guards on the gate, we loaded a few decoy boxes of supplies. Then we left the loading doors open and the heli unattended while we went to eat and rest.

From the shadows of the building I saw one of the soldiers stroll across the compound and nose around the helicopter. He clambered inside and peered into a couple of packing cases. Then, losing interest, he sauntered back to the gate and squatted down in the shade.

Just before sunset we refuelled the heli from one of the remaining bladders, using that as an excuse to reposition it with the loading door hidden from the gate.

We waited until one the next morning before making our next move. The city was still and silent, apart from the barks and snarls of scavenging dogs and the flickering of tracer from a distant gun battle in the hills to the north.

The body of the helicopter shielded the stack of fuel bladders from the view of the guards dozing in the shadows by the gate, but Boon and Tank kept watch on them while we began to load the equipment. I rammed my combat knife through the tough rubber hide of the bladder, driving it in with the heel of my hand, and forcing it upwards to extend the cut for four or five feet.

The exposed packs of gel shone grey in the moonlight. Working in complete silence, we lifted out a couple of dozen and stacked them to one side. I had partly covered the lens of my torch with insulating tape, leaving only a narrow lozenge of light, but even so I got into the space we had created inside the bladder before switching it on.

I cut through the second rubber skin facing me. As I moved forward, the bladder closed around me and the smell of rubber and the foetid odour of explosives filled my nostrils. I froze for a moment, suppressing a memory. Then I reached inside the second bladder and my hand closed around cold metal. I began to pull out the equipment, one piece at a time, passing it behind me to Dexy. It was moved from hand to hand along a chain to the helicopter where Jeff supervised its loading into cases, crates and sacks.

As soon as the last piece was loaded we began emptying the bladder of the packs of gel, forming another human chain to move them to a ruined building at the back of the compound, where we passed the packs of gel down into the cellar, which was already half full of rubble. When the last one was in place, we pushed dust and fine debris down from the floor above. It formed a thin layer, shielding the packs from casual glance, but a permanent burial would have to await daylight. The slight noise we had made set my heart thumping, but there was no movement and no challenge from the guards at the gate.

I poured a few gallons of aviation fuel into and over the empty fuel bladder, hiding any lingering smell of explosives, and we left it where it lay. As the rest of us hid in the shadow of the heli, Dexy moved soundlessly towards the gate. Ten minutes passed before Boon and Tank returned with him, moving like ghosts, flitting from each dark pool of shadow to the next.

Boon and Tank stayed with the heli, mounting guard. The rest of us stole back to the accommodation block.

Chapter 10

The next morning I found Dexy on the sat-phone to base. He broke the connection shortly after I appeared. 'They're getting very sweaty back there,' he said. 'Intercepted comms show another terrorist team is already inside the US.'

'With Stingers?'

'Not yet. But "no variation from the attack schedule will be countenanced for any reason".' He shook his head. 'Wherever that rupert went to school it wasn't Peckham, that's for sure.' He paused. 'Right, you'll take the equipment and the first group to the LUP this afternoon.'

'Who leads it — you?'

He shook his head. 'Dave. I'm coming up with the rest of the guys tomorrow. You need to make a rolling drop at the landing zone just after sunset. The timing's critical; too early and they'll be inserting in daylight, too late and you'll be in danger of being shot down for breaking curfew. You return to Kabul at first light tomorrow for the rest of us.'

The hours dragged by. We waited until we heard the muezzin calling the faithful to mid-afternoon prayer, then I fired up the helicopter. Under cover of the noise of the engines and the dust cloud raised by the whirling rotors, Dexy and Rami ran to the ruined building at the back of the compound and used an axe to smash through the single beam that held up the ceiling over our hidden packs of gel. I saw the cloud of dust as the ground floor collapsed, concealing the evidence under a thick layer of rubble.

I taxied to the far side of the compound and paddled the rudders to bring the heli around, then raised the collective, winding up the engines. The heli lifted a little and as the rotors began to take the weight, I glanced behind me into the cab. Dave's face was set, but the expressions of one or two of the guys betrayed their anxiety. In their natural element, on the ground, they felt capable of dealing with anything an enemy could throw at them. In the air they were vulnerable, not in control of their own destiny, forced to trust their lives to a pilot who was not one of them.

At full power the Hydra could climb a hundred feet every two seconds. In one minute we would be beyond the range of any trigger-happy Taliban with an AK47. We would not be out of Stinger range, however, and I had to push away the thought of what a missile would do among the mounds of explosives and ammunition in the cab.

We flew east towards the mountains, tracking the course of the river far below us. The shadow the helicopter cast on the ground stretched as the sun sank behind us and I watched the line of the sunset rising up the mountains until only the snow-capped peaks were still tinged with red light. Then they too were cast into shadow. The glow of the setting sun still lit the sky far behind us, but ahead was only darkness, the dense velvet black of the land and the twilight sky pierced by the first glimmering stars of evening.

I flipped the intercom switch. 'Take the controls and hold us steady while I put these on.'

'Okay, I have it,' Jeff said. 'Let's hope the Taliban don't choose this moment to take a shot at us.'

I changed the illumination of the instrument panels to infrared, then pulled the night-vision goggles down over my eyes and switched on the battery pack. The grey-black world disappeared, replaced by a vivid green. I counted slowly to twenty, giving my eyes time to adjust, then focused the goggles one eye at a time, fixing my gaze on the beacon of the evening star. I adjusted them until the twin images merged into a single sharp-edged one.

The thin scattering of stars I had seen by normal vision became a milky, opalescent belt covering the heavens. The twisting course of the river below us shone like a ribbon of light and the goggles even picked up the faint light of glow-worms speckling the ground along its banks.

'Taking control,' I said.

Jeff handed back, then pulled on his own goggles.

I thumbed the intercom switch again. 'Four minutes to target.'

I heard a shuffle from the back as the guys prepared themselves.

I eased the cyclic forward and the valley walls rose around us as the heli began to descend. We passed close to a village and flew on into the gathering darkness.

'One thousand feet.' Jeff's hand was clamped around the flare-release lever, ready to dump burning phosphorus and magnesium into the path of any missiles launched against us. 'Five hundred . . . four hundred . . . three hundred . . .'

Now we were well within range of any Kalashnikov pointing in our direction. I saw the small huddle of lights that marked Konarlan away to our right, and paddled the rudder to come around the shoulder of the hill into the narrow valley. Rocks and boulders loomed like green icebergs as we dropped closer to the valley floor.

'One minute,' I said. The loading door slid open behind me. My eyes raked the darkness ahead of us, lining up our navigation points: a clump of dead trees, their white, bark-stripped trunks reflecting the starlight, a sharp bend in the river and a notch in the hills. Ahead I saw a smudge of green, a small sandy beach on the inside of a bend in the river.

'This is it,' I said. 'We're going in.'

I heard Dave over the intercom. 'Yes, this is right.' Despite the tension, I smiled to myself. Special Forces never trusted anyone's navigation but their own. He'd been using his GPS and his map to track our course all the way from Kabul.

'Visual,' Jeff said. 'Height's good, stand by.'

I heard the guys in the cab scrambling to their feet and lining up near the loading door.

'Forward twenty, height's good.'

The landing zone could scarcely have been tighter. The mountainside rose sheer to our left and the bank on the other side of the river was thickly forested. There were boulders and mounds of rock, dumped by the winter floods, above and below the bend in the river.

'Down twenty.'

The river still glowed green, but the forest and the black mountain to either side swallowed every other trace of light. I was descending blind into a black-walled cavern. I could feel sweat prickle on my brow and heard the accelerating thud of my heartbeat, but I forced myself to relax my grip on the controls, making fine, almost instinctive adjustments to the cyclic and collective as Jeff talked us down.

'Forward twenty. Down ten. Stand by.'

As we dropped lower, the downwash hit the beach. One moment we were hovering in clear air, the next we were in the heart of a sandstorm of our own creation. I could still see a faint glow from the surface of the river, but nothing forward, to either side or below. A touch too far to the right and we would be in the trees, to the left the rotors would strike the mountainside. 'Get us down, Jeff. I can't see a fucking thing.' He hesitated for a moment. 'Come on,' I said. 'We have to go for a landing, let's get this thing down.'

The sand cloud was so dense around us that the velocity of the whirling rotors struck sparks from the grains of sand. The rotors were thrashing the air inches from the rockface. It was so close I could almost have reached out a hand and touched it. I touched the right rudder and eased away from the black wall.

Jeff found his voice again. 'Right ten. That's good. Down twenty . . . fifteen . . . ten . . . five . . . Go! Go! Go!'

I kept the heli in the hover, the wheels a couple of feet above the ground. The guys were already spilling from the cab. Dave was first out; he and three others went into all-round defence, taking up firing positions at the edge of the beach as the others dumped out the equipment and jumped after it.

'They're clear. Let's go,' Jeff said.

I pulled on the collective and he began counting off the ascending height as we pulled clear. As I paddled the right rudder to swing us around and head back down the valley, I glanced down. The dust storm sandbar now shone an unbroken green.

Dave and the guys had already taken their equipment and melted into cover.

I levelled at 300 feet and we flew back to the south-west, skimming the river. I pulled a wide turn around Konarlan, circling to approach from the direction of Kabul, until I saw the lights of the compound ahead of us.

We were walking across the compound towards the buildings when a Toyota came blasting up to the gate. At least twenty men were clinging to the back, using whatever precarious handholds they could find.

They jumped down and formed a hostile circle around us, shouting and brandishing their Kalashnikovs. They parted as their commander strode through them, and to my relief I saw that it was not Salan but the barrel-chested figure of Agha Shah Azuin. His son Daru padded alongside him. Daru smiled, patted his pocket and tapped a finger to the side of his nose, but his father's greeting was much less friendly.

'I warned you before, Inglisi. Why have you broken curfew? Why were you flying after dark?'

'You have every right to be angry,' I said, trying to keep my voice even. 'We should have arrived well before sunset but we've had instrument and engine trouble on the way from Kabul. We had to set down for two hours, a hundred miles west of here. I was afraid we would not get here at all.'

His piercing gaze never left my face. 'Where exactly did you set down?'

'I don't know the name, but I can show you on the map.'

I rummaged in the cockpit, produced a map, glanced at it and then stabbed my finger down. 'There.'

He took the map from me, holding it so I could no longer see it. 'Describe the place.'

My mouth dried, but I fought to hold my expression

unchanged as I struggled to remember the contours shown on the map. I kept it as vague as I could. 'It was a place where the valley narrowed a little, on the left bank of the river a few miles beyond a village.'

'You have not mentioned the ruins,' he said.

I hesitated, trying to second-guess him, but the expression on his face offered no clues. 'I saw no ruins,' I said at last.

He held my gaze a moment longer, then shrugged his shoulders. 'It is of no importance. You would be very wise not to fly after dark again.' He went to the door of the helicopter and peered inside. 'What load were you carrying that was so urgent?'

I swallowed. 'Just supplies and equipment.'

'A very small load.'

I forced a smile. 'We bring up only what we need.' I looked away from his insistent gaze.

'Where are the others?'

I had been expecting the question, but still had to suppress a nervous start. 'In Kabul. They will be returning soon.'

He was already turning away, losing interest in the conversation.

'I'm sorry for the trouble we have caused you,' I said.

He walked over to the gates and spoke to the Taliban guards there. Neither Jeff nor I moved. 'Jesus,' I said. 'I've just aged ten years in ten minutes. If he'd asked one more question I'd have been needing those toilet rolls of yours.'

Jeff didn't even try to force a smile. 'I'm getting too old for this,' he said. 'When this is over, I'm definitely getting out.'

In the temporary absence of his father, Daru seized his chance to sidle up to me.

'Not now, Daru, not now,' I said.

'But, Inglisi, I have a great bargain for you.' He patted his pocket again. 'An emerald the size of a pigeon's egg. It is a fabulous treasure, beyond price, but you can have it for 50,000 Afghanis.'

'No, Daru, I'm a poor man; such riches are beyond me.'

'40,000 Afghanis then.'

'Not at any price. I have no money.'

He gave me a sceptical look. 'You are from the West, aren't you? Of course you have money.'

I ignored him, shooting a glance towards his father who was still talking to the Taliban guards. 'Daru, your village is many kilometres away. Why were you so near here tonight?'

'There were rumours that the men who attacked Konarlan a week ago had returned.' He shrugged. 'It was the gossip of old men. They are not here. If they had been, I, Daru, son of Agha Shah Azuin, would have killed them myself.'

'Sure you would,' I said, 'or sold them an emerald.'

His father strode back to us, his long hair and beard streaming behind him.

'Will you take tea with us?' I said.

Azuin shook his head. 'Thank you, but there is work to be done.' He glanced back towards the Taliban guards at the gate. 'My allies are not pleased that you have broken their curfew. You should beware.'

He started to say something else, then changed his mind and barked an order to his men. They clambered back on to the vehicle. Daru winked at us and loped away after his father.

The warlord's black vehicle swung out of the gates and away up the hill heading north-east, but a few moments later the Talibans' red Landcruiser also started up. It took the opposite route. I watched the taillights and saw it stop in the village. I heard the murmur of voices and a few shouts, then the engine restarted and it drove on down the dusty road towards Kabul.

'Are they going to check our story?' Jeff said.

'I doubt it. They don't have to drive to Kabul to do that. The Talibans' communications aren't perfect but they must be good enough to put in a phone call.'

'Then what are they doing?'

'I don't know, probably nothing to do with us.' Just the same, I watched the red glow of the taillights appearing and disappearing as the pick-up climbed the pass at the far end of the valley. It halted at the lookout point at the top of the pass. The white headlights stabbed out of the darkness towards us as it turned round and manoeuvred to face back towards Konarlan, then the lights were extinguished. I waited a few more minutes, but it didn't move again.

The Taliban guard on the compound had been doubled by the next morning, and when I walked down to the river to wash I noticed one of them following me at a distance. Alarmed, I splashed water on my face and then hurried back to the compound.

Jeff was brewing up and scratching at his insect bites. 'Forget the brew,' I said. 'They've doubled the guard and they're definitely watching us. Let's get the hell out.'

'We still have to come back.'

'I know, but I'll feel a lot safer with Dexy and the others around us.'

There was a catch in his voice. 'I won't feel safe until I'm back in my local.'

I looked at him again. He had deep black shadows under his eyes, and his clothes were loose on his frame. 'That diet's most certainly working,' I said.

'If you don't eat or sleep, it's amazing how much weight you can lose.'

I kept a wary eye on the guards as we walked to the helicopter and began the pre-flight checks. They moved so that they could keep us in sight and I saw one speaking into his radio, but they made no attempt to interfere.

I concentrated on the preparations for the flight and heaved a sigh of relief as both engines fired and the gauges and captions gave normal readings. 'So far so good,' I said. 'Let's get out of here. One more trip there and back, then it's up to Dexy and the guys.'

I taxied slowly towards the compound gates, then swung the heli round to take off facing away from the guards. If they started firing I wanted as much metal and armoured plate between us as possible. Once airborne, I kept in a tight spiral climb over the compound until we had reached 3,000 feet, before levelling and turning west to follow the valley down towards Kabul. As we approached the pass I pulled back on the cyclic again, keeping the same margin between us and the ground as we climbed towards the summit.

I saw the red Toyota still parked at the lookout and a huddle of figures nearby. I switched my gaze forward, looking over the ridge into the valley beyond.

'Missile launch!' Jeff shouted. 'Dive! Dive! Dive!'

I stamped down on the left rudder and rammed the cyclic forward, pulling a savage left-hand break. 'Flares!' I yelled, but it was unnecessary. The ritual drummed in on a thousand training missions was paying off.

Jeff stabbed the flare release, counted down five seconds and then I heard the rattle and bang as he punched out another volley. I swung the Hydra nose-on to the Taliban lookout, masking the heat signature of our engines, and dumped the collective. The heli slid downwards in a barely controlled dive.

A pinpoint of light trailing a pillar of smoke and flame

flashed towards us. It passed so close to my face that instinct made me duck. 'Look ou—'

The rotors sucked at the grey smoke trail as it flashed past in a heartbeat and detonated in a huge ball of orange fire on the white heat of one of the flares.

The ground was now an even greater danger; we were almost in freefall. The engines howled in protest as I grabbed the collective and dragged back the cyclic. I kicked the right rudder, trying to bring us level. Still we slid downwards.

The Hydra responded to the controls with agonising slowness. It rocked slowly back into level flight and began to climb as I piled on the power. I glanced left and froze as the arc of the rotors sliced through the cedars, shredding the topmost branches. I kicked the rudder to swing us away, but our attempts to evade the missile had brought us back close to the summit of the pass. I heard rattles and cracks from below us and the whine of ricochets as rounds struck the cab. I jinked the heli right and left, then pushed the cyclic forward again, forcing the collective against the stops, racing to put the ridgeline between us and our attackers.

I heard more rounds puncturing the cab and there was a crack and a shout of fright from Jeff as a round smashed through the Perspex of the side window and exited through the screen of the cockpit. Then we were skimming over the trees on the far side of the pass. I kept the heli at treetop height; another few seconds and we would be out of range of the guns.

The heli juddered and lurched. At the same moment a warning siren began to whine and the smell of burning oil filled the cockpit. My eyes darted to the instruments, but Jeff was already calling it. 'Engine fire. Shut-down sequence. Fuel cock.'

Another couple of rounds ricocheted from the tail. 'Shut.'

'Extinguisher.'

'On.' I snapped the switch, the heli again juddered and slowed. I heard the engine note change and the beat of the rotors alter as gas flooded the engine. The stench of hot metal and burning oil intensified then began to fade and the cloud of smoke and steam was chopped away by the rotors.

The rattle of rounds against the fuselage had stopped, but we were still banked steeply and descending. Vortices from the blades were throwing up plumes of dust from the ground beneath us. 'Up, you bastard, up!' I shouted, trying to coax every ounce of power from the one remaining engine.

The Hydra righted and began to climb. I levelled almost at once, at just fifty feet. My eyes darted to the readings on the panel, looking for more trouble before it happened. The noise was deafening, the normal bass beat of the engines and the whoosh of the rotors undercut by a high-pitched, chattering whine.

I gave it twenty more seconds at maximum power, then lowered the collective, nursing the engine a little. 'Three options,' I said. 'Set down here, make for the compound at Kabul or take off for the border. Fuel?'

'We're okay for Kabul,' Jeff said. 'Maybe for the border too, but it's very tight.'

I checked the readings once more. The oil temperature was high. 'Setting down here looks like the worst option to me. The Taliban would be on us within half an hour. They've tried to shoot us out of the air. I'm sure they'd have just as much fun shooting us on the ground.'

I waited a few seconds, but Jeff was silent. 'If we run for the border we may run out of fuel and have to come down inside Afghanistan anyway, and if we do that we're blowing the mission.'

'But if we go to Kabul, what are our options?' Jeff said.

'It's for Dexy to call,' I said. 'If he wants to risk it, then that's what we'll have to do. You don't know if those guys were shooting at us out of irritability or because we're blown. If we are, then Dexy and the other guys, and Amica, are all in deep shit too.'

I felt sick at the thought.

I checked the gauges again. The oil temperature had risen a little further and the hydraulic pressure had dropped. I lowered the collective a fraction more.

'So we're going to Kabul?' Jeff said.

'What else can we do?'

He didn't reply.

I kept the Hydra in level flight, doing my best to minimise the twists and turns as we followed the course of the river down the valley. Goats and a herd of sheep scattered as we flashed overhead. A few figures ran with them, the survival instinct hammered into them over years of raids by helicopter gunships. Other people remained motionless, so close below us that I could see their mouths opening and shutting as they stared upwards.

Another Taliban position loomed on the ridgeline ahead. I eased the heli even lower and hugged the far side of the valley. I could feel the sweat trickling down my neck, and my hands were clenched rigid on the controls. I glanced sideways at the Taliban post and could see a row of heads outlined against the sky, but there was no firing. I breathed out as we crested the ridge and dropped into the next valley.

The oil temperature was still rising, and twenty miles out from Kabul I heard an arrhythmic rattle beneath the chattering whine of the engine. It grew steadily louder, clanking like an old banger with its big end gone. The pulse of the engine began to slow and quicken, the heli decelerating and accelerating in time with it.

I coaxed a little more height, my eyes fixed on the horizon, willing the Hydra towards Kabul. Neither of us spoke lest we broke the spell that was holding the heli in the air.

Finally the Kabul skyline pierced through the dusty haze ahead of us, but I dared not relax. The engine noise forced any thought other than survival out of my head. I picked out the grey slab of the Qarga dam above the city, the curve of the sports stadium and a flash of sunlight reflecting from the tiles of a mosque.

The engine coughed, faltered, then picked up again. The heli dropped like a stone, slowed and strained to climb once more. I was whispering under my breath, 'Come on. Come on. Come on.'

I could see the perimeter of the compound ahead, the diamond pattern of the fence and the vicious coils of razor wire laid along the top.

'Nothing fancy,' Jeff said. 'Let's just get this crate on the deck.'

I didn't reply. I juggled the controls, making minute adjustments to our trim, all the time straining my ears for any change in the engine noise. I eased the cyclic forward, dropping the nose of the heli, as I saw the compound begin to open up ahead of us.

The engine faltered again, rallied, and then there was an explosion as if a grenade had detonated over my head. There was a flash of silver, and a broken piston lashed out through the edge of the casing like a steel javelin, pursued by a shower of fragments.

The sudden silence was broken only by the slowing beat of the rotors. The heli began to slide down and to the right. Instinct made me stamp on the rudder and fight the controls, but there was no engine to power them. The earth floor of the compound was barely thirty feet ahead of us and the same distance below.

'It's all right, we're going to make—'

The right wheel clipped the top strand of the perimeter wire and the heli toppled over. The still-flailing rotors knifed into the ground and shattered one by one. Shards of broken metal flew through the air around us, gouging the walls of the cab.

A second later we hit the dirt. The tail collapsed and snapped off, and we rolled over twice as the cab bounced and slithered to a halt in a cacophony of shattering metal and Perspex. My helmet smacked against the side-strut and I blacked out.

I came to, hanging upside down in my seat harness. I could hear the drip of leaking fluid, the hiss of steam and the ticking of hot metal as it cooled. I turned my head and winced as pain drilled through my temples, and a wave of nausea swept over me.

Bile flooded the back of my throat. I swallowed and yelled at Jeff, 'Out! Out! Out!' I took a grip on the side-strut, punched the release buckle on my harness and swung down on to the inside of the roof, gashing my shin in my haste to get my feet down first. I took most of Jeff's weight as he released himself and slithered down alongside me. There was no door on his side, just a battered hole where one used to be. We crawled out, jumped to the ground and stumbled away from the heli as fast as we could.

Boon and Tank sprinted out with fire extinguishers and doused the still smoking engine. Dexy grabbed my arm. 'What the hell happened?'

'Not here,' I said, moving away from the circle of AMCO personnel who had gathered to gawp at the wreck. To my relief, the Taliban made no move as I limped away across the compound.

Dexy and the others huddled around as we told them what had happened. When we had finished, he walked to the corner and called up base on the sat-phone, his voice low and his back turned. He broke the connection and sat silent for a couple of minutes. When he looked up, his face was set. 'Right. The only reason why the Taliban here are not on our case already must be their lousy communications. We can't expect that situation to last. Take only essentials.' He glanced at me. 'Make sure you bring those forged passes. We'll toss everything in the back of one of the AMCO pick-ups and fuck off in that.'

'To the border?' Rami said.

'No way. The operation isn't blown yet, and the rest of the guys are still in the LUP. We'll head south-west out of the city, as if we're heading for Qandahar and the border, then go covert and double back on our tracks towards Konarlan. We'll link up with the others, carry out the assault and then exfiltrate overland to the border.' He glanced at me. 'You and Jeff can take your pick. I don't think that heli will be flying again. You can either E & E direct to the border and take your chances on your own, or you can travel with us, wait at the RV while we carry out the assault, and then E & E through the mountains with us.'

Jeff's expression was unreadable. I waited a few moments for him to speak, then shrugged my shoulders. 'I've always preferred mountains to deserts. We'll stick with you.'

'Then let's get to it.'

'What about Amica?'

'What about her?' Rami's tone was hostile.

'If we're blown, so's she.'

'That's her problem. We're here to carry out a mission, not rescue civilians.'

I clenched my fists. 'Amica has risked her neck for us for the last six years.'

He ignored me, speaking directly to Dexy. 'This mission is too important to be jeopardised by amateurs and women.'

Dexy held up a hand. 'We don't have time for this.' He glanced from Amica to Jeff and me. 'We're not leaving you here for the Taliban. We'll take you with us, but if at any time I' – he stressed the personal pronoun, without looking at Rami – 'I feel that you are in any way putting us at risk, you will be ditched and left to find your own way home. Now let's go. Make your way to the pick-up in ones or twos. Make it look casual and don't carry so much kit that it looks like we're moving out. Rami, give me a hand.'

Rami shot him a furious look, but did as he was told.

Dexy rummaged among the piles of AMCO stores. 'No paint, damn it,' he said. 'This will have to do.' He picked up a five-gallon drum of oil. They carried it out to the pick-up, and leaned on the tailboard. Rami smoked a cigarette and the two of them began chatting, apparently without a care in the world.

The rest of us sauntered over to join them a couple of minutes later. Amica was a few paces behind, shrouded in a blue burka. As the others stood in a circle, blocking the view of the guards at the gate, Jeff and I slid half a dozen jerry-cans of petrol into the back.

Dexy yawned and stretched and moved round to the driver's side. I stopped him. 'Best if I drive. If the shit hits the fan, we'd be better off with my hands on the wheel and yours on a rifle.'

He nodded and got in the passenger side, the rest of them perched in the back.

The guards stood up as we approached the gate and I slowed as if about to speak to them, then raised my hand in a wave and spun the wheel, slewing the pick-up around, out of the gate.

I drove through the outskirts of Kabul and along the Qandahar road for about forty minutes, the road tracking the left-hand bank of the river. Then we began to climb into the hills and the fields gave way to scrubby woodland. The road ahead of us lay empty as far as the next ridge. I glanced in the mirror, then jerked the wheel to the right. The pick-up bumped down a track between the trees, down towards the river.

I touched the brakes and without a word of command, Tank and Boon jumped down and ran back up towards the road. Each tore a branch from a sapling as they ran and brushed away the tyre tracks from the verge.

I turned the pick-up around on the bank of the river, then parked among the trees, invisible from both the road and the river. Dexy looked at his watch. 'We need to work fast. I want to be well east of Kabul before curfew.'

While Tank and Boon covered the entrance to the track, Dexy and Rami huddled together studying maps and satellite images. Jeff, Amica and I used rags to smear oil all over the bodywork, the roof of the cab and the number plates. As soon as the pick-up was covered, we scooped up handfuls of dust and sand and tossed them over it. The white paint and AMCO markings disappeared under a thick layer of honey-brown dust.

When we'd finished, Jeff and I stripped off our flying suits. We knotted the arms and legs, filled them with rocks, and tossed them into the river. I changed into drab brown clothes and began to wind a turban around my head.

Amica peered at me for a moment. 'Your roots are showing. Give me the dye and I'll fix it.'

'Shit,' I said. 'I've left it behind.'

She glanced towards Rami, but he was still absorbed in studying the maps. 'It doesn't matter,' she said. 'I'll fix it the same way as the pick-up.' She poured some oil into her hand, scooped up some dust and rubbed it into a filthy brown paste. She smeared it around my hairline and the edges of my beard, frowning with concentration, her face only a few inches from my own. Then she stepped back, tilting her head to one side to study her handiwork. 'That should do,' she said.

'Are you all right?' I said.

She paused, as if the question surprised her. 'Doing this, you mean? Why, do we have a choice?'

'We don't. You might have had.'

She shook her head. 'I don't think so.'

'Anyway, you're safer with us,' I said.

She shrugged. 'Perhaps it's safer for you as well. If the Taliban had come for me . . .' She left the sentence hanging in the air.

'You did counter-interrogation training, just like us.'

'But if they tortured me, I would betray you.'

'No, you wouldn't.'

She held out her hand towards me. 'Look at my nails.' There was a curious ridge across each of them. 'When I left Afghanistan six years ago, I was stopped at a Taliban checkpoint near the frontier. I was wearing the burka, but in my haste to leave I'd forgotten to remove my nail polish.' There was a catch in her voice. 'One of the Taliban soldiers, a boy of sixteen, perhaps less, saw them. He grabbed my arm, dragged me away from the other refugees and punched me in the stomach. I dropped to my knees. More of them held me as the boy produced a pair of steel clippers. He didn't cut the nails, though, he began tearing them out, breaking them off at the root. He paused between each one to abuse me, calling me a whore and a traitor. When he had finished he put his foot on my back and forced me down into the mud. He ground my face into it and then walked off and left me. No one moved to help me, even after the Taliban got in their vehicle and drove off. The column of refugees just began to move on again. Except one women who stayed behind and helped me up. She tore strips from her underwear to bind my fingers and stayed with me as we walked on towards the frontier. I lost sight of her in the crowd at the frontier and though I searched and searched for her on the other side, I never saw her again.' She had been staring over my shoulder as she spoke, but now she turned her head towards me. 'If they torture me, I know I will break.'

'Even the toughest soldier only promises that he'll try and give the others twenty-four hours to get away before he starts to talk.'

'I don't know if I could even last that long.'

'If you have to, you will.' I touched her arm. 'And don't let Rami hear you talking that way. He's looking for an excuse to dump us as it is.'

She smiled back, despite herself.

Dexy stood up, folded the maps and looked over the pick-up. 'It'll have to do.' He glanced at Jeff. 'If we hit any checkpoints, leave all the talking to Sean, and if any shooting starts, hit the deck and leave it to the experts.'

He whistled to Tank who moved up the slope to the edge of the road. He remained motionless, listening for two or three minutes, then raised his arm. We jumped in and I gunned the engine and set the pick-up racing up the slope. I slewed out on to the road, paused a moment while Tank and Boon jumped on board, then put my foot down and sent us speeding back towards Kabul.

I threaded my way through the back streets, making a loop around the west and north of the city, keeping well clear of the area around the AMCO compound. Once beyond Kabul, however, there was no real choice of route, only the pitted dirt road leading through the mountains to Konarlan.

The heat was ferocious. There was no shade to be found anywhere on the broad valley floor as we headed east. A thick pall of dust surrounded us, covering my clothes, face and hair, choking my mouth and nostrils. I had a scarf wound around my face and chewed the end between my lips to try to stop them cracking in the heat.

I drove flat out, bucketing over the ruts and potholes. The guys remained on maximum alert, one peering through the window of the cab, scanning the road ahead, the others raking the hillsides to either side or watching the rear, though at the speed we were travelling the road behind us could largely be left to look after itself.

Chapter 11

It took three hours to reach the shelter of the hills, veering around bomb craters in the road surface, still unrepaired ten years after the last Soviet air-raid.

As we left the worst of the heat and dust of the plain behind us and began to climb into the foothills, we stopped in the shade of a grove of trees, by a ford across the river. The rusting skeletons of a convoy of Soviet vehicles lined both banks.

All the usable metal from the vehicles had been removed, but the twin barrels of the machine gun of an armoured car still pointed at the sky. Built to withstand the intense heat of continuous fire, the tempered gun-barrels had been twisted and blackened by the white heat of the explosion that had consumed them.

Shell casings, water-cans and even an old seat still protruded from the sand on the far bank of the river. 'I'm surprised the

Afghans missed them,' I said. 'They seem to have taken everything else.'

Amica shook her head. 'It's safer to leave them. The Soviets often booby-trapped them. Unfortunately, children are always the most curious. They're usually the ones who suffer.'

The remains of the convoy were part-buried, as if sinking slowly into quicksand. Each year's snow-melt and monsoon floods carried a fresh tide of sand and silt down from the mountains to bury them a little deeper. The doors of one truck gaped open and sand had filled the interior to the line of the bonnet. Stunted shrubs and grasses had taken root there.

In the fields near the river, I saw stepped mud-brick towers and pyramids crumbling slowly back into the earth. The faces of them were pierced with small rectangular holes.

'What are they?' I said. 'Forts? Watchtowers?'

Amica shook her head. 'Pigeon towers. Farmers used to eat the birds and collect the droppings for manure.'

'What happened to the pigeons?'

She shrugged. 'The men were killed and most of the irrigation system was destroyed. Until the fighting stops it will never be rebuilt, perhaps not even then.'

A few miles along the road we came to a halt at the first of a succession of checkpoints. They were manned by villagers, not Taliban, and marked the border of rival domains.

At each one I showed our documents and the forged pass purportedly issued by the Taliban, with crossed Kalashnikovs beneath an inscription from the Koran. A bribe of a thousand Afghanis also changed hands at each checkpoint. In return we were issued with another scrap of filthy paper, decorated with more Koranic inscriptions and the thumbprint of the local warlord, enough to guarantee us safe conduct as far as the next checkpoint.

As we climbed higher into the mountains, the sides of the valley closed in around us and the debris of battle became more and more frequent. The ditches at the foot of the steep hillsides were littered with the rusting remnants of trucks and tanks.

At one former Soviet outpost, overlooking the point where two roads met, a dozen shipping containers had been buried three-quarter deep in the ground. There were rows of narrow, blackened, vertical apertures near the top of each one.

Dexy grinned and pointed to them. 'The Sovs thought they could use them as miniature forts, but that thin metal couldn't withstand anything, machine guns, grenades or rockets. The Muj used to blast them apart with rockets, or they would pin the defenders down with gunfire while one man ran up and dropped a grenade inside. It opened them up like a tin of beans.'

A few miles further on, the valley walls receded and we drove on across a broad flood plain alongside the river. The fences or low mud walls dividing the fields had collapsed. In places a few had been repaired using pieces of armour plating, some still with fading Soviet markings.

But the fields flanking the river were still green and fertile. Boys and a few old men worked in them, cutting the last of the wheat with sickles. Others goaded on bony mules, dragging wooden ploughs and harrows across the cleared earth. Others still diverted water down the few remaining irrigation channels, using wooden shovelfuls of mud to stem or direct the flow.

We climbed higher. Through the suffocating fog of dust that surrounded us, I could smell the resinous tang of cedarwood as the forest closed in around the road. The sweat began to cool on me as the heat of the day faded and we climbed the first of the chain of passes that stood between us and Konarlan.

The shadows were lengthening and the sky growing dark. 'It's almost curfew,' I said.

Dexy nodded, his eyes flickering between the map, his GPS and the hillsides around us. 'Not far now.'

A few minutes later he checked his GPS again and pointed to the entrance of an overgrown track – little more than a path – into the forest. I pulled off the road and paused as Tank and Boon again jumped down and obliterated our tyre-marks.

The grassy track curved around the hillside and opened into a clearing. Around the edge stood the ruins of three houses. After I cut the engine I could hear the whisper of water; the river was somewhere among the trees below us. It would have been an idyllic scene had the houses not been scarred by shells and bullets, blackened by fire.

'Tank, Boon, take the first watch till we get sorted,' Dexy said. 'Rami and Jeff will take the second one, and Sean and I the third.'

'I should do my turn as well,' Amica said.

'You don't need to; three won't go into seven. You can get some sleep.' He paused. 'It's not because you're a woman. You're not trained for this.'

Tank and Boon were already moving back up towards the road, taking up firing positions among the trees overlooking the junction with the track. Jeff had begun to walk towards the only house with some semblance of a roof when Dexy stopped him. 'These places may have been empty since the Sovs left. There could be mines, booby-traps, anything.'

Jeff blanched as Dexy moved slowly towards the house, parting the undergrowth to scan the ground. He felt around the doorframe for wires, then disappeared inside. We waited in the silence of the gathering dusk.

He showed himself again fifteen minutes later. 'All clear,' he said. 'We'll get a brew on and eat some food, then get what rest we can. From tomorrow we'll be travelling by night and lying up by day. Make the most of this, it could be the last decent sleep we'll get until we hit Pakistan.'

The unspoken thought, 'If we hit Pakistan,' showed on every face. The interior of the house was covered in dust and rubble, but it was dry and offered some protection from the cold. Dexy left it to us to get a brew on, while he tried to contact the rest of the assault team on the net.

We cleared a sleeping area, then made black, sweet tea and sat sipping it in silence with our backs against the wall. I looked around the room. Jeff was sunk in introspection, tracing an endless pattern with his finger in the dust at his feet, his jaw moving slowly as he chewed at the inside of his cheek. Rami seemed hot-wired, starting at every small sound, his dark eyes darting everywhere. Only Amica looked calm and poised, as motionless as stone, her hands folded on her lap.

There was a faint noise from outside. Jeff stiffened and Rami slipped the safety-catch off his weapon. Amica merely turned her head to watch the door. A moment later Dexy slipped inside.

'All right?' I said.

He nodded. 'Dave and the boys were out last night. They've recced to within a couple of miles of the target. I told them to lie up where they are tonight and we can push on together at last light.'

We shared the fresh rations we had brought and drank some more tea, then Rami and Jeff relieved Tank and Boon and the rest of us settled down. I winced as I bumped my gashed shin against a piece of broken timber, then lay still. The silence was broken only by the sound of our breathing and the whine of mosquitoes. I closed my eyes and fell asleep almost at once.

I was back in the Q-shed in the Falklands. I could hear the rumble of aircraft, faint at first like distant thunder, but swelling to a deafening roar. Bombs began falling. The line of explosions marched towards us, growing louder and louder, shaking the ground. The roar of the aircraft and the blasts of bomb-bursts merged into a continuous wall of noise. I clapped my hands to my ears but could do nothing to stop the sound. My body was jerked, lifted and thrown sideways against the wall.

I woke and lay for a second, staring into the darkness. It was a familiar nightmare, but this time it did not fade. I tried to get to my feet, but my legs seemed unable to obey me and I stumbled and fell.

I saw a blacker shape in the darkness, the archway leading to the ruined interior of the house. I tried to reach it but the ground seemed to shake and buck beneath my feet. My foot caught something soft and I heard Amica cry out. I reached down and pulled her to her feet, dragging her with me, my arm around her shoulder.

'Incoming!' I heard Dexy yell. 'Get down! Get down!'

A torrent of rubble was crashing down around us. I moved Amica into the doorway and we cowered in the shelter of the lintel, pressed together. Dexy flattened himself against the other side of the doorframe a moment later.

A battery of sharp, snapping, explosive sounds was undercut by a thunderous roar, an avalanche of sound so deep it seemed to come from the bowels of the earth. The ground jerked upwards.

'What the hell's happening?' Dexy shouted, his voice almost buried in the din.

Amica's voice was close to my ear. 'It's an earthquake.'

As she spoke, the ground gave beneath my feet again and there was a massive crash. The roof was torn apart and the jagged, broken end of a huge beam speared downwards, impaling the blanket on which Amica had been lying. A wall of dust blotted out everything except the noise. All I could hear were the rumble and crash of falling rock and the explosive crack of huge cedars snapping like matchsticks.

As suddenly as they had begun, the tremors faded and died. I was still pressed against Amica's trembling body, shielding her as I clung to the doorframe as if it were a liferaft.

The silence seemed almost as oppressive as the noise that had gone before it. The dust began to settle around us, but I remained where I was, too scared to move. Then I felt Amica's hand on my arm. We both looked up.

The roof had disappeared and the room lay open to the stars. I stepped away from her and began to pick my way uncertainly through the mounds of fresh rubble. 'Dexy?'

'I'm all right.' He stepped out of the shadow of the lintel. I saw movement in the outer doorway and Tank took a few cautious steps away from his sanctuary.

'Where's Boon?'

There was a muffled reply. Half-buried by rubble, he was lying face-down on the ground, his arms in a protective cradle over his head.

'Are you all right?'

'I will be when you get this shit off me.'

Relief from the fear and tension made us laugh. Then I remembered Jeff and Rami. I ran outside and saw a figure coming down the slope towards me. 'Jeff?'

'Rami.'

'Where's Jeff?'

He spat. 'Up there, crying like a baby.'

I could hear the tremor in his own voice and fought down the urge to punch him. I stumbled up the hillside, clambering over toppled trees and fallen rocks. Jeff was sitting at the base of a huge cedar, which was now leaning precariously down the slope.

He was facing away from me with his arms wrapped around the trunk. His face was pressed into the bark, his shoulders shaking.

His rifle lay on the ground, half-buried by debris. I picked it up and brushed the dirt from it, then put a hand on his shoulder. 'Come on, Jeff. It's okay, it's over.'

He didn't move.

'I nearly shat myself there,' I said. 'I thought our time was up.'

He turned his head to look at me. 'I'm going to die here.'

'Don't talk crap. It was just an earthquake; they happen all the time here.'

I took hold of his hand and prised it away from the tree. 'Now get a grip. We've a job to do.' I took his arm and led him back down to the clearing.

A fine dust still hung in the air, softening the pink light of dawn. Pale-lit, the clearing had been transformed. A torrent of rock had scythed down the hillside, sweeping away almost everything in its path to the river. I could see the silver glint of water among the tangled boulders and shattered trees. The other two houses had collapsed completely. Only a single wall still stood, like a gravestone above the mounds of rubble.

The pick-up was where we had left it, but a fallen cedar had buried the rear of the vehicle to the axles.

The others were grouped around it. 'The quake could be our ally,' Dexy said. 'Taliban communications aren't that good at the best of times. After this they can only be worse, and most of their soldiers will be on rescue duty. We can turn it to our advantage, if we can get this bloody tree off and the suspension hasn't collapsed completely.'

'Even if it hasn't,' I said, 'how are we going to get it back to the road?' I pointed along the track. It was blocked with boulders and fallen trees.

Dexy looked towards the scar on the hillside. 'We'll get it up there.'

'And how do we get the tree off?' Amica said. 'We've no saws or axes.'

'We don't need them,' Dexy said. 'You guys dig our kit out while Tank and I fix some charges.'

We dug our bergens out of the rubble, then I watched as they laid two necklaces of small charges around the trunk on either side of the pick-up and ran a det-cord back to the shelter of the ruin. 'What if the Taliban hear the explosion?' Jeff said.

Dexy smiled. 'We'll be long gone before anyone gets round to investigating, and I think they've enough to worry about right now.'

There was a roar as the explosives detonated and splinters whistled through the air above us. The tree had been severed as neatly as if it had been cut by a circular saw, but a six-foot section still lay across the back.

Boon and I climbed in behind it and pushed and shoved, our feet struggling for grip on the dusty floor of the pick-up. We moved the trunk a little, then it stuck fast. Tank lashed a rope around it and we lined up like a tug-of-war team and began to heave on it. The trunk rocked and fell back again a couple of times, then toppled off the back with a crash. The pick-up rose a couple of inches on its springs.

'Thank God for that,' said Dexy. 'We're in with a chance.' He grabbed a broken branch and began to lever the twisted bodywork away from the tyres while Tank and Boon dug away the soil. Then Dexy gunned the engine as we pushed against the back, choking on the dust as the wheels spun and then gripped, and the pick-up lurched clear.

Dexy paused, revving the engine as he studied the path of the landslide, looking for a way up. It had scoured the soil down to the bedrock in places; in others boulders and tree stumps littered the slope.

The rest of us watched from the clearing as he let in the clutch and sent the pick-up careering up the slope. It hit each bump with a dull thud and a groan of tortured metal. A third of the way up, as he fishtailed between a tree stump and a huge boulder, he lost momentum and slid to a halt. He revved the engine hard, but the wheels spun and he could get no higher.

As he slid back down for another run, I again felt the earth shift beneath my feet. There was a deep bass rumble and I swayed, rocked and dropped to my knees. As the aftershock began to fade, I saw a boulder further up the slope jolt free and roll downhill. It gathered speed, taking a small avalanche of rocks with it.

Dexy was still reversing down the hillside. I yelled a warning, even though I knew he could not have heard it above the noise of the engine and the rumble of the quake. The boulder smashed into a ridge of exposed rock and took off, cleaving an arc through the air towards the pick-up.

Still oblivious, Dexy spun the wheel to take him back across the clearing. I saw his face change as the shadow of the boulder darkened the cab. There was the crack of metal and shattering glass as it struck the corner of the cab above his head. It hurtled away, smashing its way down the hillside to shatter in a thousand pieces as it hit the rock face on the other side of the river.

The pick-up had ground to a halt in front of us, the windscreen crazed and opaque. For a moment no one moved, then a fist punched through the screen, and Dexy's face appeared, framed in the hole. 'There goes my no-claims bonus.' He grinned, but not as convincingly as before.

The impact had dented the roof and jammed one of the doors. I slid along the seat, kicking out the rest of the windscreen with my boots. 'Right, let's get the hell out of here before anything else falls off the mountain.'

I reversed right to the edge of the clearing, revved the motor until it screamed, then let in the clutch and hurtled at the slope. The pick-up was airborne clearing the low ridge, and I almost lost it as I landed. I fought it back under control and kept the revs high, swerving around the tree stumps and boulders. I caught one huge rock a glancing blow, but still had just enough momentum to reach the top.

The rest of the team saw the glow of brakelights and began running up the slope after me, while I grabbed a piece of sacking and rubbed oil and dust over the fresh white scars on the bodywork.

Before we moved off, Dexy tried to raise Dave on the net, repeating the call-sign over and over again. The only answer was the hiss of static. 'They're probably just holding radio silence,' Dexy said. 'Maybe there's a Taliban patrol nearby.' The others nodded in agreement, but I could tell that nobody bought into it.

I drove at a crawl into the gathering dawn, unsure what might be around the next corner. Stretches of dirt road had been buckled and fissured, and half-blocked by rock falls. We paused before every bridge.

There was a stream of people fleeing the mountains, shoulders bowed. They raised their faces to peer at us as we passed, but there was no curiosity in their eyes, only resignation.

Along one stretch, half the road had been carried away. We crept past, the offside wheels an inch from the edge. I looked down a sheer drop to the river, a gash in the red earth.

Dexy had tuned the car-radio to the Taliban 'Voice of Sharia'. The normal diet of martial music and prayers was interrupted by a special announcement. 'The Army of the Islamic Emirate of Afghanistan is already working to rescue those trapped and injured in the earthquake which struck the Emirate in the early hours of this morning. It is believed that the epicentre was in the mountains north of Konarlan.

'The religious people of Konarlan and Badansan provinces are providing with love every assistance they can to the forces of the Islamic Emirate. They are thanking Allah for their salvation. The officials of the Islamic Emirate are in touch with the people and are helping to solve their problems swiftly.

'Mullah Muhammed Omar has sent his condolences but has issued a warning that when corruption festers in an Islamic area, Allah becomes angry and punishes the people. Unless they follow the Taliban and Sharia law, the punishment of Allah will continue.'

Dexy made me pull off the road at once and again tried to contact Dave on the net. Once more there was no reply. Jeff caught my eye and gave a slow shake of his head.

Tank saw him and reacted angrily. 'Don't be so quick to write them off.'

We worked our way onwards into the mountains. By midday the stream of humanity had dwindled to a trickle. We saw no traffic or livestock and very few people. The blasted landscape through which we passed was now all but deserted.

By mid-afternoon we were climbing a steep pass, the engine of the pick-up groaning. I pulled off the road into the cover of the trees two miles short of the summit and the Taliban guard post overlooking Konarlan.

The near end of the valley looked almost untouched by the earthquake, but in the distance beyond Konarlan I could see grey and yellow gashes of bare earth on the slopes, rents torn in the fabric of the forest.

Dexy was staring beyond Konarlan towards the hidden valley where his troops were lying-up . . . if they were still alive.

'What's the plan?' I said.

'We have to get to the LUP, link up with the other guys if they're there and then press on to the target. We've only got forty-eight hours and there's a lot of miles to cover.' He paused. 'But first we have to deal with that guard post.' He stabbed his finger at the map. 'If we're not back by 20.00 hours, make for the emergency RV at grid 352683. The window is 22.00 to 22.10. After that, if there's no show from us, you're on your own.'

Rami, Boon and Tank followed him up the hillside, moving silently through the trees. We were invisible from the road, but I could not have felt more exposed. I closed my hand around the butt of the Kalashnikov, but it offered little reassurance.

I glanced at the others. Their expressions seemed to mirror my own. 'We're too vulnerable here. We'll lie up in the woods where we can watch the road and the pick-up. Here we're just sitting targets.'

We worked our way in among the trees. We couldn't risk making a brew, but we drank some water and divided the last of the naan bread and fruit we'd brought with us, putting aside a share for the other guys. 'That's it,' I said. 'From now on it's emergency rations and what we can scavenge.'

We settled down to watch and wait as the sun sank the last few degrees to the horizon. At last the approach of dusk purpled the hillside with shadows and the birds in the wood behind us began to fall silent.

I heard a vehicle approaching from the west. We flattened ourselves in the undergrowth as the engine note grew louder and a red Toyota pick-up flashed into view. I could make out more than a dozen Taliban soldiers clinging to the back as it raced past and disappeared up the hill.

I caught Jeff's eye. 'Don't worry. We've heard no shooting, so the guys can't have been compromised. The Taliban are probably just on their way to help out in the earthquake zone.'

His expression didn't change. 'Or they're looking for us.'

'Well, they haven't found us, have they?'

He shrugged. 'But I wish they were still behind us instead of somewhere in front.'

Another hour dragged by, then I heard a voice further up the road. I slid off the safety-catch and peered into the darkness, picking up the white flash of a turban. I took aim at a point two feet below it and tracked the single figure as it approached.

I saw the outline of an old man's bearded face as he drew level and staggered past, his wavering voice rising and falling in an endless lamentation. He stumbled frequently in the dark and once fell full length in the dirt. He pulled himself up again and carried on, moving away until the darkness swallowed him up again. The sound of his voice faded to a whisper and then died away altogether.

I glanced at my watch. 'Fifty minutes before deadline.'

No one replied.

Forty minutes later there was still no sign of the others. I inched my way over to Amica and Jeff. 'We need to get our shit together. If there's no sign of them in ten minutes, we have to take off.'

'Shouldn't we wait a bit longer?' Amica said.

I shook my head. 'It'll take us all of two hours to get to the Emergency RV.'

'And if they don't show there?'

I shrugged. 'Like Dexy said, we'll be on our own.'

'No you won't, we're here.'

I had seen no trace of sound or movement, but Dexy and the guys were standing in the trees just behind us.

'You guys had better improve your sentry skills. If we'd been the Taliban, you'd be dead by now.'

It took me a moment to calm my nerves. 'What about the guard post?'

'It's unmanned . . . now.'

'And the red Toyota?'

'Stopped for a look around, found the post deserted and went straight on. It stopped a couple of miles down the other side, though. Either something's going on down there or the road is out. We'll get a bit closer, then have a look. Let's go.'

He touched my arm as I got behind the wheel. 'It's after curfew and we're a long way from home. Use the moonlight to steer by, and as soon as you clear the summit start freewheeling. Only use the engine when you have to. I'll tap on the cab when I want you to stop.'

He jumped in the back. I drove past the deserted guard post and began to freewheel down the other side of the pass, bump-starting the engine to clear a couple of rises. I'd just shut off the engine for the third time when I heard Dexy's tap on the cab roof. I braked to a halt at once.

He sent Tank and Boon forward to recce the road ahead. They came back some twenty minutes later, silent as shadows. 'The Taliban vehicle's still there,' Tank said, 'but there's no sign of the soldiers. The road's been swept away just beyond it. They must have gone further up the valley on foot.'

'We'll have to do the same,' Dexy said.

As we began to unload the bergens, Rami glanced towards us, then touched Dexy's arm. 'Dexy, a word. Over here.'

The two of them moved a few yards away. A minute later Dexy shook his head and began to walk back towards us. 'Get ready to move out.'

'What about the pick-up?' I said.

'It's served its purpose. Send it the same way the road went.'

I got back in, released the brake and let the pick-up freewheel down the road. I saw the shape of the Toyota outlined against the sky ahead of me. I eased past it, then braked at the edge of the landslip. Fifty yards away I could see the road continue, a gray ribbon in the moonlight.

I pulled the wheel over, but kept my foot on the brake as I opened the door and eased myself out. At the last moment I released the brake and threw myself back as the pick-up rolled over the brink and vanished from view. I heard it tumbling down the mountainside long after it had disappeared from sight. 'If the suspension wasn't knackered before,' I said, 'it sure as hell is now.'

The weight of my bergen made me stagger as I hoisted it on to my shoulders. We roped ourselves together and then began to inch our way out across the rock slide. Darkness made the cliff seem even more sheer. Stones and small rocks slipped away from under my feet at each step, bouncing away down the mountainside.

I'd crossed far worse traverses in my climbing days, but I could tell that Jeff, in front of me on the rope, was badly frightened, and it made him lean towards the mountainside, trying to hug the slope. 'Stand more upright, Jeff,' I said. 'You may feel safer at that angle, but your weight's actually pushing your feet sideways and it's more likely you'll slip.'

As I spoke, the rope jerked and tightened as he slid away down the slope. I grabbed a handhold and braced myself to take the strain, but as the rope snapped taut, it almost dislodged me as well.

I heard a muffled curse as Tank, on Jeff's other side, struggled to hold on. I waited a few seconds. 'It's okay, Jeff. Climb back up. We'll take the strain.'

He didn't move. He was gripping the mountainside, staring straight ahead of him into the rock an inch from his nose. I had seen people freeze before at times like this. Sometimes they could pull themselves out of it, but usually they had to be helped.

Rami was just behind me on the rope. 'Brace yourself,' I said. 'I'm going to climb down to him.'

'Be quick,' he said. 'If we're spotted here, we're finished.'

I ignored him and began to work my way down. I dug in next to him, holding myself against the cliff with my feet and knees, then reached over, took Jeff's right hand and tried to move it. He was rigid.

'Come on,' I said. 'Just move your hand a couple of inches and put it down again.'

He didn't even turn his head. 'I can't.'

'You'll have to. If we can't move you, we'll have to cut the rope and leave you here.' The tone of my voice as much as my words got his attention. He turned his head a fraction as I forced his hand away from the rock. He gave a gasp as it came free. I pushed it upwards. 'Find a handhold, find a hold. All right?'

Without waiting for a reply, I reached across him and advanced his left hand a couple of inches. We moved with painful slowness, inching our way up the slope to the ledge where the others stood waiting. I shortened the rope between us and guided him on across the scarred mountainside. He grew in confidence as we reached the other side, and made the last few yards to the road unaided.

As soon as he realised he was safe, he sank to the ground and shook uncontrollably. I grabbed him by the arm. 'Don't show weakness,' I said. 'That bastard Rami has already tried to ditch us. We must move on.' I didn't give him time to think about it. I pulled him to his feet and shoved him down the track in front of me.

We moved in 400-yard stages. Dexy was lead scout, Tank at number two. Jeff, Amica and I came in the middle, with Boon and Rami at the back. We moved in silence, communicating only in whispers or clicks of the tongue. Before each stage we would pause to look and listen, then move on again.

Konarlan was just visible lower in the valley, but there was not a light to be seen. Half a mile short of the village we left the road, working our way round the north side through the tangled cedar forest. The guys moved in complete silence. Jeff, Amica and I struggled after them, trying not to snap twigs underfoot or scuff our feet.

In the darkness it was impossible to see how much of the village was still standing. Twice we froze as dogs barked. It was the only sign that the village was still occupied.

We had passed the last houses and begun moving back towards the track when dawn started to break. Dexy checked his GPS and we began to search for a place to lie up for the day. After twenty minutes, we found a huge toppled cedar, its broken roots standing clear of the soil.

We moved another 400 yards past it, then looped back. We dragged brush and undergrowth against the roots, then crawled wearily into the hide as Tank and Boon took the first watch. The guilt I felt at resting while they stood guard did not last long.

Dexy glanced across at Amica and grinned. 'If the Taliban find us, you're in deep shit, Amica, lying with six men and not married to one of us.'

She didn't smile back. 'If the Taliban find us, we're all dead.'

She lay down next to me in the cramped space, so close I could feel the warmth of her breath on my cheek, and closed her eyes. I lay watching her in the gathering light. The scars across her nails made my jaw clench.

She opened her eyes and smiled gently, then closed them again. A few moments later her breathing slowed and she was asleep.

Dexy was trying to raise Dave on the net, but yet again all he got was white noise. He hesitated for a moment, then contacted base on the sat-phone. 'Base, this is Raider Three. There has been an earthquake. We've lost radio contact with eight members of our patrol in an LUP near the target.'

There was a silence as the base controller digested the news, then an American accent came up through the static. 'Roger, Raider Three. The mission remains paramount and you have less than forty-eight hours to accomplish it. What do you propose?'

'To go to the LUP and investigate, and then carry out the mission with whatever personnel we have.'

'Roger that.'

Chapter 12

I dozed for a few hours, then took a turn on watch in the early afternoon. A trickle of people was still moving down from the mountains towards Konarlan. A few clutched tattered bundles; most were empty-handed, their dirt-encrusted faces weary, their eyes downcast. One old man slumped at the roadside, too exhausted to carry on. He accosted every passing person. Each one shook his head and moved on.

As soon as it was dark, we prepared to move. Jeff disappeared, heading for the rough scrape of a latrine Boon had dug a few yards away. When he came back a few minutes later I saw a flash of white in the darkness as he stuffed something into his bergen.

'For Christ's sake, Jeff. You haven't brought those bloody toilet rolls?'

He looked up, his expression defensive.

We shouldered our bergens, but paused for five minutes at

the edge of the road, watching and listening, before we moved out in single file. Hunger gnawed at my guts and I felt tired before we'd even started the night's march. The straps of my bergen sliced into my shoulders, and every time we paused to listen and watch I slipped my hands under them to ease the weight.

As we moved closer to the heart of the earthquake zone, the silence of the night became complete. We paused at midnight to drink some water and eat a few mouthfuls of our rations. An hour later we passed the ruins of a walled garden. The grapevines that had sprawled over the domed earth mounds had been pulverised and buried in rubble, but a few unripe apricots still clung to the branches of a tree, the only one still standing in that valley of desolation. We ate some and filled our pockets before moving on.

As dawn approached, I was stumbling with tiredness, but Dexy still forced us on. A large village lay between us and the LUP where we'd left the rest of the troop and where the valley walls converged.

We stopped short of the outskirts and held a whispered conference. 'We can work our way around the cliffs,' Dexy said, 'but it looks hard going. I think we should risk the village.'

'What if we're compromised?' Tank said. 'Do we fight or bluff?'

'Bluff,' Dexy said. 'We can't afford to shoot it out this far from the target.' He glanced at Rami. 'Agreed?'

Rami said nothing.

Dexy studied him for a moment. 'If you have a problem with this, now's the time to say so. Don't come to me afterwards and say we should have done something else.'

Rami looked up. 'Agreed.'

We began to move towards the village. There was a network

of fissures and crevasses across the ground. The houses at the western side had simply disintegrated into the soil from which they were built. We picked our way through the rubble of what had once been living rooms and courtyards.

Nearer to the centre of the village many of the buildings were intact, and a maze of dark, high-walled alleyways confronted us. Dexy led us away from the main track and through the narrow side alleys. High above us I could see the stars, but ahead was a dark tunnel, unbroken except by wooden doorways, and small barred windows.

We huddled in the shadows at the entrance to a small square. Dexy checked his compass and led us across, towards another labyrinth. We passed a break in the façade where a house had collapsed, then were hemmed in again by the fortress walls.

Whether through tiredness or inattention, Jeff tripped and stumbled and his boot dislodged a pebble. It rattled away across the cobbles. We all froze. I could feel the rapid beat of my heart as I waited, straining my ears for any answering sound.

After five minutes we began to advance again. I could see the open ground at the end of the alley glowing a faint grey in the starlight. There was a sudden guttural shout from the rooftops above us. I glanced upwards and saw a figure outlined against the night sky.

I slid the safety-catch off my rifle and heard the faint metallic clicks as the others did the same. The challenge was repeated. I looked up again. More figures had joined the first and I saw the glint of gunmetal.

I looked ahead, towards the end of the alley, where more dark figures blocked our way. I heard footsteps in the dust behind us.

A figure on the rooftop challenged us again, first in Pushtu and then in Farsi. 'Who are you?'

There was a moment's pause. 'We are travellers seeking shelter,' I said.

I heard a whispered conversation above us then there was a flare as a lantern was lit. It swung in the wind as they lowered it into the alley towards us. The watchers were now invisible to us, but we were sitting targets.

I heard Amica's urgent whisper close behind me. 'Don't be defensive. Take the initiative. They're Muslim, demand hospitality.'

I swallowed. 'Is this the way your village receives guests? Enough of this foolishness, we travel under the protection of the Taliban.'

They swung the lantern towards me. 'You are not Afghans,' the voice said.

'We are Arab fighters for the cause. We speak the language of the Prophet.' I gave them a sample of my best Arabic to prove it, then waited, my scalp pricking, sweat trickling down my neck.

There was a long pause, then another shout and the lantern was jerked upwards. 'Walk to the end of the alley,' the voice commanded.

I saw Tank turn to say something to Jeff who then whispered to me: 'Stay spread out, we'll be harder targets.'

We came out into a broad square and stood facing a circle of villagers training Kalashnikovs on us. A ladder carved from a single tree trunk was propped against the end house. The men on the rooftop clambered down and the leader walked towards us. 'Brothers, if you are what you say, you are welcome in our village.'

He held up the lantern so that he could see our faces. By its light I also saw him for the first time. His beard was grey, but his thick eyebrows formed jet-black bars across his face, accentuating his piercing gaze. 'You have papers?'

I fumbled in my pocket and produced the dog-eared, forged Taliban pass.

He stared at it in silence for some time and did not hand it back. 'You are breaking the curfew,' he said.

'We are doing it to try to save men's lives.'

'What is your business here?'

'We are fighters,' I said, 'but we have come to help rescue people trapped by the earthquake.'

'On whose authority did you travel here?'

'With the permission of Mullah Nur of Konarlan.' I held my breath. If the man had a radio or even a cellphone, one call would reveal the lie.

There was a long silence. 'You have travelled far, I hope you are not too tired.'

The tension eased as he began the ritual greetings. His men even laughed and joked with us as we walked across the square towards the mosque. It appeared to have survived the earthquake almost intact, but as we were led inside I could see starlight through a jagged crack snaking out towards the apex of the dome.

Amica was led away by two women, the rest of us propped our bergens against the wall and were ushered to a low table. We sat on cushions as black tea, cold rice and cucumber were laid before us. The hospitality was offered without resentment, though from the meagre offerings they put before us, they had little enough to spare.

When we finished, we spread our hands palms upwards and said grace, thanking Allah for the food, then wiped our hands on our beards and turbans.

The villagers asked about the destruction that the earthquake had wrought lower down the valley and discussed their own losses without rancour or self-pity, brushing away the destruction of crops, buildings and lives with a shrug of the shoulders.

There was a shuffle of feet at the entrance to the mosque. I glanced up and saw two of the villagers leading in a white-bearded figure in the black turban and robes of a mullah. He limped heavily across the floor and lowered himself on to the cushions.

He peered at each of us in turn, staring over the top of his round, wire-rimmed glasses with unblinking concentration. He put out his hand and the elder passed him the forged Taliban pass. He studied it with minute care, turning the paper over and over in his hands. 'You are under the protection of Mullah Nur, you say.'

We nodded our agreement.

'Yet this is not his seal.' The villagers stopped talking among themselves and moved closer to the table, fingering their weapons.

'No, it is not,' I said. 'Two weeks ago we were in Kabul. The seal is that of Taliban commander Salan. That is his mark.' I pointed to the thumbprint pressed on to the corner of the pass.

He looked at it again. 'I do not know this man.'

'We are a long way from Kabul,' I said, 'but I am surprised that his name is not known here, for he is a brave fighter and a fine leader.'

Dexy and Rami picked up their cue, nodding sagely.

'He killed many Soviets,' I said, 'including a garrison commander.' There were more nods of approval, this time from the villagers and accompanied by calls of 'Allah Akhbar'.

The mullah remained motionless.

'We are grateful for your hospitality,' I said, 'but we have travelled far and are tired. It will soon be dawn and we must sleep a little then move on. Every hour's delay in reaching the heart of the earthquake zone may mean more lives are lost.'

'Our leader has travelled up the valley today,' he said,

lowering his voice as he said the name. 'He will wish to talk with you on his return.'

I bowed my head. 'Then we shall meet him on the road.'

His gaze still held mine and he continued as if I had not spoken. 'He will wish to see you here on his return.'

'And when will that be?'

'Today, Insh'Allah.'

I glanced at Dexy, who gave the faintest of nods. I spread my hands. 'We are your guests.'

One of the villagers walked forward and whispered in his ear. He fixed me with his heavy-lidded gaze. 'You are carrying explosives.'

I looked behind me at the bergens. One had been opened and I could see detonator cord and slabs of PE. I struggled to keep my face neutral. 'We may have to blast our way through rockslides or into buildings to rescue survivors.' I held his gaze.

He stood up and placed his hand on his heart. 'May your rest be comfortable. We will talk again later.' His voice was friendly, but his eyes remained cold.

We made a move towards our packs, but the Mullah held up his hand. 'They will be looked after.'

I hesitated and then bowed. 'You are truly kind.'

There was just a trace of a smile across his face before he turned away to talk to one of the villagers.

'What do we do?' I said in Arabic.

Dexy shrugged. 'We have no choice, we wait for their leader.'

'We could take these peasants easily,' Rami said. 'They've got our bergens, but we've still got our pistols.'

Dexy shook his head. 'Even if we get away, we'll have blown the mission. We'll have every Taliban soldier for miles around on our tail. All we can do is wait.'

'But we've got less than forty-eight hours——'

'And we can manage it in twenty-four if we have to,' Dexy said.

The villagers led each of us to separate low-ceilinged cells, their floors sunk below the level of the rest of the mosque. There were no windows to the outside, only a small barred opening high up on the inside wall, looking back into the interior of the mosque.

There was a rug in the middle of the floor, but no cushions, and I made myself as comfortable as I could. A moment later the door closed and I heard the clack of a latch. There was no handle on the inside. I lay down and closed my eyes.

I was woken by the voice of the muezzin, calling the faithful to prayer. Some time later, a mug of brown water and a tin platter containing a few grains of rice were pushed inside the door.

'Has your leader returned?'

The man shrugged. 'He will be here soon, Insh'Allah.'

The door slammed shut again. I put two-thirds of the rice in my pocket, saving it for later, and then forced myself to make a ritual meal of the remainder, first washing my hands with a little of the water and then eating the rice one grain at a time.

The calls of the muezzin punctuated the long day, summoning the village to prayers at noon, before sunset, before last light and once more when darkness had fallen.

The whole day had passed with no sign of the warlord's return. After the last prayers, the villagers remained in the mosque, and the mullah began to chant.

Slow at first, the chant began to quicken, 'Allah Hu, Allah Hu.' It became higher and faster. I could hear the mullah's followers striking their heads and chests with their open hands. They carried on for an hour or more, their shouts reverberating across the dome. At last the mullah called a halt, his voice hoarse and cracking. The men roared out a last chorus: 'Allah Hu. Death to traitors. Allah Akhbar. Death to our enemies.'

There was a sudden flurry of movement, the latch was withdrawn and the door swung open. We were marched across the mosque and lined up standing in a row, facing a familiar warlord, who had finally returned.

Agha Shah Azuin's keen hazel eyes missed nothing as his gaze ranged over each of us in turn. He raised an eyebrow as he recognised me, but said nothing for the moment. His expression changed when he saw Dexy. He sat motionless for a moment, then stood up and strode around the table to embrace him.

Dexy cracked a broad grin as the warlord turned to his men. 'This is a brave fighter. He fought alongside me in the war against the Soviets and killed many men. I learned much from him. He and his companions are our honoured guests.'

He led Dexy back around the table and sat him in the place of honour on the cushions to his right-hand side. Then he called his son, who was standing in the shadows by the wall. 'Daru, you have heard me speak often of a brave *faranji* warrior. This is the man.'

The boy greeted Dexy and the rest of us gravely, touching his hand to his heart, then took his place at the table between Dexy and me. Food and sweet black tea were brought and laid before us.

While the warlord and Dexy traded reminiscences of the Soviet war, Daru told me of the devastation further up the valley — villages wiped out, tracts of forest swept away and whole hills obliterated without trace, leaving him struggling to find a familiar landmark. Then he glanced around him and lowered his voice. 'I know what you are. My father has spoken often of the brave *faranji* warriors who helped us against the Soviets.'

Seeking a safer subject, I pointed to the figure seated on the far side of his father, as tall and powerful as the warlord himself. 'Who is that?'

'My uncle. He leaves tomorrow on a *haj* – a pilgrimage to Mecca. His house was destroyed in the earthquake. He thinks it was a punishment from Allah because he has not been a good Muslim.'

I smiled. 'You should go with him, Daru. Think of the fortunes to be made supplying the pilgrims with food, drink and souvenirs.'

'My father has forbidden it.' Daru's voice showed his injured pride. 'He says I am too young to cross the mountains to Dir.'

'But that's in Pakistan. Why not Kabul?'

He tapped the side of his nose. 'The charter planes that fly pilgrims to Mecca from Dir also carry lapis.'

'And when they return they also bring back other things than pilgrims?'

He smiled. 'You ask too many questions, Inglisi.'

It was now almost dawn. We breakfasted on naan bread and green tea and then walked to the door of the mosque. Our bergens were laid out in a neat row outside, the contents undisturbed. His men lounged on the steps nearby, but Azuin led us across the square alone. 'I will walk with you to the edge of the village and guarantee your safety with my body.'

Daru tried to join us, but his father sent him back. The boy gave him a reproachful look, then smiled at us, touched his hand to his heart and walked away.

Azuin shouted a command and a group of women led Amica from a nearby house. She kept her head down and her gaze averted, and took her place a few paces behind us as we filed out of the square.

There was a volley of shots. I flinched, my heart pounding, and Jeff ducked. There was more ragged firing, as the warlord's men gave us a traditional farewell, loosing off rounds into the sky. Jeff straightened again, avoiding my eye.

At the edge of the village Azuin turned to Dexy. 'The debt of hospitality that I owe to you has been repaid. You were once my friend and ally, but now your country is the enemy of mine. You are free to leave my territory and I will not pursue you or betray you to the Taliban, but if you return in the future, I will have to kill you.'

He touched his hand to his heart as we filed past him and moved away up the dusty track. He remained motionless as we climbed the hillside and raised a hand in farewell just before we passed beyond the ridge.

We held a quick council of war at the side of the track. 'We're blown,' Rami said. 'We have to abort.'

Dexy shook his head. 'I know Agha. He's a man of his word. I say we go on.'

Rami shrugged. 'We're screwed either way.'

'So let's get on with it, then.' Dexy glanced at Tank and Boon. 'Okay with you guys?'

They nodded.

'And the Air Force?'

'I'd rather take my chances with you lot than the warlord and his mates back there.'

He turned to Amica. 'I am a mere woman,' she said. 'What can I do but follow my men?'

We shouldered our bergens and moved on up the road. It forked after a mile, the left branch following the track of the river towards the target, the right one curling away across a ridge into the valley beyond. Without a pause, Dexy led us up the right-hand track.

'This is the wrong one,' Jeff said.

'He knows that,' I said. I pointed behind us at the marks of our bootprints impressed in the dust.

We followed the track for almost a mile up the hillside. As we climbed, it became more stony and when we reached a broad band of rock, Dexy checked and then led us back down into the forest. Boon dropped back to obliterate any trace of our tracks. We worked our way down through the forest, grateful for the shade.

I caught a glimpse of the other road below us, and we began to make our way parallel to it. Dexy paused to check his map. 'We'll be able to see the LUP from the next ridge.' He made one more attempt to call Dave on the net. There was still no response.

When we reached the ridgeline, he frowned and re-examined the map. I moved up alongside him and glanced down into the valley.

The site chosen for the hide had been the face of a rounded hill on the opposite side of the valley. Stands of larch and cedar had covered the hillside, bordering a stream. It now looked like an open-cast mine. Topsoil and rock had been ripped away in an ugly gash half a mile wide. The stream had disappeared completely, choked by boulders, broken trees and rubble.

The shape of the hill was still just recognisable, but the trees, the undergrowth and every other living thing had been swept away. 'Maybe they were out patrolling,' I said.

Dexy remained motionless.

'Maybe they were recceing further up the valley.'

He shook his head. 'I told them to stay here.'

We moved down the hillside in silence, pausing to listen and watch at the side of the road. We climbed on to the moraine of loose rubble at the foot of the slope – the burial mound of eight men.

I stared stupidly at the ground beneath my feet. Then I glimpsed a smudge of khaki among the chocolate-brown dust. I tugged at it and uncovered a webbing strap. As I pulled away more of the rocks and soil, the corner of a bergen began to emerge.

Galvanised, the others began to rip and tear at the mound of rubble. Tank and Boon used broken branches like crowbars, levering out the larger rocks. Every few minutes we stopped to call and listen. There was no reply.

Dexy found another bergen a few minutes later. The discovery made Boon and Tank redouble their efforts. They sent a large boulder toppling, setting up a small avalanche of smaller rocks and dirt, and a human hand stuck out of the newly exposed patch of earth. I bent towards it, praying that there would be some response from the fingers. There was none. More earth and rubble slid away, exposing the rest of the arm and a head.

Dave's sightless, dust-rimmed eyes stared at the sky, his mouth hanging open in a silent scream. I pressed my fingers to his neck, but I already knew there would be no pulse.

I heard Dexy cursing behind me. 'Shit. Shit. Shit.'

He worked alongside me as we pulled away more soil and rock. Dave had died upright. Two other bodies were sprawled around his feet, engulfed and suffocated by the landslide before they even had a chance to get to their knees.

I could see Dexy's jaw clenching and unclenching as he looked at them. One was SAS, the other Delta Force. Tank and Boon were still digging frantically, but Dexy called them off. 'Forget it,' he said. 'They're dead and buried already. Let's leave them that way.'

We stood in a semi-circle, with our backs to the bodies behind us. 'Well?' Rami said.

'We go on.'

Dexy raised base on the sat-phone. 'This is Raider Three. We've found the others. They're dead.'

'Compromised?'

'No, killed in a landslide.'

There was a pause. 'And the mission?'

'Will be carried out to schedule,' Dexy said. He broke the connection.

Rami stared at him. 'We've got four trained men, two pilots and a woman. We're going to attack one of the best defended targets in Afghanistan. Be realistic. We haven't got a chance.'

Dexy's eyes were cold. 'The smaller the force, the greater the chance of getting through. And we can still carry enough kit to do the job.' He paused. 'Be glad you still have the chance, instead of lying there dead.'

Rami turned back to the mound. 'We're dead anyway.' He looked around for support, fastening on Jeff when the rest of us blanked him.

Jeff cleared his throat. 'Dexy's right. If these guys have taught us anything, it's how to die like men.'

'You can say that?' Rami said.

Jeff ignored the sneer. 'I was frightened before, I admit that. I'm not now.'

Tank slapped him on the back. 'You're the man, Jeff. Spoken like an American.'

We retrieved the bergens from beside the other two bodies and Dexy began sharing out the explosives and detonators between us. 'Carry the maximum,' he said. 'Maximum explosives, maximum ammunition. Ditch anything we don't need. Amica, you'd better lose that burka, it'll be no protection where we're going, anyway. Rami, you're about her size – give her your spare trousers and jacket.'

Amica took the clothes from Rami without a word. I saw the sheen of her olive skin and the curve of her breasts as she shrugged her burka over her head and shoulders. She pulled on the shirt and trousers, and handed me her knife. 'Cut my hair,' she said. 'Crop it as close to the scalp as you can.'

I made a few careful cuts, remembering the agony as mine had been hacked off by Salan in Kabul. She reached up and took my hand, pressing the blade down harder. 'Quicker,' she said. 'You won't hurt me.'

I sawed at the hair until her feet were buried under the mound and her scalp showed through the black stubble. Then she wound a turban around her head. The looseness of the shirt hid the contours of her body and from a distance she might have been taken for a boy. She smiled at me, as if reading my thoughts. 'If they get close enough to challenge us, it will make no difference.'

I tried to lift my bergen on to my shoulders but then set it down again. To save weight, I discarded all my spare clothes and some of my rations. I ripped the sleeves off my spare shirt and made shoulder pads from them.

'Let's go,' Dexy said.

Tank held up his hand. 'Wait a minute. Let's at least rebury them.'

Dexy shook his head. 'Sorry, mate, we need all the time we've got.'

We recrossed the river and moved off parallel to the track. As the walls of the valley narrowed around us, the trail we were following petered out, ending at the collapsed wall of an irrigation channel carved out of the side of the mountain.

We clambered over the rubble and walked along the bottom of the channel. The water was low and we worked our way along the edge, climbing over the biggest of the rocks.

Finally the way was blocked by a barrier of boulders through which the river roared in a series of torrents. We climbed out and worked our way on through the fringes of the woods, trying to balance the use of cover against the need for speed.

The village at the head of this section of the valley had disappeared. In its place was a mound of earth and rock like the one we had left behind us. Screened by the trees, we saw a handful of villagers digging into it with their shovels, picks and bare hands, searching for the dead. As we watched, a body in a dirt-smeared mauve burka was pulled from the rubble and carried away. The cries of the men and the shrill keening of the women echoed across the fields.

We passed by unseen. Beyond the ruined village, my eye was caught by a crumbling monument in the undergrowth above the track. Unlike the dry-stone graves of the martyrs, this was a single massive stone, a carved obelisk. I parted the bushes and peered at it.

The inscription was weathered, covered with lichen and pocked with bullet marks, but parts of it were still legible. '. . . ory of the three thousand British fighting men . . . down their lives for Queen and Country during the retreat from Kabul 18 . . .'

Dexy avoided my eye as I turned away, but I knew that he too had read the inscription.

He led us on towards the head of the valley. Three miles beyond it was the target we were seeking.

Chapter 13

It took several hours to cover those three miles. We advanced in short stages, lying up while Dexy proved the ground ahead of us, then closing up to him again. The heat was savage and clouds of insistent, biting flies buzzed around our heads.

We lay up in the last of the cover, overlooking the point where the track narrowed and disappeared into the gloom of the ravine. There was a sangar on the cliff top above the entrance to the ravine, but it appeared to be unmanned. 'I don't know if that's a good sign or a bad one,' I said. 'Either the Taliban have got complacent or there's nothing worth guarding.'

'We'll know soon enough,' Dexy said.

We ate some rations, then he gathered us around him. 'This will be the first RV. Emergency RV here.' He jabbed his finger at the map. 'And the War RV here. Moonrise is at 23.04. We'll aim to be in and out before then.

'As soon as it's dark, Tank, Sean and I will recce the target. If we can find a route up or down the cliff face, we can bypass the sangar guarding the steps leading to the cave entrance. If we're lucky, we might be able to lay the charges before the Taliban even know we're there.

'The rest of you wait for a signal on the net, then follow us in. Jeff and Amica will lie up close to the target with Rami, ready to give covering fire. Boon will watch the sangar. If we can't find a climbable route, we'll have to take out the guards in the sangar and do a frontal assault on the cave.'

I knew that desperation rather than admiration had made Dexy trust me with a key role, a thought that made my nerves tighten as the shadows lengthened. By the time it was dark my heart was pounding.

At last Dexy gave the signal to move. He led the way with me at his heels and Tank bringing up the rear. We crept on all fours through the last of the undergrowth, then flattened ourselves and belly-crawled towards the ravine. I could hear the river thundering over the rocks below us

Part-natural, part-blasted from the rockface, the track wound round the wall of the ravine. We moved in short stages, in total silence. With the moon still below the horizon we had only faint starlight to guide us. I saw little ahead of me but the dark shapes of Tank and Dexy hugging the ground, worming their way forward along the track.

We crawled, stopped and then crawled again. Finally I heard Dexy's quiet voice. 'Target in sight. I'm going to recce. Wait here, and check the cliff face for a climbing route. Tank, call the others forwards.'

As he moved away, I saw the dim outline of the sangar beyond him. It was about a hundred yards away. A rough-hewn flight of steps led up the rock face, ending in a black hole sixty feet above the track, the entrance to the cave. I began to search the face of the cliff for handholds. At the top, half-hidden by a clump of mountain cedars, I glimpsed the curve of a satellite dish.

Dexy was gone for fifty minutes. Even though I was looking for him, he moved so slowly and moulded himself to the rocks so well that he was only a few yards away when I saw him.

'Three guards,' he said. 'All awake, but not very alert. What about the cliff?'

'There's a route,' I said, pointing. 'As far as I can tell there are only two tricky moves. About twenty feet up you have to make a lateral move right to catch that crevice. It looks a full armspread, for you certainly.'

He nodded. 'That's all right, what's the other problem?'

'There's an overhang just below the cave entrance.' I indicated the bulge in the rock. 'There's a crevice right under the overhang. If you wedge your hand in there and swing out and up, you should be able to catch the lip of the cave and pull yourself up . . . providing there's no sentry in the mouth of it.'

'The way I feel at the moment, I don't fancy his chances.'

A double click on the net showed that the others were now in position behind us, their weapons set. Dexy, Tank and I carried nothing but demolition charges in our bergens, with our Kalashnikovs slung over our shoulders.

Dexy led the climb, following the route I'd picked out. The rock was rough and fissured, but to my relief there were few loose flakes to worry us. I inched upwards through the darkness, feeling as much as looking for the next handhold. Dexy braced himself before the lateral move, then swung out to the right, his arm fully extended. His fingers scrabbled and caught on the edge of the crevice, he paused, shifted his grip, then completed the move. I made it more easily, Tank did so only after two false starts.

As Dexy moved on up the cliff face he dislodged a fragment of rock that skittered off the surface of the cliff above me. I thrust out my right hand, clinging on with the other. The rock hit my hand, then bounced away, but I stretched again and caught it on the tips of my fingers.

I clamped myself to the cliff, my heart beating wildly, and it was a moment before I could recompose myself enough to transfer the rock to my pocket. I didn't dare turn my head to look towards the sangar, but there was no sound, no challenge.

We climbed on until Dexy reached the overhang. He was now no more than four feet below the entrance to the cave, separated from it only by the ledge. The steps were just to our left, but there was an expanse of rock in between, without the faintest trace of a handhold.

Dexy paused and I heard his indrawn breath. He swung himself out and threw his hand up, but it fell short by a couple of inches. He swung back with a thud that forced the air from his lungs. His feet slipped, but his left hand held. He regained his position and tried again, but once more fell short.

I reached above me, tugged at his leg and motioned him to the right. He hesitated, then moved out of my way. I climbed up in his place and jammed my left hand into the crack at the base of the overhang, using my thumb as a wedge to lock it into place. My bones would have to break before I could fall.

The cold barrel of the Kalashnikov over my right shoulder touched my cheek. I glanced at Dexy's face a couple of feet away and saw a flash of white as he bared his teeth in a smile of encouragement. I took three deep breaths and forced myself to focus only on the move I had to make, not the danger that might lie beyond it. Then I launched myself outwards and upwards. My right arm flailed through the air, my hand scraped against rock – but it dug in and held. I released my left hand and hauled myself upwards, the muscles in my arms screaming in protest at the extra weight of the bergen on my back.

My eyes came level with the floor of the cave. I saw nothing ahead, only blackness. I groped with my left hand like a blind man, until I found a grip that would hold me. Then I was up and crouching on all fours, trying to quieten my breathing as I swung the Kalashnikov from my shoulder. There was still no noise or movement from inside the cave.

I hesitated for a moment, unsure of my next move, then swung round and took the rope coiled around my waist. I lowered one end to Dexy and braced myself as he hauled himself up. A moment later Tank followed. We inched our way inside, out of sight of the guards in the sangar below.

Dexy passed me his torch. 'Count to three,' he whispered. 'Switch on, count three and then off again.'

I heard the faint click as he and Tank slid the safety-catches off their weapons. I flicked on the torch, the beam of which was narrowed by black tape to a thin strip. Two men lay sleeping on the floor of the cave, otherwise it was deserted. Tank moved silently to within a yard of them. He drew his combat knife and remained motionless as I played the torchlight around the walls.

The cave was a single chamber, barely forty feet deep. A rough fireplace had been built near the entrance and the walls were blackened with smoke. A few sacks and crates were stacked against one wall. Dexy and I examined them in silence as Tank kept watch over the sleeping guards.

I used my combat knife as a jemmy, prising open the lids of the crates. There was a squeak as a rusty nail came free and I froze and glanced behind me. One of the guards stirred in his sleep. I saw Tank lean down, one hand hovering above the man's mouth, the other holding his knife an inch from the guard's throat.

The man's breathing settled again. We waited a further minute, then resumed our work. I eased open the lid of the last crate and then exchanged a look with Dexy. The sacks and crates were full of plastic-wrapped blocks that looked like brown sugar. I felt sick. The cave was a storeplace all right, but for the morphine base the Taliban traded for guns, not the Stingers we were seeking.

Dexy's shoulders sagged for a moment, then he put a hand on my arm and steered me to the entrance. 'Back the same way,' he breathed.

'The guards?'

'Sleeping dogs.'

Tank stole after us to the cave mouth and I took the strain as first Tank and then Dexy slid down the rope. As soon as I felt the weight go from it, I coiled it around my waist again, slung my rifle over my shoulder and began to lower myself over the ledge.

I hung at full stretch from the fingertips of my right hand and began to swing myself backwards and forwards. Three times I scrabbled at the rock with my left hand but failed to catch hold before I swung away again. The fourth time, as I felt my grip loosening, I caught the edge of the crack, forced my hand into it and swung down beneath the overhang. I winced as the rock tore my fingers, but held on and worked my way back down the cliff face. Dexy was waiting for me at the bottom. The others had already begun to retreat the way we had come.

Back at the RV, no one spoke for some minutes. We were all too dispirited. I looked at Dexy. 'What now?'

'We have to assume that the other attacks have gone in on schedule,' he said. 'The Taliban will know what we're trying to do. It may take them a little longer to move troops up to this area because of the earthquake, but as soon as they can they'll quadruple the guard on the Stingers – wherever they are – and then disperse them to other sites. If we don't find the right cave in the next twenty-four hours we're fucked.'

'So what do we do?'

He thought for a minute. 'We go and see Agha Shah Azuin.'

'Are you crazy?' Rami said. 'He told us he'd kill us.'

'It's a chance we have to take.'

'He's allied with the Taliban, for Christ's sake.'

'But it's a marriage of convenience.' Dexy looked around the circle of faces, trying to convince us. 'I know him. His first priority is his family and his own people. We have to persuade him their safety depends on him helping us.'

'And how do we do that?'

'We haven't got a carrot, so that just leaves the stick.'

Rami stared at him. 'We can't compromise the security of the operation.'

'It's compromised already. Agha Shah Azuin recognised me and Sean. He knows we're both British and he knows I'm SAS. When he hears about the other two attacks going in – assuming their intelligence proved more accurate than ours – he's going to know exactly what we're doing here and why. But he won't blow our cover because I'm going to make him an offer which is as much in his interest as it is in ours.'

Before anyone else could argue, he'd shouldered his bergen and begun the trek back down the valley.

We walked for the rest of the night and reached the village again just after dawn. A few farmers were already in their fields, but we made no attempt to hide ourselves. They ran ahead of us shouting a warning as we marched up the hill towards the mosque.

Azuin strode out to greet us, his face red with anger. His men stood behind him, fingering their rifles. 'Is this how you heed my warning?' he said. 'You insult me.'

Dexy held up a hand as the rest of us kept a wary eye on his men. 'Agha Shah, I swear on the friendship we have shared and the respect I have for you that only the most dire emergency would have brought us back here. Let me tell you our problem in private. After that, I will accept whatever you decide.'

'Even if it is your own death?'

Dexy spread his hands wide. 'Our lives are no longer in our hands, but in yours.'

The warlord hesitated, then nodded. 'Very well then, follow me.'

He led us to his house, a fortress-like building on the outskirts of the village. Daru grinned and clapped his hands as he saw us approach, but his father ordered him away. The boy pretended to comply, but when I looked over my shoulder he was padding along behind me. He grinned and put his finger to his lips.

Azuin led us through the house into a courtyard and shouted at his wives to bring tea. We sat in silence as they served us and withdrew, then he turned to Dexy. 'Now you will tell me what has brought you here.'

Dexy took a deep breath. 'The Stingers that we supplied and trained the Mujahedeen to use in the war against the Sovs have now been turned against us by the Taliban. They are being used to shoot down not fighters and bombers, but planes carrying civilians – families, wives and children. Our mission is to destroy the Stingers before more innocent people die.'

The warlord nodded. 'And why have you come back to my village?'

'Because the intelligence we were given is flawed. We went to attack a store cave last night but it contained no Stingers, only morphine base.' He paused, studying Azuin's face.

'Why do you assume that my knowledge is any better than yours?'

Dexy grinned. 'Because I know you. This is your territory. Nothing happens here that you do not know of.'

Agha Shah smiled, flattered. 'And if I have such knowledge, why should I use it to help you against my allies, the Taliban?'

Dexy's tone was suddenly sombre. 'Because if you do not, the Americans will rain down bombs and missiles from the skies until they have obliterated not only the Stingers but the surrounding land as well. Thousands of people – your people – will die.' He glanced at me for support.

'The power of the Americans has no limits,' I said. 'There will be no soldiers you can fight against; you will not even see the aircraft that attack you. There will only be endless attacks from the air against which even the Stingers will be no defence. Your people will be maimed, killed, poisoned. Those that survive will starve. That is why we ask you to help us spare your own people from such suffering.'

He looked from me to Dexy. 'How do I know that you're speaking the truth?'

'You have heard of the attacks on Iraq and the cruise missiles the US fired against the desert camps of Osama bin Laden?' Dexy asked. 'That is nothing to the destruction that will pour down on here. The Americans have nuclear weapons too. If they have to use them to destroy the Stingers, they will.'

Azuin's expression had grown more grim as he listened. When we had finished speaking, he sat in silence for several minutes. Then he raised his head and looked us each in the eye. 'I will help you,' he said.

Dexy was already spreading out our maps. 'This is the cave that we entered last night.'

Agha Shah leaned over to look. 'It is a store cave, one we used in the war against the Soviets. The Taliban still make use of it, but I believe the cave that you are seeking is . . . here.' His broad finger stabbed down on the valley immediately to the south.

'How can we be sure?' Dexy said.

'I also used that cave during the Soviet war,' the warlord said. 'Since the Taliban took over, the area has been forbidden territory even to their allies. There are sangars at both entrances to the gorge where the cave is located, and there are many guards.' He smiled. 'I know, because the food convoys that supply them pass through my territory.'

'But it still could be drugs stored there, not Stingers,' I said.

He shrugged. 'It could, but precious though morphine base is to the Taliban, they do not normally defend it with anti-aircraft guns. There are two on the ridge above it and my men have told me that they have also seen men armed with Stingers in the sangars above the ravine. So at least there will be one or two there, no?' His powerful shoulders shook as he chuckled at his own joke.

'What of the interior?' Dexy said. 'Is it one cave or many?'

'I do not know. Much work has been carried out there by the Taliban. The river was discoloured for many weeks with the spoil from their workings.'

'What about the approach?'

'The track is on a broad rock ledge on the north face of the ravine. Above and below it, the walls are sheer.'

'Could they be climbed?' I said.

Azuin turned to look at me. 'I am regarded as a brave man,

but I would not do it. The track runs behind a waterfall; it is broad enough for only two men to pass. The cave you are seeking lies four to five hundred metres beyond the falls.' The warlord looked up from the map. 'It is a dangerous journey, my friends. There are many Taliban patrols and they fight like Afghans, not Sovs.'

'We'll make it,' Dexy said.

Daru's voice piped up as he stepped out from behind a pillar at the side of the courtyard. 'And if the Stingers were destroyed, the Americans might be grateful?'

I laughed. 'They might be very grateful.'

A smile spread across Azuin's face. 'Then be sure you survive to tell them.' He paused. 'I will escort you to the boundaries of my territory, but beyond that I cannot go. If the Taliban discover I have betrayed them . . .' He left the sentence unfinished.

He led us away from the village and up the track we had used to lay a false trail the day before. Had I not been so exhausted, the irony of pointing it straight at the very target we were seeking might have raised a smile.

He led us on to the point where the river forked. To the left was the valley we had penetrated during the night, to the right lay the one we were now seeking.

'Go with God.' Azuin touched his heart, then turned away.

We moved up the valley, using the cover of the wooded lower slopes. A shoulder of rock compressed the river into a narrow gorge. We had to climb above it before we could see the upper valley. A corridor some 200 yards wide had been carved down the mountain by a landslide, stripping it of trees and cover. We had no option but to cross it, though it was horribly exposed.

Dexy and Tank went first, then gave cover as the rest of

us followed. I crouched low, the weight of my bergen pushing me down. I measured each footfall on the loose, shifting surface.

We emerged on to a high, sloping plateau ten miles in length, and broadening to some four or five miles in width, before the steep walls of the valley began to converge again. They culminated in a narrow cleft breaking the line of the mountains, a black ravine carved by the river. If Azuin was right, this was our target.

The earthquake damage was much less severe here, but the devastation of war was all around us. The plain was littered with craters, and the trees on the slope where we stood were scarred by the shells that had fallen there. The edges of the dirt road winding across the plateau below us were lined with the skeletons of trucks and armoured vehicles, punctured by bullet holes and still blackened by fire.

As we advanced up the valley, the tree cover gradually grew more sparse. Soon we were walking along the margins of the plain, hugging the valley wall. Dexy raised a hand. The fierce sunlight made the rock-face hot to the touch, but it also cast our shadows, black against the red-brown stone. We dropped to our hands and knees and began to crawl along a ruined irrigation channel. Our footmarks scored the surface but there was no time for better concealment.

We flattened ourselves against the ground as we heard a shout. I raised my head enough to peer over the rim and saw an old man a couple of fields away cursing his mule as he tried to drive it forward. It moved a few yards, dragging a wooden plough through the parched earth, then stopped again. The old man paused long enough to look at something away to our right. I followed his gaze and saw two shepherds driving a handful of sheep further down the valley.

The channel ended in a bomb-crater twenty feet deep. Clouds of flies hovered over a trickle of scummy water at its base. The ground rose on the far side of the crater, but there was no trace of cover.

'It could have gone underground,' Amica said. 'Our ancestors dug tunnels under the plain from the bed of the river to irrigate the fields.'

We climbed the far side of the crater, then wormed our way forward to a low ridge, pausing just below the edge. As I stared across the plateau, I began to realise that the stippled pattern of craters and holes in front of us was too regular to be random.

Among the bomb craters were lines of neat holes surrounded by low cones, protruding a couple of feet above the level of the plain.

'They're like bell-pits,' I said. 'Shafts linked by tunnels. They use them for irrigation.'

'Very interesting,' Rami said, 'but —'

Tank held up his hand then pointed towards the road. We lay motionless, straining our ears. I waited a couple of minutes, raised my head a fraction of an inch at a time, and peered through the strands of dry grass.

Back across the fields I could see the mule still hitched to its plough, but the farmer had left it to walk to the roadside. A red Toyota pick-up was parked there, and a large group of Taliban soldiers was talking to him. As I watched, he raised an arm and pointed towards the low ridge we had just crossed.

Half a dozen soldiers began moving towards us, while the rest advanced slowly along the road. I looked around. The ground ahead of us was as bare as a beach at low tide. There was no cover, no way of escaping without being seen.

'We can take the first group, no problem,' Dexy said. 'But

that will bring some serious shit down on us.' He thought for a moment, then nodded to Tank. 'Fix up a diversion in that ditch back there; we'll break cover and leg it as soon as you're back. If we're split, RV at that clump of trees, thirty minutes after sunset.'

Tank shrugged his bergen off his shoulders and pulled out a detonator and some explosives. Holding his Kalashnikov in his hand, he flattened himself against the ground and began crawling back the way we had come, towards the Taliban.

They had fanned out and were moving slowly across the fields in a line. Tank was outlined against the sky for a moment as he crossed the ridge. There was a shout and one of the Taliban soldiers swung up his rifle and fired. The shot struck a rock a couple of feet from Tank and whined away. He disappeared from sight, dropping below the level of the ridge.

The Taliban soldiers changed course, racing to cut him off. I raised my head a fraction more and saw Tank running, bent double along the bottom of the irrigation ditch. The soldiers were now also out of sight, but they must have reached the ditch. I heard the crack of rifles, then there was the boom of an explosion. Clods of earth were flung into the air and a cloud of dust drifted away on the wind.

We waited, ready to move at a moment's notice. Then Tank wormed his way over the ridgeline. Still stooping, he sprinted down to join us.

'Sorted?' Dexy said.

He nodded.

'It's bought us a bit more time,' Dexy said. 'And if they're stupid they may think that was a mine and slow down. Even if they don't, they still have to guess which way we've gone. We might have doubled back or moved on up the valley, and we might have split our force. Ready? Let's go.'

We moved out fast. I was bent double, running with the crushing weight of the bergen on my back. I ran blind, following the footsteps of the man in front, gasping for breath, my muscles burning with the effort. We crossed one field, and another, then I heard the rattle of rifle fire.

'Down!' Dexy shouted. No orders were given or other words exchanged, but he and Tank immediately began to wriggle back along the ground in a wide loop to one side, while Rami and Boon did the same on the other. I raised my head. The Taliban were no more than a hundred yards away and closing fast.

There was a burst of fire and the earth was whipped around me. Amica was ahead of us, already in the cover of a low mound, but Jeff and I were pinned down in the open. The mound was only twenty yards away, but if we ran for it, we'd be cut to pieces before we'd covered half that distance.

'I'll distract them,' Jeff said. 'You make a dash for the mound, then cover me.'

'Don't be stupid,' I said, 'you'll get yourself killed.'

He ignored me, scrambling to his knees.

'Get down, you idiot.' I grabbed at his arm, but he shrugged me off.

'Run,' he said, then took off in the opposite direction.

There was the crack of gunfire as I sprinted for the mound and dived into cover beside Amica. As I raised my head, the brief, savage barrage of fire fell silent. A blizzard of white flakes like snow was drifting down around me, pouring out of a clear blue sky. I shook my head, trying to clear my vision.

I heard a groan. A hole had been blown in Jeff's bergen and I could see the shredded remains of one of his precious toilet rolls, a red stain spreading across the white paper. The rest was still fluttering to the earth around me.

I belly-crawled to him and turned him over. There was a wet, dark hole in the pit of his stomach and I could hear his breath bubbling through a torn lung. 'You stupid bastard,' I said. 'Why did you have to—'

There was a noise and I whipped round in fright. Dexy and Tank dropped into cover alongside me. 'The Taliban?' I said.

'Out of it, but there are others back down the track.' He glanced at Jeff and then at me. 'We can't take him,' he said.

I began to argue, then stopped myself, knowing he was right. I looked down at Jeff. His eyes were fastened on mine and he tried to say something, but choked and spat blood.

I laid a hand on his arm. 'Don't try to talk. I know what you want. I'll go and see them. I'll make sure they're all right. I'll do it, I swear.'

Dexy took out his knife, cut the straps of Jeff's bergen and eased it out from under him. He cursed. 'Shit, we need that explosive.'

'We can manage without it,' Tank said. 'There's no way we can carry any more.' He laid the bergen on the ground near Jeff, stooped over, connecting wires and detonators, then carefully closed the top.

'You can't leave a booby-trap there,' I said. 'If it goes off, it'll take Jeff with—' I fell silent as I met Dexy's gaze.

'It's all right,' he said. 'I'll fix it.'

I took the syrette of morphine from around Jeff's neck. 'I'll give you this for the pain.'

'I'll take care of it,' Dexy said. 'You go on.'

I hesitated, laying a hand on Jeff's brow, but Tank took my arm and pulled me away. We followed the others, who were already moving off across the field.

Amica squeezed my hand as I came up with her. 'I'm sorry,' she said.

I looked back. Dexy was still crouching over Jeff. We had gone only another five yards when we heard a single shot. Dexy was already moving towards us. 'It's all right,' he said. 'They can't hurt him now.'

Chapter 14

We moved on across the plain. Dexy and Tank were leading and Rami and Boon guarding the rear, while Amica and I struggled on in the middle. The sight of Jeff's body and the look in his eyes kept returning to me. I was sick and weary to my bones; only adrenalin kept me moving.

We scrambled through another bomb crater and paused to scan the ground ahead and behind us. There was no sign yet of pursuit. 'We don't have long,' Dexy said. 'Then the shit is going to hit the fan in the biggest possible way.'

I looked around. We were now in the middle of the plain, surrounded by the same blank landscape of empty, dust-laden fields and bare rock faces. We could keep crawling from crater to crater, but any watcher on the high ground above us would spot us in an instant.

A few yards away there was another of the conical mounds.

I grabbed Dexy's arm. 'The irrigation tunnels. We can use them.'

He thought for a moment. 'What if they're blocked?' Then he shrugged. 'What have we got to lose? Let's do it.'

Rami, Boon, Amica and I made directly for the mound. Tank and Dexy laid a false trail across the field back to the rockface and returned, walking backwards to double the tracks. Then they followed us to the mound, sweeping away the rest of our trail behind them.

I shone my torch into the hole, but couldn't see the bottom. 'How deep are these things?' I said.

Amica shrugged. 'I'm not sure, twenty feet, maybe thirty.'

I pushed the undergrowth aside and reached down inside the shaft, feeling for handholds. The walls felt cool, but smooth and dry. I uncoiled the rope from my waist and Dexy took the strain as I got ready to lower myself. 'How does the last one get down?' I said.

'Let's worry about that when we see how deep it is.'

I lowered my feet and let myself down hand over hand. It was pitch black. As I looked up, I could see Amica's face framed in the entrance, watching me. I moved my hands half a metre at a time and counted each one until my feet touched a soft mound of dust and sand.

The coolness of the tunnel was a relief after the furnace heat of the plain above. I switched on my torch. The shaft and tunnels were carved from the solid rock. I paused, marvelling at the strength and endurance of men who had hacked it out with no more than hand-tools. Then I crouched down on my knees and peered up the tunnel. I could see a dim glow of light from the next shaft.

I called up, my voice echoing. 'It's okay, we can get through to the next shaft at least. That's as far as I can see. It's about eight metres down here. The last one will have to jump. It's a reasonably soft landing though.'

'That'll be all right,' Dexy said. 'I did worse than that in parachute training.'

They pulled the rope back up and lowered Amica. Dexy came last. He lowered his bergen, then dropped the rope. The circle of light disappeared as he lowered himself into the opening. He hung from his fingertips and then let go, landing with a thud that drove the breath from his lungs.

'Are you all right?' I said.

'Sure.' He took a compass reading and then we moved off into the tunnel. It was about five feet high and wide, and I had to stoop to clear the roof, adding to the ache in my thighs. Underfoot was bare rock, earth, wet sand and a few pools of brackish water. In places, rockfalls had brought down parts of the wall and roof of the tunnel, half-blocking it with mounds of rubble.

I extinguished my torch, trying to conserve the batteries, and we moved on through the darkness. In the distance I could see a circle of light. We paused at the foot of the next shaft, watching and listening for any sound from above before moving back into the darkness.

At intervals the tunnels forked, but each time we took a compass bearing and moved on in the direction closest to the ravine at the head of the valley. My thigh muscles were screaming with the effort of crouching for so long and I heard Amica's laboured breathing close behind me. The scrape of our boots was the only other sound.

I lost count of the number of openings we passed and all track of how far we had travelled, but the tunnels became damper and wetter as we moved on. We began to wade through shallows and pools which sometimes reached our knees.

As we approached the next shaft, we entered another deep pool. We paused in the shadows, listening for noise from above as the reflected light rippled off the walls and roof.

Dexy and Tank crossed first, then Amica. As I began to wade out through the water, I heard a voice. I shrank back into the shadows, my heart pounding. There was a splash just in front of me. Then I saw the white line of a rope tauten as a bucket of water was hauled back up towards the light.

Amica stood in the mouth of the tunnel beyond the shaft. She looked back at me and tried to smile. We waited as the bucket was raised and lowered four more times, then stood in silence for another five minutes before moving on.

I led the way over the next stretch. The tunnel ahead was in darkness; there was no reassuring circle of light from the next shaft. I moved on, my hand stretched out in front of me. After a few minutes my fingers encountered rock and I pulled out my torch. Ahead of me the tunnel was completely blocked by rubble.

'What do we do?' I said.

'Move some of it and get past it if we can,' Dexy said. 'If not, we'll have to go back.'

I slid the bergen from my shoulders, glad at least of the relief from its weight, then began to pull at the rock. Dexy worked alongside me. 'We'll do it in shifts,' he said. 'We can't all get at it at once anyway. Ten minutes on, twenty off, until we get through.'

'What if a shell's blown this in from above?' Rami said.

'Then we've got a shitload of rock to clear.'

For half an hour we got nowhere. As fast as we pulled out each piece of rubble, more dropped down to replace it. Our faces were haggard in the light of the torch. 'We'll give it another ten minutes,' Dexy said. 'Then we'll have to go back and find another way.'

A couple of minutes later we pulled a large boulder clear. In the gap it had left behind, there was a faint chink of light. I scrambled up and began to widen the opening, then shone the torch up the blocked shaft. The rubble and boulders above us seemed to be jammed, but might give way at any moment.

I reached further and further in, pulling out more and more rocks. Fine dust and earth dropped around me and twice there was a low rumbling sound as the rubble shifted. I held my breath, then crawled in still further and pushed at the rock in front of me. It rolled away and through the dust there was dim light ahead.

I wormed my way through the narrow gap and slithered down the pile of rubble on the other side. Amica was next. As I helped her down I could feel the strength in her slim frame. She must have weighed no more than nine stone, yet she had been carrying a bergen almost as heavy as mine.

Rami came next, and the other three began to push the bergens through. Then Dexy and Boon clambered through the hole, leaving Tank to bring up the rear. He had only worked his shoulders through when the rumbling began again. He threw himself forward, but when the noise died and the dust cloud cleared, he lay face-down on the rubble mound, pinned by the right leg. It was wedged in the space between two smaller rocks, jammed underneath a large boulder.

'That rock's too big to shift,' I said. 'Even if we can, it might roll down on his head.'

Dexy peered at it. 'We might be able to shift one of those two smaller ones below it and pull him out that way.'

I scraped at the soil with my fingers, then used the butt of my rifle, forcing it between the two rocks to try to force them apart. I could feel it dislodging some earth and a few small pebbles, and the gap between them widened by an inch or so.

'If you can force your leg downwards, Tank, you should be able to pull it clear.' I saw him wincing with the pain as he tried, but he was still held fast. I forced the butt of the Kalashnikov further in between the two rocks and used the barrel as a lever.

'You're wrecking your rifle,' Dexy said.

Tank raised his head. 'It doesn't matter. If you don't get me out of here, he can have mine.'

I felt the rock give a little more. I held it there, my arms shaking from the effort. 'Now, Tank, push it down.' I put all my strength into one final effort and forced the rocks a little further apart. Tank groaned with pain, but I heard his body slither down the rubble mound. Amica checked his ankle carefully and got him to put his weight on it a bit at a time. 'It's bruised, that's all,' she said.

I pulled my rifle out of the rocks and peered at it. 'It looks all right.'

'The only way you'll find out for sure is when you pull the trigger,' Dexy said. 'Either it'll work or you'll blow your own head off.'

'Tell you what,' I said. 'You have it.'

He glanced at his watch. 'Come on. We've only an hour to sunset. If we don't hit that target tonight, we've lost.'

We moved on towards the next glimmer of light. I could hear the faint whisper of water somewhere in the distance ahead. Peering up the next shaft I saw that black clouds were covering the sky. The thought of being trapped in the tunnels as a cloudburst raised the river level left me fighting the urge to break into a run. When I was a kid, my brother had once locked me for hours in the coalshed. Here in this dark, cramped tunnel, I felt an echo of those long-buried childhood fears.

The noise of rushing water grew louder and louder as we worked our way along. The ground was now permanently wet underfoot and we splashed through a serious of ever deeper pools, trapped between mounds of earth and rubble.

As we clambered over another rockfall, I sank waist-deep into icy water. There was another dim circle of light from a shaft above me, but in the distance ahead I could now see the mouth of the tunnel, and beyond it dark water and white foam.

I waded forwards, my teeth chattering. Dexy motioned for me to wait in the shadows as he scouted the entrance. Then he waved us on.

The tunnel opened into a steep gorge. Long ago the ancestors of the Taliban had constructed a channel to divert part of the river into the mouth of the tunnel by laying huge blocks of stone across the river bed. They were so massive that a hundred men could not have moved them.

Some were still held in place by other, smaller blocks, forming a ramp of stone like a flat-topped pyramid, stretching a full hundred yards up the river bed. But even that massive feat of engineering had not been enough to hold back the force of the river indefinitely. Parts of the ramp had been carried away, leaving gaps like missing teeth.

In flood, the river would still fill the irrigation tunnel at least as far as the point where the rockfall blocked it, but now it was no more than waist deep. My teeth were rattling and my legs were going numb. I looked at the sky. 'We can't wait for dark. We have to get out of this water at least.'

Dexy nodded and inched his way out, craning his neck to scan the cliff tops above us. The walls of the ravine looked black and sheer, and glistened with spray thrown up by the rapids.

Still deep in the gorge, we picked our way among the jumble of boulders at the water's edge, tracking the river eastwards until we reached a break, a fault line in the rock, marked by a band of harder stone. It formed a narrow ledge like a natural, if perilous, footpath running diagonally up the wall of the canyon.

Roped together, feeling for a grip on the slippery rock at each step, we inched our way upwards and huddled together on a ledge fifty yards below the lip of the ravine. Dexy checked his GPS, gave a frown and then checked it again. He gave a low whistle. 'We've covered eight miles underground,' he said. 'We're only a couple from the target. We might just do this.'

'Maybe,' Tank said, 'but all we've done so far is the easy bit.'

I tried to rub some warmth back into my legs. I was weary to the bone with the effort of carrying the bergen so far, and for so long and on so little food, but I was anxious to be moving again, both to keep warm and to keep from thinking about what lay ahead.

Almost an hour of daylight still remained. We sat close together for warmth, holding our rifles, our eyes fixed on the edge of the ravine. I could hear no sound but the roar and crash of the river, and sense no movement but the faint line of the rays of the cloud-covered sun inching higher up the canyon walls.

Just before sunset, I swallowed a handful of nuts and dried fruit, and a square or two of chocolate. Dexy and the other guys ate only a mouthful of their rations. 'We should save as much as we can,' he said. 'Keep it for a real emergency.'

I almost laughed.

The canyon was now in darkness, but a faint red glow still illuminated the clouds as the sun touched the horizon. We shuffled even closer together, leaning in to hear Dexy as he gave the final briefing. 'The Taliban will be on full alert. We don't have enough men, enough explosives or enough ammunition,' he said. 'But somehow we're going to get this job done. We've some idea of what's waiting for us, but without close recces of the target we're going in at least half-blind.

'We're just going to have to walk up to the front door and kick it down. I'll go lead scout, Tank is number two, Boon at five, Rami at six. You two in the middle.' He nodded to me and Amica. 'Your first job is to get your bergens to the caves.'

He handed an ear-piece and throatmike to each of us. 'We're all on the same net. I'll lead out and Tank will run liaison between you and me. Don't move until we tell you to. If it's Tank approaching, you'll hear this.' He picked up two pebbles and tapped them together in his hand. 'If you hear anything else, shoot. If you hear shots from elsewhere, take up firing positions and wait for orders from one of us.

'Close to the target, Boon and Rami will take out the guard posts on the cliffs and then give us cover. Tank and I will go in to set the charges. They'll be expecting us to exfiltrate eastwards, the shortest route to the border through the mountains. We won't. We'll retrace our steps instead.' He tried for a smile. 'We might even lie up in the irrigation tunnel again through daylight tomorrow.' He pulled out his map. 'First RV there – memorise the co-ordinates. That will be good for exactly five minutes, beginning one hour after we start the assault. The Emergency RV will be back here, open until daybreak tomorrow. The war RV will be here.' He again jabbed his finger at the map, marking a notch in the ridgeline on the south wall of the valley a few miles downstream. 'That will hold until midnight tomorrow night. After that anyone separated from the group will make their own E & E to the border. Any questions?'

We all shook our heads.

'Then that's it. From here on in, if we're challenged, we shoot first and talk afterwards. There is no way we're going to bluff our way past any guards this close to the target, especially with the Taliban scouring the area for us.'

Dexy glanced at Rami. 'I'm making Tank number two. If anything happens to me, Tank leads.'

'I outrank him,' Rami said.

'This isn't about rank, it's about who can get the job done, and Tank's a trained demolitionist, like me.' He didn't wait for Rami to argue the point any further. 'That's it, let's go.'

He shouldered his bergen and moved off up the ledge into the darkness. We waited just under a lip of the ravine for ten minutes, listening, watching and scenting the air. Then, making no sound, Tank and Dexy melted into the shadows.

The moon and stars were hidden by cloud, but enough dim light filtered through to show us the track winding its way towards the darkness of the ravine. The river boiled through it and spray hung in the gorge.

The clifftops high above us looked black and featureless, but I knew that somewhere up there someone would be watching. The track clung to a ledge on the north side, sometimes a couple of hundred yards wide, sometimes narrowing to no more than a few feet.

We moved in short stages as Dexy and Tank scouted ahead and then called the rest of us up. Every step took us further into the ravine. The walls seemed to close further around us and the cold struck an ever deeper chill in my bones.

For the moment adrenalin kept my tiredness at bay. I tried to mimic the Special Forces, moving without sound and flitting from one patch of shadow to another, but I was hampered by the bergen. My movements were clumsy, and from time to time my feet scuffed against sand and rock.

The noise of the river grew louder, seeming to bounce off the rock walls all around me. In the darkness ahead I saw a grey-white column reaching from the cliff tops to the foot of the ravine and felt a fine spray on my face.

We paused by the waterfall as Dexy scouted ahead, then began to file through the gap behind it. There was thunder in my ears and spray drenched me to the skin. The rock was wet and slippery, and I was almost paralysed by the fear of plummeting down on to the rocks far below.

Somehow I kept my feet moving, inching my way forward, searching with my fingers for whatever grip I could find. The distance was no more than ten or fifteen metres, but it took for ever to emerge into the blackness of the ravine.

We began to move on again. I lost track of how long we had been advancing, pausing, and then advancing again, but the track of the moon behind the clouds showed it had been hours since we had set out.

We paused again in a pool of shadow, and this time there was a very long interval before the signal to move on.

I tried to penetrate the darkness ahead, seeking the first sign of danger – a movement, a silhouette against the sky or the glint of moonlight on a weapon – that might save our lives. I thought of Jeff again, his life bubbling away through the hole in his chest. His premonition had come true. I pushed the image away.

At last we heard the faint chink of pebbles. We began to move forward again, inching along the track. As I drew level with Tank, he laid a hand on my arm and put his finger to his lips. He pointed towards the skyline above and slightly ahead of us.

There were black shapes against the sky, the twin barrels of an anti-aircraft gun. He bent his head to breathe in my ear. 'Get low and crawl, as close to the cliff face as you can make it. There's a guard post on the track directly ahead of you. Don't worry, we've taken care of it. Wait there.' He disappeared into the darkness.

I flattened myself to the ground and began to worm my way across the bare rock. Sharp edges of stones pressed into my body and caught in the folds of my clothing. Each time I stopped, freed myself, and moved on. I dared not look up.

At last I saw a rounded shape rising out of the darkness in front of me, a drystone sangar, built into the mountain. Pressing myself even closer to the rock, I climbed over the low, rough wall, inched along and dropped down inside.

My foot slipped on something soft and out of the corner of my eye I saw a body sprawled on the ground in the shadow of the low wall. Another lay opposite. Bloodstains marked the dirt around their heads, black as coal in the moonlight.

I pressed myself against the cliff face and lay still, waiting. There was the faintest of noises as first Amica and then the others joined me. We heard the thin scrape of metal as Boon laid a mine in the track behind us, protecting our backs.

Moments later I heard a chink of pebbles and Dexy appeared out of the darkness. He whispered to Boon, his fingers tracing a line up the hillside on the far side of the ravine. We were already caked with dirt and mud, but Boon scooped up a few more handfuls from the track, spat in it and rubbed it over his face and hands. Then he flattened himself and worked his way slowly across the track towards the edge of the gorge.

I couldn't see for a moment how he was going to get across there, but as I peered at the ravine I made out a straight line, blacker than the surrounding darkness, disappearing into the shadows. A single tree trunk had been laid across the gorge, roughly levelled along the top to make a bridge no more than six inches wide. Anyone trying to cross it would be clearly visible to the guardpost above, and the drop from the trunk to the riverbed was at least a hundred feet.

Boon disappeared over the side of the gorge. Then I caught a glimpse of him moving out along the trunk, swinging underneath it as he advanced hand over hand, using the shadow to hide himself. Only his fingers were visible, gripping the slippery wood as his hands bore not only his own weight but a 120-pound bergen as well.

I heard the faintest of noises behind me and then Rami, too, was gone, working his way up the other side of the ravine.

Dexy was resting on his haunches. I saw the glitter of his eyes as he scanned the track ahead and behind us. The waterfall hid most sounds. We would have no more than a split second's warning of anyone's approach.

The night darkened still further and I felt the first cold drops of rain on my skin. I thought of Boon and Rami scaling those treacherous paths in the pitch blackness, reaching upwards, feeling for holds on the slippery rock.

The rain grew heavier. Dexy was smiling. 'A lucky break,' he said. 'It'll keep their heads down.'

The opposite wall of the ravine had disappeared behind a sheet of rain. It drummed against the cliff and streamed down the rockface, turning the grey dust into mud.

There was a double click in my ear-piece and a second one a moment later. 'They're in position,' Dexy said.

The minutes crawled by. I stared into the curtain of rain, then jumped, startled at Boon's quiet voice over the net. 'Two men down, the south doors open. Coming back now.'

The seconds ticked by with no word from Rami. Then there was a faint, muffled report from the cliff above us. A moment later, Rami's voice came up on the net. 'North door open. Two men down.'

I slid the safety-catch off my rifle and waited, the tension gnawing at my stomach, sure that the shots had been heard, and that at any moment tracer would light up the sky.

A pebble landed beside me. Rami appeared out of the darkness, rainwater streaming down his face. Then a dark shape slithered out of the ravine by the tree-trunk, like a seal emerging from the sea. Boon.

Without pausing, Dexy signalled me to follow and moved off up the track. After a few metres, it dog-legged to the right, disappearing around the rockface. I followed, inching my way around the corner, then paused and raised my eyes. The track ran straight for a couple of hundred metres more, to a point where the ravine walls came so close together that it shrank to little more than a ledge, chiselled from the cliff face above a sheer drop to the river.

Peering into the rain, I could just discern the rounded shape of another sangar beyond the narrow ledge, guarding the approach from the east. Then the canyon veered away to the right and the track passed out of sight. Had we approached from that direction we could never have reached the target undetected. On the skyline at the far end of the ridge, the barrels of more anti-aircraft guns showed against the sky, jutting from the softer outline of another sangar.

I lowered my gaze. The cliff face was pocked with countless small craters, but there was a dark shape one-third of the way up – the entrance to the cave.

A ledge a few feet wide had been cut out of the cliff in front of it and another sangar had been constructed, guarding the cave mouth. Straining my eyes, I could just discern the blacker shapes of the heads of four guards crouching behind the sangar wall. A narrow flight of steps had been cut out of the bare rock leading from the track. It was impossible to climb them undetected by the guards above.

Dexy wriggled his way back until we were shielded by the rockface. 'Boon, take the far sangar. Rami, set up here and keep the guys on the cliff tops occupied. We can't make a covert entry. We'll have to blow them out of there.' He checked his watch.

'It's 12.42 . . . now.' He glanced at Boon. 'I'll give you forty minutes to get there. Blast-off at 1.22. My shot the signal. Sean, Amica, when you see me and Tank go in, get on our heels as fast as you can. Don't draw attention to yourselves by firing, but if you are targeted, use short bursts – fire and movement. Maximum six minutes to clear those caves and set the charges. 1.28 we're pulling out.'

Rami checked his gun and Tank assembled a grenade launcher, both working in complete silence. Boon had already disappeared into the night, working his way like an eel along the edge of the wet track. I watched him until he disappeared into the darkness. He had advanced inch by inch, moulding his body to the contours of the rock and offering no outline or discernible movement to the guards watching above. It would take him every minute of the forty to cross those 200 yards.

The rest of us waited, the tension palpable. I checked and rechecked my rifle, and kept touching the spare clips and the grenades at my belt. I slid back alongside Amica and put my mouth close to her ear. 'Go ahead of me this time, just behind Dexy and Tank. It's your best chance. They'll deal with anything in front of us and it'll take the guys on the cliff tops a few moments to get their range and bring fire to bear.'

She whispered a reply, her mouth so close to my ear that her lips brushed along my cheek. 'No, you'll be faster than me.'

I turned my head to argue again, but she put her finger on my lips and shook her head.

Dexy checked his watch. 'Time to move out. Stay on our boot-heels. When we move, you move. When we freeze, you freeze. Safety-catches on. We haven't come this far to blow it with an accidental discharge. When I fire that first shot, go like fuck behind us.'

The rain was still hammering down, streaking our faces.

Dexy dug his fingers into the mud and smeared more over his face. Then he flattened himself and wormed forward along the track. I followed Tank so closely that now and then my head scraped against the sole of his boot.

The rain lashed off the rockface and cascaded into the ravine. I was soaked to the skin, but barely aware of the cold. I worked my way forward, inch by painful inch, driving myself on with my elbows and feet, my face turned slightly to the side to keep my nose and mouth clear of the water. I had no sense of how far we had travelled or how far we had to go. At one point we paused for so long that I thought we'd reached the foot of the steps, but then we moved on again.

At last we stopped once more and I heard a faint scraping sound, like a steel whetting a knife, as Tank slid the RPG from his shoulder. I peered forward through the curtain of hair plastered against my forehead and saw him lying full-length, RPG at the ready, held in his half-extended arms.

Chapter 15

The sudden chatter of a machine gun broke the silence. There was a curse from Dexy, a burst of answering fire from further up the track and a movement from the sangar above us. Then Dexy and Tank leapt to their feet, the barrels of their RPGs swinging up in unison. There was a double report, so close together it merged into one blast. Twin streaks of fire flashed upwards towards the cave and there was a flash that lit up the night and threw the canyon into stark relief, followed by a massive explosion.

I had closed one eye to save my night vision. As the flash faded and fragments of rock and debris fell around us through the rain, I saw Dexy and Tank sprinting to the cave entrance above me. There was more gunfire from in front and behind, the whipcrack of assault rifles and the rattle of heavy machine guns etching lines of tracer across the darkness.

I felt Amica push my back, and began to scramble up the steps. My mouth was dry and the weight of the bergen dragged at my shoulders. The risers were high and the steps barely wide enough for two feet to stand together. I held my assault rifle at the ready in my left hand and dug the fingers of my right into the cliff face to propel me upwards.

Dexy had already reached the entrance. I saw his arm outlined against the glow from the still-burning bodies in the sangar. It arched back, then forward, and a small black shape lobbed into the mouth of the cave.

There was another blinding flash. I tried to up my pace, but stumbled and almost fell as my foot slipped from the edge of a step. Bullets were now striking the rockface around me. Tracer sliced across the cliff, seeking me out. Dexy and Tank dived through the cave entrance, firing bursts from their weapons. There was a flash and a bang from further up the ravine. The tracer died for a moment, then resumed.

A blizzard of fire riddled the cliff face around me. I threw myself across the edge of the sangar and rolled over and over. The cave floor was littered with bodies.

I was in a huge arched chamber. There were numerous recesses and small rooms opening off it, and two dark tunnels. Dexy and Tank were working their way along, tossing grenades and firing bursts into each. I scrambled to my feet and glanced behind me. There was no sign of Amica. I stared into the darkness, willing her to appear.

Bullets ricocheted from the rock, screaming past me. Then a dark shape hurled itself through the wall of fire and rolled across the floor. It seemed impossible Amica had not been cut to pieces, yet somehow she rose and half-ran, half-stumbled towards me.

Dexy was still working his way deeper, clearing each recess and entrance with a grenade and a burst of fire. Ignoring the explosions, Tank was working his way along a line of cases and chests piled against one wall, cursing and swearing as he threw open the lid of each one.

There were stacks of boxes full of ammunition, grenades and shells, and crates of rifles and small-arms. 'Where are the fucking Stingers?' he shouted.

Dexy was firing down one of the tunnels. Tank flattened himself against the rock alongside and unclipped a grenade. I hardly saw him throw it. A second later there was a roar and the blinding flash of white phosphorus. I heard screams from the tunnel, drowned by more bursts of fire from Dexy and Tank.

I fired down the other tunnel and sprinted into another huge chamber. A generator powered the lights strung across the arched roof. Wooden crates were stacked against one wall. Inside were rows of flat plastic packs, containing morphine base.

I cursed, then swung round as I heard the sound of boots in the tunnel behind me. Tank appeared, with Amica following a couple of paces behind. 'The Stingers?' Tank said.

I shook my head.

He swore again and turned to run back through the tunnel.

Just then I saw the glint of metal among a pile of rocks by the opposite wall.

'Wait,' I said.

I pulled a few boulders out of the stack, exposing a dull green barrel the diameter of a drainpipe. A yellowing but still legible sticker was fixed to it: 'Confidential National Security Information. Unauthorised disclosure subject to US criminal sanctions.'

Tank pushed past me. 'Give me the charges from your bergens.'

He began laying them all the way around the base of the mound. He worked with precision and blinding speed, packing each explosive charge into the mound, fixing a detonator, setting the timer and then moving on to the next.

We ran back through the tunnel into the first chamber. Rounds were still screaming across the entrance, but the firing from the other tunnel had stopped.

Dexy ran back towards us, his face black with smoke and bloodied by a score of cuts from rock splinters. There was a dark stain on his shoulder and his left arm hung limp by his side. 'Two minutes,' he said.

'What's through the other tunnel?'

'Living space, dormitories, kitchens.'

'The enemy?'

'Not any more,' he said. 'Only twelve men. No officers.'

We stared at each other. Something was wrong. Tank was still moving around the chamber laying more charges against the grenades and ammunition.

'One minute.'

I ran through to the third chamber. It was strewn with more bodies. Some had died where they slept, on rugs now stained with blood. I glanced round the chamber. At first I saw nothing unusual, then I noticed the faintest rectilinear outline on the back wall. A door? I stared at it again, then yelled to Tank and Dexy.

Tank took one look, then motioned us into cover and fixed two charges on minimum fusing. He dived for cover just before the blast and the camouflaged steel door flew open, blown from its hinges.

The chamber beyond it was empty, but a long, sloping tunnel led away from it: a rat-run for the officers' escape.

Tank threw himself flat in the entrance and fired his RPG up the tunnel into the darkness. As the echoes faded away, I could hear groans and screams through the ringing in my ears.

'Twenty seconds,' Dexy said. 'Let's go. Let's go.'

Tank paused long enough to slide a detonator and timer into the remaining explosives in his bergen. He pushed it into the mouth of the tunnel, then we turned and ran.

The firefight still lit up the cave entrance. We paused just inside, Dexy and Tank at either side holding white phosphorus grenades.

'Dump everything but your weapon, ammunition and belt kit,' Dexy said. 'I'll count us down. Five . . . four . . .'

They pulled the pins together, then threw the grenades in a high arc, out towards the far end of the canyon. As he reached zero there was a double blast and a blinding flash of white light.

'Go! Go! Go!'

We burst from the cave entrance, half-running and half-falling down the flight of rough stone steps. There was the briefest pause, then the firing intensified. Dexy tripped and crashed the last few feet, landing heavily on his wounded arm, but he dragged himself up at once and loosed off a burst at the machine gun on the cliff top.

I saw a line of tracer cutting through the night towards me and hurled myself flat. Then I pulled myself up to a crouch, fired, rolled sideways and fired again. Amica and Dexy ran past me, then turned and fired, giving Tank and me cover as we dropped back.

I saw Tank stagger and fall as a round tore into his thigh. He hauled himself up at once and hobbled away. A round tugged at my sleeve, another creased my hair and smashed into the rockface behind me. The noise was deafening, overwhelming, the firing so continuous that it merged into an endless cacophony.

There was a flash of answering fire from the track behind us. The next moment Boon sprinted past. We kept moving back a few yards at a time, giving each other what cover we could.

I flattened myself against the ground. Taliban soldiers were running along the narrow ledge at the far end of the ravine. We picked off three or four but at least a dozen ran on, firing as they went. They reached the foot of the steps leading to the cave. Careless of their own lives, a few sprinted towards us, shooting from the hip. The rest began climbing the steps.

I felt sick. They still had time to disarm the charges.

I heard the crack of Amica's rifle, then there was a movement beside me. Tank was up and running back towards them, dragging his wounded leg, his weapon spitting out a continuous stream of fire. The two leading Taliban soldiers were cut to pieces. They fell back, dislodging a third behind them. And then suddenly it seemed that every enemy weapon was concentrated on Tank.

I paused for a second, watching in horror.

'Come on.' Dexy yelled.

But I couldn't take my eyes off what was happening. Tank's body was torn apart; his massive frame disintegrated as the rounds ripped into him. I froze for a moment, then sprinted away, dropped and fired, and then sprinted again. The rattle of the machine gun ahead of us fell silent as we approached.

Rami emptied a magazine in one burst, turned and ran straight back down the track, then threw his machine gun into the ravine. I saw the darkness on the track between us and the waterfall pierced by a score of muzzle-flashes. We were trapped. There were troops in front of us and behind us, and we were pinned between the rockface and the ravine below.

We threw ourselves flat again. There was a roar as Boon detonated the mine by the sangar, but the volume of fire barely altered. Then I heard Boon's gasp as if he had been kicked in the gut. He sank to his knees, clasping his stomach.

There was a tremor like the beginning of another earthquake. I felt the earth buckle and twist as a monstrous explosion lit up the night sky, reverberating from the canyon walls. A blast of hot air, fiercer than a desert wind, swept over us.

As the shockwaves began to fade I heard another sound, a terrible grinding, crushing noise from the mountain behind us. With a roar even louder than the explosion, the entire face of the ravine peeled away in a massive avalanche of rock.

I raised my head. The track behind us now ended in a black void no more than five metres from where I lay. Then a cloud of dust and debris, dense as fog, swirled down the canyon and enveloped us.

'Get down in the ravine,' Boon shouted. 'It's your only chance. I'll hold them off.'

The mess that had been his stomach showed he had no hope. He propped himself against a rock, laid his spare clips alongside him, and put his Browning pistol in his lap.

I hesitated for a second, then uncoiled my rope and looped one end over a boulder. I tied a rough knot and threw the rest into the ravine. The black dust still swirled around me as I swung myself over the edge.

The rope burned my hands as I tried to slow my descent. I looked back and could make out three dark shapes above me, as Amica, Rami and Dexy followed me. Dexy lowered himself one-handed, his left arm dangling useless at his side.

There was an eerie silence. Rather than fire blind, the Taliban were waiting for the dust to clear.

It was a few moments before I realised that the one constant sound that had been accompanying us throughout the long night – the thunder of the river – had ceased.

I looked below me. At first I could see nothing, but as the wind and rain began to disperse the dust cloud, moonlight filtered back into the ravine. There was no trace of the river. It had simply disappeared.

I felt the end of the rope slip between my feet and jerked myself to a halt, ignoring the stabbing pain in my hands. I lowered myself to the very end, hesitated and then let myself go with a silent prayer.

My landing knocked the breath from my body, but I was unhurt. I saw the dark shape of Amica swaying above me. 'Let go, I'll catch you!' I called, but slipped as I caught her and we fell in an awkward heap.

Rami thudded down a moment later. Dexy must have dropped the last few feet of the rope almost in freefall. He crashed down, stifling a cry of pain. I took his good arm and pulled him to his feet.

He jerked twice on the rope and a moment later it came snaking out of the darkness above us and landed in a pool with a splash. 'It'll not delay them for long,' he said. 'Even if they don't have ropes themselves, they'll be able to scramble down where the side of the ravine's blown in.'

Firing broke out again above us. It seemed faint and remote, but I thought of Boon alone on the track, waiting until the magazine of his Kalashnikov was empty, then pushing the barrel of the Browning into his mouth.

I glanced upstream. A massive barrier blocked the ravine, blotting out the light. 'We can use the riverbed. The rockfall's dammed the river.'

Dexy nodded. 'And if we're still in the ravine when the dam breaks . . .' He didn't complete the sentence.

The firing above us reached a crescendo, then ceased. Boon had fulfilled his last obligation to his mates.

'Come on,' Dexy said.

We turned and ran downstream, the sound of our pounding

feet echoing off the rocky walls. We splashed through pools and vaulted over rocks, making no attempt at concealment. Our only hope lay in speed, not secrecy.

There were a few isolated shots in the darkness behind us, but they seemed to be random rather than aimed. I slipped and fell, crashing into an icy pool, and Rami sped past me, churning through the water. I got up and chased after him. Amica was close by, as sure-footed as a cat in the darkness. Hampered by his arm, Dexy brought up the rear.

Whenever I could risk raising my eyes from the ground in front of me I scanned the sides of the ravine, searching for a way up, but the black, glistening walls seemed sheer and featureless. My mind was fuddled with exhaustion and I began a stupid prayer for dawn, even though the light which might guide us to safety would also expose us to the Taliban.

I ran on, straining my ears for the sounds of pursuit, or the noise of the rock dam giving way. I imagined the water level rising higher and higher behind it as millions of gallons continued to flow down from the mountains.

At my feet was the first ominous sign. Water was beginning to flow along the bed of the river again. It was no more than a trickle at first, but it began to swell just as we reached the point where the riverbed disappeared into a narrow cleft of rock. There was no alternative; we had to go through it.

There was no sand or gravel underfoot, just huge slabs of smooth, slimy, water-worn rock. The walls of the ravine pressed in so close they seemed almost to meet over my head. As I began to clamber over the rocks, I heard the crack of rounds from behind us. I slid down the far side of a boulder and peered back. The firing was coming not from the rim of the canyon but from the floor of the ravine. 'Come on,' I said, 'they're on the riverbed.'

The Taliban soldiers were gaining rapidly, advancing over

the smooth floor of the river as we struggled through the rocks. I heard the crack and whine of rounds ricocheting around us, and felt rock splinters tearing my skin. The noise seemed to grow in volume, echoing and reverberating from the walls of the ravine.

The black walls of the cliffs had just begun to open out again and the floor of the riverbed started to level, when I was caught by a wall of water. I lost my footing and fell heavily. I struggled upwards, gasping for air, my arms flailing. I managed to grab hold of a rock and drag myself clear of the surface so I could look back up the canyon.

The rising tide beyond the dam must have made a small breach, no more, but it was clear that our time was running out.

I stumbled on. The blood was pounding and roaring in my ears and my breath was ragged. Amica was just about keeping pace, but she was staggering and her head was lolling on her shoulders. Dexy seemed to be running from memory, his face ghost-white, his expression vacant.

More rounds speckled the water around me. I splashed through the shallows, accelerating as I felt grit and sand beneath my feet. There were more shots from our pursuers, but they were now caught among the rocks while we were increasing our distance from them.

A faint greying of the sky marked the dawn. I could now see that the rim of the ravine was lower below the cleft than above it. I scanned the wall and saw a dark, jagged line – either a fault or a crevasse opened by the earthquake – running down towards the river. If we could scale the cliff, we might be safe.

Rami was twenty yards ahead of me. I shouted and pointed. He swerved and began to climb.

I waited for the other two to catch up, expecting our pursuers to come through the barrier of rocks at any moment. Then I began to climb. I had made many more difficult ascents in my mountaineering days, but never when exhausted, in semi-darkness and soaked to the skin.

With only one arm, Dexy was struggling. I paused to help Amica, then Dexy, over a smooth, almost featureless block of rock. I heard a crack above me and flattened myself against the rock face, shouting a warning.

A boulder the size of my head, dislodged by Rami, smashed down the cliff, so close to my face that I felt a rush of air as it passed. Amica threw herself sideways to avoid it, her arms clawing at the air. I threw out a hand, caught her sleeve and held her until she regained her balance.

We began to climb again. Above me I saw Rami outlined against the sky. 'Come on,' I said. 'He's almost at the top. It's not much further.'

There was the sound of firing from below and bullets struck the cliff around me. The Taliban soldiers were closing fast. Half-hidden inside the crevasse, we were protected for the moment, but soon we would become more exposed.

I pulled myself upwards, the muscles in my arms and legs screaming. Above the rasp of my own breath I could hear Amica sobbing with the effort as she dragged herself up behind me. More rounds smashed into the rock, ever closer to me.

Then I felt a stabbing pain in my leg. I swayed and almost fell. I was only a few feet from the top.

Rami was leaning over the edge looking down at us. Beneath the rattle of gunfire I heard a low rumble. I stared back up the valley. A tide of foam sped along the floor of the ravine. Behind it came a wall of white water, filling it from brim to brim.

The soldiers on the riverbed were swept away, driven like matchwood by the avalanche of water.

I threw myself upwards and my hand caught the edge of the

ravine. I dragged myself up and twisted around, leaning back over the edge as I shouted at Rami to help.

Amica reached out her hand towards mine. It fell short. There was terror in her eyes. I inched forward, hanging over the cliff from the waist, still screaming at Rami to help.

I saw Dexy's face below Amica. Then the water engulfed him.

Amica threw herself forward and her hand met mine. I gripped it with all my strength and dug the fingers of my other hand into a crack in the rock.

Before I could brace myself or take another breath, I felt myself lifted and shaken, crushed by the weight of water. Pain tore through my left hand as the flood tried to sweep me from the rock.

I was dimly aware of the touch of Amica's fingers, still clasped around my right hand, but the roaring water drowned every other sense and my chest was bursting.

Then my head came clear of the surface. I choked, coughing and spitting, and filled my lungs with air. I felt the rock beneath me and pressed myself against it.

Amica's face appeared, water pouring from her nose and mouth. Her eyes flickered and I felt her grip tighten. Rami was only a metre away. 'Help me,' I said. 'For God's sake, help me.'

He looked me in the eye, then turned and ran. I heard another roar and saw a fresh line of white water careering down the canyon towards us.

Amica's grip weakened and I felt her start to slip away.

My worst nightmare had returned. I saw Jane's hand slipping from mine, the waters closing over her face for ever.

'NO!' I lunged forward and grasped Amica's wrist. I pulled her arm with all my might, hauled her back over the edge, and dragged her to the rock Rami had used to save himself. I shielded her body with mine and braced myself as the second wave broke over us.

I felt as if I was sinking, the pressure building in my ears, my heart pounding, my tortured lungs screaming for air. The water was tearing at me, dragging me inexorably away. I fought against the urge to breathe, but as my consciousness faded, freezing water filled my mouth and nose.

Then, as quickly as it had come, the wave had swept past. I collapsed to my knees, retching. If a third one came, I was dead. I dragged myself upright.

Amica had slumped forward, face-down on the ground. I felt ice in my heart. I called to her, rolled her over and then began thumping her chest with the heels of my hands, driving water from her lungs. She lay corpse-still for a moment longer, then convulsed, coughing and choking, as more water poured from her mouth.

Her eyes flickered open. I put my arms around her and we sobbed on each other's shoulders.

The flood water started to drop back into the ravine. I looked around. We were alone; not a figure moved in the whole of the valley. Rami had either escaped or drowned, I no longer cared which.

I looked at Amica. She was deathly pale and trembling with shock and cold. 'Can you stand?' I said. 'Can you walk?'

She nodded.

As I put my weight on my left leg, I felt a stabbing pain. I looked down. One of the rounds fired by the Taliban had ripped across my calf, gouging its way through the flesh.

Arms around each other, we hobbled away from the edge of the ravine. The narrow plain was barely recognisable. All trace of the track had disappeared and the force of the flood had stripped the vegetation from the fields, leaving a glistening surface of wet mud and bare rock.

We stumbled on as it got lighter. On the far side of the plain, against the mountain wall, a mound of boulders had been washed from the cliff face and then dumped by the flood. There was a narrow gap behind them, just wide enough for the two of us to squeeze into.

Amica took the shell-dressing from my belt kit. The wrapper had been perforated and the dressing was sodden and stained. She hesitated, then squeezed out as much water from the dressing as she could and bandaged my wound. Then we huddled down together, hidden from sight, crying with relief at our own survival and with grief for the loss of our friends.

We had succeeded in our mission, but at what cost? I thought of all the deaths – Dexy, Boon, Tank, Jeff, Dave and the other guys buried alive by the earthquake – and of all the bereaved wives and fatherless children left behind.

Other deaths weighed on me too. No one waited for me or depended on me, yet I seemed to be condemned always to survive while others, more deserving of life, did not.

Too exhausted to keep watch, we closed our eyes and fell asleep, Amica's head still resting on my shoulder.

Chapter 16

The sun was high in the sky when I woke. I was still cold and tired, my bones ached and the wound in my calf was throbbing. Amica slept on, huddled against my shoulder. I kept my movements slow, trying not to wake her as I raised my head a fraction to peer from behind the shelter of the rocks.

Beyond the valley wall, thin cloud trailed from the peaks of the mountains to the north and east of us, like smoke in the wind. I saw vultures spiralling on the thermals high above us. The feathers at their wingtips clawed at the piercing blue of the sky.

I could see no movement, no living thing, on the floor of the narrow plain that separated us from the ravine. It was littered with flood debris — broken branches, tree trunks, even huge boulders — dumped as the water receded.

Depressions and shell craters in the floor of the plain were flooded with water that steamed in the heat of the sun. The soil, reduced to patches of chocolate-brown mud, was already crazed with cracks as it dried. Trapped once again in its rocky gorge, the sound of the river had faded to a sullen roar, but a dark stain about three metres up the cliff behind us told a different story.

My movement was enough to wake Amica. She sat up, her face blank, staring at me as she tried to piece together the events of the previous night. Her cropped hair was matted with dirt and mud, her face grey with fatigue.

I stood, still crouching behind the boulders, and tried to rub some life and warmth back into my limbs. I fumbled at my belt for my emergency rations. My belt kit was still sodden, but the foil packets were unbroken. I opened one and ate a couple of mouthfuls, then passed the rest to Amica. She ate even less than me. The effect was almost worse than having no food at all.

'How is your leg?' she said.

'It hurts, but it'll be all right. You?'

'Okay. Should we wait for dark?'

I hesitated and scanned the plain again from end to end. Nothing moved. 'We should.'

'But?'

'We need to make whatever time we can while the Taliban are reorganising. When they realise what's happened they'll be piling troops in here. If we're still in the area, we're dead.'

'Then let's take our chance.'

I moved out of our shelter and took a few hesitant steps. The pain in my leg flared with each one, but I gritted my teeth and kept moving. It eased to a dull ache, but I could see a spot of fresh blood staining the bandage.

Amica followed me as I limped along the edge of the plateau, hugging the valley wall. Our footprints made an unmistakable trail through the mud but there was nothing we could do about it. Our only hope was to be long gone when the first Taliban soldiers set eyes on them.

I had formed no coherent plan, driven more by the urge to keep moving than anything else. To head down the valley was inviting capture, but to move back towards the caves seemed even more suicidal. Had I been alone and uninjured I might have tried to scale the sheer walls of the valley and escape over the ridge, but carrying a leg wound and with Amica alongside me, it was impossible. Our only hope seemed to be to keep on past the natural barrier where the granite outcrop cut the valley in half, and then seek a way up the gentler cliffs beyond.

My movements became easier and the pain in my leg lessened as a little warmth crept back into my bones, but it did nothing to ease my weariness, or the despair that threatened to overwhelm me. We were alone in a hostile country and every hand would be raised against us. There seemed so little hope, so little point in carrying on, that I felt a powerful urge simply to give up, lie down and await the end. I tried to bury the thought, but it returned again and again. Only fear of what Amica would suffer at the hands of the Taliban if they found us, and the ice-hard glint of determination in her eyes, kept me moving.

We walked in hundred-yard stages, pausing between each one, crouching down to look for any movement and listen for any sound. The silence was total. There was only the empty plain and the sky above.

We paused in the shadows of the ridge barring the way to the lower half of the valley, ate another mouthful of rations and took a few mouthfuls of water. I refilled my canteen from a flooded bomb-crater, though the water was as brown and muddy as the river from which it had come, then I wormed my way forward and raised my head. I was totally unprepared for what I saw. We had passed through here just the previous day, but it was as if I had never set eyes on this landscape before.

The steep ravine that had channelled and curbed the worst impact of the flood broadened into a valley below it, and the wall of water it had unleashed had hit the valley like a nuclear bomb.

The thin covering of earth had been stripped away, laying the bedrock bare. Not a single tree, not a building remained standing. The entire village of Agha Shah Azuin, the blue-tiled mosque and the rows of houses as squat and strong as forts, had disappeared. All that remained were low mounds of mud-covered rubble dumped by the flood and boulders so massive that even its ferocious power had not been enough to dislodge them.

The only movement came from the vultures and ravens gorging themselves among the detritus abandoned at the edge of the flood as the waters receded.

'What have we done?' Amica said. 'We have destroyed the Taliban's missiles, but killed more people than if they had used them.' She lowered her head to her arms and wept.

I put a hand on her shoulder, but could find nothing to say, no way of denying the truth of her words. I led the way in silence to the valley floor. We kept close to the edge of the plain, skirting mounds of rubble and pools of mud and slurry that sucked at our legs like quicksand. I averted my eyes from one mound of rubble where a group of vultures were bickering over their spoils, their heads stained crimson.

Amica trudged on, her face white, keeping her gaze fixed on the ground. On the outskirts of what had once been Agha Shah Azuin's village, the foundations of houses protruded through the mud and silt. We walked on. A quarter of a mile ahead of us, I could see a faint grey line rising from the high water mark. A path, little more than a goat track, led upwards, disappearing behind a shoulder of the hill. I pointed to it and urged Amica on.

We had perhaps two hours of daylight remaining; long enough, I hoped, to reach the ridge dividing this valley from the next and make out a safe route we could take across it during the night. Fatigue dragged at me, but I was reluctant to rest in case my leg stiffened up. Occasional spots of fresh blood still showed on the bandage.

As we left the site of the village, I saw tracks in the mud ahead of us, leading towards the path up the hillside. I crouched down to examine them. They had been made at least a couple of hours earlier; the edges of the footprints had dried in the sun. I hesitated, but could see no choice but to follow them up the hillside.

We moved on with greater caution. As we rounded the shoulder of the hill I pulled Amica down into cover. A building stood at the side of the trail, above the floodline, perhaps a hundred yards away. It had been hidden from us until now by the fold in the hills. The window apertures gaped empty and the roof had fallen in. The remains of a crude stone chimney stack poked up from the ruins of one wall.

We watched for five minutes and then began to move forward. As we approached, I heard a noise, as faint at first as the wind whistling through a cracked window-pane. I turned my head, trying to pinpoint the source of the sound, then eased my rifle from my shoulder and slid off the safety-catch.

I went on, one step at a time. The noise grew louder. I motioned Amica to get down into cover, then wormed my way through the dirt below a gaping window-frame and flattened myself against the wall by the door.

I took three deep breaths to steady myself, then swung round the door-frame and levelled my weapon. The room was a mess of rubble and fallen timbers, but a boy was crouching in the far corner, in the crook of the wall. A Kalashnikov lay on the ground alongside him as he sat hunched, his arms wrapped around his knees, rocking slowly backwards and forwards, keening to himself.

Daru stopped and stared at me in silence. Keeping my eyes fixed on him, I called to Amica.

'Where is your father?' I said to the boy.

He shook his head.

'Your mother?'

'Gone, all gone.' He began to cry again.

Amica ran to him and held him until he quietened. 'How did you escape?' she said.

'I got up before dawn to take the goats to the high pasture.' He spoke in a low monotone. 'The muezzin had just begun to call the faithful to prayer when I heard a sound like thunder. The goats scattered. I tried to chase them, but they kept running.

'When I looked back, the village had disappeared, buried under the water. Later, I climbed back down the track. My father, my mother, my brothers and sisters, all had gone. I could not even find where our house had been, so I came back here to my uncle's house. But he left yesterday morning on the *haj*. I've been waiting here for someone to come back.'

Amica hugged him to her again, tears pouring down her face. 'They won't be coming back, Daru. You know that, don't you?'

'Where are the other survivors?' I said. 'I saw more than one set of tracks in the mud back there.'

'The Taliban killed them,' he said. 'Two other boys from the village escaped the flood because they had been herding their goats. We went down to the village together. Once I had seen it, I came back here; they said they would wait in case anyone came back.

'An hour later I heard shots. I ran out of the house and hid in the trees. When I looked down towards the village, I saw two Taliban soldiers standing over the other boys' bodies.'

I was thinking hard. 'Were the men officers?'

He nodded. 'They had a missile. Only officers fire them.'

I froze. 'How do you know it was a missile?'

'I know all weapons, Inglisi.'

'Describe it to me.'

'It was dark green, with a wide, round top.' He used his hands to sketch the size and shape in the air. 'And it had letters on the side in your language.'

I felt sick. 'There was definitely only one?' I said.

He nodded.

Amica met my gaze. 'They must have escaped from that tunnel with one—'

I finished the sentence for her. 'Or they kept it with the anti-aircraft guns in one of those sangars on the cliff top.'

'But what can they do with one?'

'The same as they did to BZ169.'

Daru sat silent, watching us.

I avoided his eye. 'We have to get moving.'

Amica gave the boy water and some of our rations, then stood up. 'Wait for a moment,' she said. 'I must speak with my man.'

She led me back outside and studied my face for a moment. 'He comes with us.'

'Are you out of your mind? Our only hope of finding that Stinger is to move as fast as the Taliban we're chasing. And you want to bring a kid with us?'

'If we don't, he'll die.'

'If we do, we will.'

There was not a glimmer of doubt in her eyes. 'His family are all dead because of what we did, Sean. Enough have died. No more.'

I gave a guilty glance towards the house.

'He won't be a liability,' Amica continued. 'His family and his name are known. He can speak for us, vouch for us to the Taliban, and he'll be good camouflage; we'll look more like a man and wife with him.'

Daru was now leaning out of the empty window-frame. 'Please take me with you,' he said. 'I can guide you through the mountains. I can track the Taliban, I can shoot, I can run, I can steal, I can find food. Take me with you. Take me to America.'

Still I hesitated, lowering my voice so he could not overhear us. 'What if he finds out what caused the flood? He could betray us.'

'He won't.' She stared at me. 'I mean it, Sean. He goes with us. If you're not happy about that, then you must go alone.'

'I guess that settles it, then.' I gave a weary smile. 'Let's go.'

'All three of us?'

'All three of us.'

'Wait a minute.' She glanced at Daru. 'Let's see what we can find in the house – clothes, food, anything.'

I began sifting through the debris in the first room as Amica clambered through a rubble-filled doorway. I found an old Soviet ammunition box in a corner. Inside was a rusty tin half-full of raisins, a handful of rice grains, an onion and two discs of naan bread, green with mould. I put the onion in one pocket, emptied the rice and raisins into the other, and was about to throw the tin and the naan bread away when Amica stopped me.

'Wait. We can use those.'

She had found a pale blue and a mauve burka and a torn, threadbare blanket. She put them down on the floor and took one of the naan. 'Let me see your wound,' she said.

I hesitated, then sat down and took off the soiled dressing.

'It's going to get infected if we don't do something,' she said.

She tore a couple of pieces from the disc of bread, then

rubbed them where the wall met the ceiling in the corner of the room.

'What are you doing?' I said.

'Getting cobwebs.' She walked back and knelt down in front of me.

'Why?'

She gave me a patient look. 'We've lost our medical kit, Sean. We have to do it the Afghan way. They don't have antibiotics or dressings.'

She placed the fragments of bread over the two wounds, tore a strip from the blanket and bound it tightly around them.

'It feels better already,' I said.

She gave a half-smile, the first I had seen from her in days. 'Then let's go.'

She made a loose bundle of the clothing she had found, added the empty tin and the rest of the naan bread and tied it across her back, using another strip from the blanket.

We moved off up the track. Daru led the way, his Kalashnikov slung across his shoulder. He hurried ahead, then waited for us to catch up.

'How much do we tell him?' I asked as he ranged ahead of us again.

'Not everything,' Amica said. 'But if he's going to help protect us, he needs to know that we're on the run from the Taliban and that a wrong word could give us away.'

'What were you saying?' Daru had moved back down the track to chide us for our slowness.

'That we should tell you the truth,' Amica said. 'If any Taliban – not just the two who killed your friends – find out who we are, they will kill us.'

He studied me for a while as he digested the information. 'I already knew that,' he said. 'We shall say you are my uncle. My father's name is well known. My word will be enough.'

Amica frowned. 'But if they hear his accent, they will know he is not of your tribe. They'll know he is *faranji*.'

Daru considered that for a moment. 'Then we shall say he is dumb,' he said. 'There was an old man in the village who could not speak.' He imitated the grunting noises he made, then winked at me. 'Leave the talking to me, Inglisi.'

He turned and ran on again.

I shook my head. 'Two hours ago he was broken-hearted at the loss of his family. Now he's running around like a kid without a trouble in the world.'

'Don't think his pain is any less.'

We reached the ridge about half an hour before sunset. There was no sign of the Taliban soldiers on the slopes below us. A caravan of mules and camels moved slowly along the track in the bottom of the valley and I could hear the tinkle of bells as a shepherd led his sheep down from the hills. Compared to the valley of devastation behind us it was a different world.

We passed a group of three windswept larches as we made our way down. Nearby were the ruins of a sheepfold, a rough, dry-stone semi-circle, and a crumbling shepherd's hut roofed with twigs. The last rays of the sun were still warming us, but I thought of the cold night ahead.

My body cried out for rest and sleep, and my mind was so fuddled with fatigue I could no longer think clearly. I looked at Amica. 'Do we stop or move on?'

She thought about it in silence as she stared down into the valley. 'We stop,' she said. 'We can't track the Taliban in the dark, and if we're caught breaking the curfew we have no real excuse. If we move openly by day, we can stick to Daru's story.' She gave another half-smile. 'You see, he's already paying his way.' Then the smile faded. 'There is no one from his village to contradict us.'

We dropped below the skyline and moved round to the sheepfold. A soft rain of yellowing larch needles fell around us as we sat with our backs against the wall. I reached into my pocket and shared out some of the raisins. I began to eat them one at a time.

Daru looked at me. 'This is all we eat?'

'This is all we have. It may have to last us several days.'

He unslung his rifle. 'I will find us food.'

'No.' I laid a hand on his arm. 'No shooting, that will attract too much attention.'

He shrugged and laid down the gun. 'You found rice in the house, yes? Give me some.'

'We have to save it, Daru.'

He shook his head, exasperated. 'Not to eat.'

Puzzled, I dug my hand back in my pocket. He removed the thin cord tied round his jacket, searched among the litter of larch needles and twigs until he found a large stick, then ran off down the hillside clutching a handful of grains.

I looked at Amica. 'Do you think we'll see him again?'

'Of course we will.'

I lay back against the wall, too weary to speak again.

I woke with a start and scrambled to my feet when Amica laid her hand on my arm.

'It's all right,' she said. 'I've been keeping watch. Daru's back.'

Through the gathering dusk his teeth showed white as he smiled at me, and something hit the ground with a soft thud.

I looked down. Two partridges lay in the dirt. 'How did you—?'

Daru grinned in triumph. 'My father taught me this. You lay a trail of grains of rice across the ground to a flat rock propped with a stick, then you sit very quiet, holding the end of the cord tied to the stick. The partridges come and eat the rice grains until—' He clapped his hands together.

Amica smiled. 'The first decent meal in days, even if it is raw.'

'Let me show you my trick,' I said. I moved around in the last of the light, gathering larch needles, lichen, moss and small twigs.

Daru climbed one of the larches and hung from a dead branch until it snapped, sending him crashing to the ground. He picked himself up unhurt and began breaking it up.

'How are you going to light the fire?' Amica said.

'Special Forces kit. Every piece has a dual purpose. One of the buttons on the jacket is a compass, there's a tungsten saw blade sewn into the seam and then there's this.' I undid my belt and worked the buckle loose. 'The edge is sharpened steel, you can use it as a knife, but the prong of the buckle is a softer metal – aluminium. Strike them together and you make a spark.'

I knelt down in the shelter of the wall, out of the wind and the line of sight from the valley, and plucked a handful of feathers from the chest of one of the partridges. I held the prong in the middle of them and struck it a few times. Sparks flew and the feathers began to smoulder. I blew on it and dropped fragments of lichen, dry moss and larch needles on to it until it glowed red and then burst into flame.

As the flames strengthened I added dry sticks, then sat back on my haunches, embarrassed at my glow of achievement. 'The Boy Scouts meet James Bond,' I said. 'Sorry, you wouldn't know—'

Amica interrupted me. 'Even the Taliban have heard of James Bond, Sean.'

While Daru fed the fire, I plucked and gutted the partridges, then impaled them on a couple of sharpened larch sticks. The smell of the birds cooking over the fire sent saliva flooding into my mouth. We devoured every scrap of the flesh and then chewed on the thin, brittle bones.

We had no tea, but Amica took the empty tin from her bundle, filled it with water and boiled it in the embers of the fire. We passed it round, holding it in a scrap of blanket.

I was still exhausted, but the black, debilitating depression that had hung over me had lifted. I knew that the odds against us were still astronomical, but I no longer had the slightest thought of giving up.

The need for us to rest outweighed the risk of not mounting a guard. We let the fire burn itself out and huddled down together in the cold of the night, sharing the warmth of our bodies.

I was woken by Daru shaking my shoulder. 'It is almost light,' he said. 'We must go.' I smiled at the way he was assuming the leadership of the party.

Before we left, I rekindled the fire and boiled some more water. We shared it, sitting against the wall, watching the dawn flow from mountain to mountain and across the ridge around us. The valley floor below was still in shadow, but I could see smoke rising from a few houses and figures already moving out towards the fields.

I hobbled around, trying to force some movement back into my leg. Amica watched me for a moment. 'Let me see it.' She peeled away the bandage and stinking fluid oozed from the wound. 'Sit down and wait,' she said.

'We must move.'

'We can wait half an hour.' She took the onion we'd scavenged from the ruined house, pushed it into the ashes of the fire and left it to bake. When she scraped it out of the fire, she cut it in half and left it to cool slightly, then pressed it against the wound on my leg.

I let out a yelp of pain as I felt the heat burning into me.

She ignored me, binding it tight with the bandage. 'This will draw out the poison.'

'And then we eat the onion, right?'

She gave a weak smile, then stood up and pulled on one of the burkas we'd found in the house. She reached up inside it to remove her trousers. I turned my back as she did so and cuffed Daru, who was watching with great interest. 'Perhaps this is the last time you will have to wear it,' I said. 'When we reach the border you can take it off and burn it.'

'If we reach the border,' she said, her voice already muffled and her eyes invisible behind the lattice screen.

We collected our belongings and moved out. 'Any people we meet,' Daru said, 'or any checkpoints, I'll do the talking. Whatever happens, don't say anything.'

I smiled. 'I'm being ordered around by a twelve-year-old boy.'

'No,' Daru said. 'You're being ordered around by a twelve-year-old man.'

We made good time down the side of the valley, keeping pace with the line of the sunrise, as the villages below us came to life. People herded animals out into the fields and a steady stream of foot-traffic moved along the road. Further down, we passed a villager working in his field. I held myself alert, my fingers twitching on the butt of my rifle, as Daru exchanged the ritual pleasantries. 'Have you seen two Taliban soldiers?' Daru said.

The villager spat. 'An hour ago. I offered to share my breakfast with them. They took it all. I have nothing left to offer you.'

'Which way were they heading?' Daru said

'Down the valley, towards Mazar,'

We moved on. Our pace slowed more and more as each person we passed had to be greeted, his state of health enquired after, his livestock admired, his offers of hospitality politely declined. From every dwelling, no matter how poor, even those devastated by the earthquake, the owners would hasten to offer us something – tea, bread, grapes, a handful of raisins – or would offer to share their meal. Refusal took longer than acceptance.

Merchants driving a mule train down the valley pressed ropes of nuts threaded on string around our necks, as if they were garlands of flowers. It was a gesture of pure hospitality to fellow travellers; they had no hope or expectation of selling anything to us.

The leader stopped to talk as his sons moved on down the road, driving the mules before them with thin, whippy branches. 'What goods are you carrying?' Daru said.

'We are Blue Men.'

Daru smiled and pointed to the bundles of rifles tied on either side of the mules swaying past us. 'They don't look like lapis lazuli to me.'

'We must trade for what we want – guns for lapis.'

'And is that all you're carrying?'

The merchant smiled. 'There are other things one can buy in Pakistan, which are highly valued in Afghanistan.' He turned to move on down the road.

Amica leaned close to Daru's ear. 'Ask him where he's bound.'

'Where are you going?' Daru said.

'To Mazar to trade. Then back to Peshawar.'

'May you travel safely,' Daru said.

'And may you not be tired,' the man said. He touched his hand to his heart and then hurried after the mule train.

Amica was watching me. 'What do you think?'

'About what?'

'We could travel with the merchant. Any checkpoint we pass

on our own could mean the end for us. We have no papers, no right to be in this area.'

'We've a good story.'

She shrugged. 'Maybe. But if we travel with the mule train, we're just three more nomads. He will pay his usual bribe so that they let him pass and they'll look the other way.'

'But why should he take us?' I said.

'Because merchants love money above everything else and we will pay him well to do so.'

I saw the sense in what Amica had said, and after a moment I nodded. 'All right, let's do it.'

I unbuttoned my shirt and pulled out one of the Saudi gold riyals from the money belt next to my skin. I laid it on a stone and cut it in half with my knife, the blade biting through the soft metal. I pocketed one half and gave the other to Daru. 'Run after the merchant and tell him he can have that now and the other half when we're across the border, if we can travel with him.'

Daru took the half-coin and spun it into the air, watching the sunlight glitter from it, then caught it and ran off, shouting and waving. He rapidly overhauled the slow-moving mule train and spoke to the merchant for a few minutes, then whistled and signalled us to follow him.

'I told him you were injured and my aunt is tired,' Daru said as we came up to him. 'He and his wife will walk, you can ride their mules, but he wants to see the other half of the coin first.'

I took it out of my pocket and handed it to the merchant. He tested it with his teeth, put the two halves of the coin together and then tossed it back to me, nodding and smiling. I clambered on to a mule; Amica sat side-saddle on the one behind, and Daru padded alongside us in the dust, chattering and laughing with the merchant.

We moved at a bare walking pace, the bells around the mules' necks clanking at each step. It was a relief not to be walking on my injured leg, but the heat, the slow pace, the dust thrown up by the hooves of the mules and the clouds of flies took their toll. Not only this, but the hard wooden saddle, covered with only a thin blanket, chafed my legs.

As I shifted my weight, trying to ease the discomfort, my knee banged into one of the saddle-bags and I heard the chink of glass. I undid the strap. A bolt of cloth lay across the top of the bag. Underneath it were rows of bottles of whisky.

I glanced around. The merchant was ahead of me, deep in conversation with Daru, and the other members of his family trailed well behind. I slid down from the saddle, leaving the mule to plod along, and dropped back to walk alongside Amica. 'This guy is smuggling alcohol. I think there's more risk in travelling with him than there is in going it alone.'

She turned to look at me and I peered through the mesh of the burka, trying to read the expression in her eyes. 'You're right,' she said. She jumped down from the mule. 'Get Daru.'

'I can't speak, remember,' I said, but I ran to the front of the column and tugged at Daru's arm and then beckoned him back away from the merchant.

'What is it?' he said.

I beckoned again, then froze. Some distance ahead along the track, I could see a dust cloud moving fast towards us and the sun glinting off a windscreen. I took his wrist and pulled him away. The merchant muttered something to himself and then called to the eldest of his two sons, who hurried forward to stand alongside him.

'What is it?' Daru said.

'He's carrying alcohol. It's not safe for us to travel with him. If the Taliban find it they might shoot the lot of us. We need to get away.'

'What about the gold?'

'To hell with the gold. Let him keep it.'

The outline of a vehicle was now clearly visible and I could hear the note of its engine. 'Shit!' I said. 'It's too late. We'll be spotted if we try and run for it.'

We hurried back along the line of animals. Amica dropped into step with the wives and daughters and began talking to them, but I could hear the strain in her voice. Daru and I walked a few paces in front of them.

When I raised my head again the vehicle was almost upon us, its red bonnet shimmering in the heat haze. It skidded to a halt and a group of black-clad soldiers jumped out, surrounding the merchant and his son. The merchant exchanged a few words with the Taliban leader, then passed him a bundle of Afghanis. As the man licked his thumb and counted them, I saw his face. I pulled my turban lower on my forehead and wrapped the trailing end around the lower part of my face.

Salan slipped the money into his pocket. Then he began walking along the line of animals, pulling at their packs. He pulled out one of the rifles from a bundle, raised it to his shoulder and pretended to fire at the merchant. His men laughed. 'Why are you still bringing Kalashnikovs? The Soviets left us plenty. We need Armalites,' he said. 'The Americans are dogs and infidels, but they make good weapons.'

He slapped the saddle-bags on the next mule and his smile faded. He ripped the strap from it, pulled out the bolt of cloth and threw it in the dirt, then brandished a bottle over his head. His voice rose to a scream.

His men grabbed the merchant and his son, and dragged them back to where Salan was standing. He smashed the bottle over the merchant's head. Blood and whisky streamed down his face as he sank to his knees. His son received the same treatment.

The Taliban piled the rest of the bottles in a mound in front of them.

Salan emptied his magazine into the bottles, smashing every one. Glass fragments flew like shrapnel in all directions. Then he shouted an order to his men. They stripped the terrified traders to the waist, then pinioned their arms as two other soldiers strode up to them. They wore lengths of electric cable wrapped around their waists like belts, which they untied, twisted around their wrists a couple of turns and began to beat the merchant and his son. The cables rose and fell, whistling through the air, and the men writhed and screamed as the lashes bit into their flesh.

I looked away, but the obscene sounds of the beating continued. Even after both men had lapsed into unconsciousness the Taliban continued to rain blows down on their bodies. When Salan at last called a halt, the traders lay inert in a puddle of spilt whisky, blood and broken glass. Salan took something from his pocket and stooped over them. As he straightened up and put his gunmetal lighter back in his pocket, I saw blue flame envelop the two motionless bodies.

Salan watched for a moment, then strolled down the line of mules towards us, his men at his shoulders, their cables still dripping with blood. I felt sweat prickle my brow. Despite my tanned face and dyed hair and beard, I was sure he would recognise me. He stopped in front of me. 'You are merchants?'

I kept my head bowed, but gestured towards Daru. 'We are not merchants but travellers,' he said. 'My uncle cannot talk, he is a mute. I will speak for him.'

'He hears well enough though,' Salan said. He pulled the cloth away from my mouth. 'Open your mouth.'

As I hesitated, Salan swung his fist and pain exploded in my head.

'Open your mouth.'

I did so, and felt an agonising pain in my tongue as he clamped a pair of rusty pliers on it and pulled. Frozen with fear, I made inarticulate gargling sounds. He pulled out a curved knife and laid it across my exposed tongue. 'As he can't speak, he won't need this.' His men bayed with laughter. The edge of the blade stung my tongue and I tasted blood.

'Please do not hurt him,' Daru said. 'He is the brother of my father, Agha Shah Azuin, a great warrior and ally of the Taliban.'

I felt the pressure from the blade stop and a moment later Salan released the pliers. I tried to stand motionless, still keeping my eyes averted from him as I struggled to suppress the fear that was shaking me.

'I know your father's name,' he said. 'He is a brave man and a great fighter for the cause. Why are you not at his side?'

'My father is dead,' Daru said. 'Killed with all my other family by the great flood that swept our valley two nights ago.'

'And were there strangers in your village before the flood?'

I held my breath, but Daru shook his head. 'I saw none. Why do you ask?'

'There are traitors and enemies in our midst. We will search everywhere, under every rock until we find them. You have seen no strangers on your journey here?'

'They are all strangers to me here, but apart from those men' – he gestured to the merchants still lying motionless in the dust – 'all those we have met were Afghan and good Muslims, as far as I could tell.'

The answer seemed to satisfy Salan, for his stance relaxed a little. 'Where are you travelling?'

Daru shrugged again. 'To Mazar, Konarlan, even to Kabul. Anywhere I can find work. My father is dead and our lands are now worthless. The soil has been stripped away by the flood. But I am the head of the family now and I must support my aunt and uncle. They are all I have left — save for my other uncle who, Allah be praised, left on a *haj* the morning before the flood.'

Salan's expression changed. 'I know of no *haj* from Kabul. From where is he flying?'

'From Dir in Pakistan, in four days' time.'

Salan smiled and turned to one of his men. 'He will be truly blessed.'

Salan reached out and stroked the boy's cheek. 'Go to Qandahar,' he said. 'We are building a new capital of the Muslim Republic there and the Taliban always has need of brave fighters.'

Daru touched a hand to his heart. 'Thank you, perhaps I will go there.'

The Taliban walked on to the rear of the mule train, checking all the saddle-bags. The women huddled together around the younger son, keeping their eyes averted and heads bent. The soldiers turned and moved back towards their vehicle, past the smoking bodies of their victims.

The truck stopped alongside us and Salan reached out to ruffle Daru's hair and again pat his cheek. 'We shall meet in Qandahar,' he said.

I turned my head away, still fearing recognition, and found myself eye to eye with a soldier in the back. I hurriedly dropped my gaze and as I did so I saw an olive drab shape protruding from a piece of sacking on the floor of the Toyota.

The Taliban drove off up the valley in a cloud of dust.

'I saw the two soldiers,' Daru said.

'I know. I saw the Stinger.'

I paused. 'Wait one minute.' Even though I knew it was hopeless, I ran along the mule train and felt for a pulse in the necks of the two traders. I stood up and shook my head. There was a wail of grief from the women as they ran forward to claim the bodies of their men.

I handed Daru the other half of the gold coin. 'Give it to them,' I said.

'But we may need it.'

I shook my head. 'I have plenty more. Give it to them.'

He handed it to the merchant's younger son, who stood bewildered at the edge of the group of women, clutching the coin in his palm.

The fate of the men was nothing to do with us. They had died not because we were with them, but because they were smuggling whisky. Still it felt a betrayal to walk away from them. I hesitated, then signalled to Daru.

'Let's go.'

Chapter 17

We moved away from the road, across the fields towards the wall of the valley. 'What will happen to them?' I said.

Amica shrugged. 'They will bury their dead and then move on. The lapis dealers will express their sorrow and then try to rob them. The young son will grow up very quickly, Insh'Allah.' Her voice was matter-of-fact. Daru nodded his agreement.

I was caught between admiration and revulsion for a people who could bear the most appalling suffering and accept every cruelty of fate. 'Where do you think the soldiers are heading?'

'I don't know,' Amica said. 'They could be making for another cave in the mountains, but more likely they're making for the border and Peshawar.'

'It's the easiest route. The passes north of there are 5,000 metres high and winter is coming on. And Peshawar is where the Taliban was formed; they have many friends there.'

'What about us?' Amica asked.

I thought about this for a minute.

'North-east?' I said.

She hesitated for a second, then nodded. 'North-east.'

We followed a small trail through the foothills, keeping clear of the main track along the middle of the valley. Towards sunset we climbed higher into the hills, looking for a safe place for the night, but we could find no building, not even ruins, and had to settle for a night in the open, huddled in a hollow in the ground, sheltering from the biting wind.

We waited until full dark before risking a fire. As I boiled water, after we had eaten, Daru reached back into his pocket and produced sugar and green tea in twists of paper. He looked very pleased with himself, and I knew exactly how he'd procured the supplies. 'Daru,' I said, 'I can't deny it's wonderful to have these things, but you're taking a terrible risk in stealing them. Every person we meet offers us hospitality anyway. They give us the food from their table without even being asked. Why steal from them?'

He stared back at me, his face sullen. 'You are not my father. You do not tell me what I can and cannot do.'

'If I speak to you as a father might, it's because I've come to respect and like you. And I don't want to see you hurt. I've been in the sports stadium in Kabul when they have cut off men's hands for stealing. I don't want it to happen to you.'

'If they are stupid enough to be caught, they deserve to lose their hands. They will never catch me.'

'I hope not. But please – no more stealing unless I say so. All right?'

He shrugged. 'Okay. Okay. No more stealing.'

Amica changed the bandage on my leg before we settled down for the night. To my surprise the primitive medicine had worked and the wound was already cleaner and much less painful. I kicked earth over the ashes of the fire and kept watch for an hour as the others slept, in case it had been spotted from the valley below. Then I too lay down and slept next to Amica, huddling into her to share the warmth of our bodies.

We moved on at first light. After a few miles, the trail we had been following led into another, slightly broader track. We had gone only a hundred yards along it when we came to a checkpoint manned by a man and a boy. They could have been a grandfather and his grandson.

'A hundred Afghanis to pass,' the old man said.

'We are refugees,' Daru said, 'made homeless by the earth-quake and the great flood that swept our valley.'

The man's face remained impassive. 'A hundred Afghanis to pass.'

'I am Daru, son of Agha Shah Azuin.'

'And I am Omar, son of Abdul,' the old man said. 'A hundred Afghanis to pass.'

Amica whispered to me. 'Give him fifty.'

I turned my back on the old man and peeled a few grubby, damp-stained notes from the bundle I still carried, and handed the old man the money.

Daru was staring at the man with fierce hatred. 'My father would have killed you for this.'

'He would have had to,' the man said in an even voice. 'No one passes here without payment.'

I put my arm around Daru's shoulders and led him past them. 'I should have killed him,' he said, his jaw clenched.

'You should,' I said, 'but then we would have had to fight his relatives too. Are the Taliban not enemies enough for now?'

We moved on, past fields of opium poppies, their seed heads already milked of sap, dried brown and hard in the sun. A row of golden poplars by the river shimmered with light as the sun struck their leaves, and the last summer flowers flared from the fields around us in slashes of crimson, turquoise, purple and blue. Birds and clouds of butterflies darted among them, drinking the nectar and feeding on the seed heads, their own vibrant colours accentuated by the barren brown of the hills around them.

The valley began to narrow and the air was sharper and cleaner as we climbed into the hills, leaving the baking heat and dust of the plain behind us. Bands of parched grass and dusty scrub alternated with cool forests of cedar and larch.

I saw another rough barrier ahead. The twisted barrel of a Soviet artillery piece had been dragged from its grave in the undergrowth and lain across the track between two boulders. It was manned by four Taliban soldiers. I slowed almost to a stop.

'Come on,' Daru said. 'There is nothing to fear. Give me some money, I will need maybe 200 Afghani.'

He strode to the barrier, announcing his name and lineage as he walked. He spoke to them for a few minutes, gesturing towards Amica and me, and then produced his bundle of notes.

The Taliban leader inspected it, weighing it in his palm, but made no move to pocket it. He looked again at Amica and me. He was so young he had no more than a few stray wisps of beard, but he stroked them thoughtfully. 'How do I know this man and woman are who you say they are? My commander was here not two hours ago. He warned me of enemies loose in the country – *faranji kafir.*'

'Do I look like a foreigner or an infidel?' Daru said.

The Taliban soldier ignored him, pushing him aside. He stopped directly in front of Amica. 'Take off your burka.'

Daru swung round, cursing him, but one of the other soldiers pressed a rifle to his stomach.

Amica's voice cut through the silence. 'You call yourself a

Muslim? You would shame me in front of my husband and my nephew, expose what the Prophet – may his name be blessed – has said is for the eyes of my husband alone?'

He blushed crimson, averting his eyes, but his voice remained firm. 'Sister, in a time of jihad, all is subordinate to the fight against the infidel. The Holy Koran tells us we may break the Sabbath or we may lie to our enemies. If I ask you this, it is because of the jihad we are fighting to rid our Muslim republic of traitors, infidels and enemies.'

'You lie,' Amica said. 'It is because you wish to see what is forbidden. I am unclean, I am menstruating, would you defile me further?'

He blanched and I could see beads of nervous sweat form on his brow, but he would not back down. 'I wish only for proof that you are what you say and that you and this man are truly man and wife. If you have papers, a marriage licence . . .' His voice trailed away.

I fumbled in an inside pocket and pulled out a crumpled piece of paper. It was torn and tattered and the green ink had run after its soaking in the flood, but the pictogram and the lines of wavering script were still just visible. I held it out to him.

He opened it, fumbling with his thick farmer's fingers and tearing it still further, then began to study it, his brow furrowed, the tip of his tongue protruding from his lips.

The seconds dragged by. At last he raised his eyes from the paper, folded it and handed it back to me. 'That is in order,' he said. 'May you travel safely. I meant no offence to you or your wife.'

I inclined my head in acknowledgement and moved past, stooping under the barrier. Daru followed, but turned to spit on the ground. I took his arm and dragged him away. None of us spoke until we had turned a bend in the track and passed from their sight.

'Never have I heard a woman speak so strongly,' Daru said.

The release of tension made me laugh. 'Get used to it. Where we're going they're all like that.'

I glanced at Amica. 'That was very brave. He could have killed you for it.'

'What did you show him?' she said.

'The forged pass. Lucky he was illiterate.' I glanced at my watch. 'It'll be curfew in an hour. We need to get off the track and find somewhere to spend the night before then, but I don't want to stop too close to those guys. Let's give it another half-hour and then start looking.'

The gradient of the track was growing steeper. We zigzagged around escarpments and across narrow, rock-strewn valleys, then climbed again through forested hillsides rich with the scent of cedarwood. A shrike – the butcher bird – flew out of the bushes, chattering its anger at being disturbed. It left the bloody remains of its half-eaten prey impaled on a spiky thorn. I looked away.

We hurried on up the mountain, Amica's burka billowing behind her. Where the sun struck the face of the mountain and we climbed in the shelter of the ridge, sweat poured from me and the glutinous mud caked my boots. Where the slope was in shadow, our breath fogged in the cold air and our feet slipped on the rocks as the water dripping from the cliffs above the track began to freeze.

As the sun sank towards the horizon, the snow-capped peaks looming ahead of us were bathed in rose pink light. It deepened to russet and gold as the sun set. Aquamarine ice-fields and glaciers high on the slopes caught and refracted the last rays of light.

'If we keep going,' Amica said, 'we will find a *chai khana* – a tea-house.'

'Even in a desolate place like this?'

'Especially in a place like this.'

'What about the curfew?'

'Let's risk it a little longer.'

We climbed still higher. A bitter wind knifed through my clothes, and flurries of snow stung my cheeks. We must have passed a handful of isolated houses in the dusk, though their location was revealed only by the barking and snarling of the dogs that guarded them, but I had heard nothing more than the moan of the wind and the crunching of ice beneath my boots for over half an hour. I was wearing every piece of clothing I had, but the cold bit like a dog and my breath froze into icicles on my beard. Only the thought of the unpleasant night that awaited us if we had to sleep in the open kept me going forward, my lungs labouring for breath in the thin mountain air.

As we crested another small rise, I saw a shape in a hollow ahead of us, black against the snow. I caught the whiff of woodsmoke on the wind and saw a faint glimmer of light.

The building was a ramshackle stone hut with a lean-to at one end. The roof was made of twigs and branches, weighted down by large flat stones. A battered tin trough nailed to the wall served as a sign.

We paused just outside the door. 'Keep your ears open in here,' Amica said. 'If Salan has passed this way we may get word of it, and if we meet anyone who has come down from further up the valley, we can certainly find out about the checkpoints ahead.'

The door was salvaged from a truck, riddled with bullet holes and still emblazoned with Soviet markings. As I pushed it open, an acrid stink filled my nostrils. The room was low-ceilinged, filthy with smoke and smelt of damp wool and hides, dirt and dung. A score of sheep and half a dozen mules were penned at one end of the room and a handful of people sat around the stove in the middle. A small boy sat by the fire, feeding it with branches and dried animal droppings. The blaze under the samovar flared and subsided as the wind whistled through chinks in the walls. It blew fine snow into the room, forming miniature drifts which melted slowly in the heat.

A half-partition, again made from cannibalised Soviet truck panels and topped by a torn curtain, divided off the women's area. Amica immediately walked to it, while Daru and I took our places near the stove. The conversation stopped and every face swivelled to scan the new arrivals. There were perhaps a dozen people, but there were no Taliban soldiers, just the usual collection of old men and young boys.

A shrivelled, toothless old man with a jagged scar running down the side of his face laid two cups before us, ladled sugar into them and filled them with black tea. He slopped down two tin bowls containing some grey rice, a piece of gristle and a lump of fat, laid some naan bread alongside them, then stomped back to his place by the fire.

I ate slowly, my eyes fixed on my plate, as the hubbub of conversation resumed. Daru kept up a stream of chatter with those around us. He flashed me a cheeky grin as he explained that I was a mute, then tapped his forehead and rolled his eyes, winning laughs from his audience.

There were two shepherds bringing their flock down from the mountains for winter, a couple of refugees making their way towards Peshawar, and a Blue Man and his two armed guards returning to Peshawar with a consignment of lapis lazuli. He sat with a proprietorial hand resting on a sack at his side. At Daru's prompting, he opened the top and let the flakes of brilliant blue cascade between his fingers, shimmering in the glow from the fire.

'Are you not worried?' Daru said. 'I have heard many tales of robbers and foreigners.'

The trader shrugged. 'All I am worried about is that every new Taliban checkpoint costs me another hundred Afghanis. Each one gives me a pass that will take me to the border, or so they say. Each time the next one tears it up and sells me another.'

'And is the border open?'

The owner of the tea-house stirred himself. 'I hear not,' he said. 'A great Taliban commander and his men honoured my *chai khana* today. They are hunting for *faranji kafir.*'

'What have they done?'

'They destroyed a mosque and killed many people. I should like to have them here.' He drew a finger across his throat. 'We would do to them what we did to the Soviets.'

I felt my heart begin to beat harder, but I kept my eyes downcast. I relaxed again as the conversation turned to the earthquake and the scarcity of rice and sugar. The old man refilled our cups a couple of times, the tea tasting increasingly bitter the longer it steeped. The warmth of the place was heightening my weariness.

When I had finished my meal I huddled down to sleep on the pile of filthy mats and torn sacking piled against the wall. There were no mosquitoes at this altitude, but I could feel the bites of fleas as soon as I lay down. Still scratching, I fell asleep.

I jerked upright, suddenly alert, as I heard another sound beneath the murmur of conversation. The talk faltered and died as the others strained their ears to listen.

The noise of vehicles grew louder. They were labouring on the steep gradient, the engines whining in low gear, the wheels slipping and crunching on the ice.

They stopped outside. One of the drivers gunned his engine

once or twice, then we heard the slam of doors and feet stamping through the snow. The door banged open. Six black-clad figures, dragging a bound and manacled man, stooped under the low doorway. As they straightened up I saw the black turbans with long forked tails and the black, kohl-rimmed eyes of the Taliban. Two of them wore the insignia of officers.

I raised my eyes and once more found myself looking into the face of Salan. He glanced from me to Daru. 'This is not the way to Qandahar.'

'I— My uncle wished to join his brother on the *haj*,' Daru said. 'I am taking him to the frontier before returning to Qandahar.'

Salan's one good eye continued to fix us with a baleful stare. 'Then you must make sure he is on that flight.'

I thought of the Stinger, unattended on the back of one of the Toyotas outside, and got to my feet.

'Nobody leaves this building,' Salan said.

I mimed taking a piss.

'Sit down or I will do to it what I almost did to your tongue.' He turned to the other officer. 'Two men will come with me to the frontier. Take the prisoner back to Qandahar. But keep him alive; when we have finished this business, I shall have more questions to ask him.'

His captive's head remained down, staring at the ground between his feet, his shoulders sagging. His face was a bloody, bruised pulp and there were ragged holes caked with blood on either side of his head where his ears had been hacked off. The nails of his filthy hands were also torn and bleeding.

The owner of the tea-house hurried to grovel before Salan, pushing some other customers aside to clear the cushions nearest to the fire. Salan ignored him, took a handful of naan and hurried out into the night followed by two of his men. A moment later I heard his vehicle drive off up the pass.

The other officer surveyed the room. He shouted at the women beyond the dividing curtain, waited no more than a moment, then pulled it aside and hustled them through to join the men. They stood huddled together, their faces averted, staring at the wall.

'Your papers,' he said.

Some of the old men began rummaging in their pockets or the folds of their garments, others started to stammer explanations. The officer silenced them with a gesture. The two soldiers began moving through the room, checking each person's papers. Those who had none were kicked and punched to one side.

While pretending to search for his papers, Daru was inching away from me. My rifle was propped against the wall behind me. There was no way I could reach it. Hidden by the table, I put my hand down and eased my knife from my belt.

The soldiers were working their way fast around the room. I heard Amica answer a question from one of them and point towards Daru and me.

The captive raised his head at the sound of her voice. I saw the spark of recognition flare in Rami's eyes as he saw me. He pointed his hands towards me, mumbling through his broken teeth. 'Those are the ones,' he said. 'They are the Americans. The terrorists.'

There was a moment's silence. Then I heard the roar of a gun and the front of Amica's burka was punched with holes. I yelled in rage and despair, throwing the table upwards and outwards. It struck the nearest soldier and the burst from his Kalashnikov smashed into the roof.

I launched myself and was on him before he could fire again.

I hit him under the ribs with my shoulder and he grunted as the air was driven from his lungs. He crashed backwards on to the ground with me on top of him. I drove my knife in under his rib-cage, twisted it and pulled it out.

As I rolled clear I heard another burst of fire behind me. I was looking straight down the barrel of the second soldier's rifle, but he had not fired. His body was convulsing, jerking and twisting, as Daru emptied his magazine.

I hurled myself back towards the wall. My fingers curled around the butt of my rifle, expecting the impact of shots from the officer behind me. I threw myself into a tumbling roll across the floor and swung up my rifle to fire a burst. There was no target to be seen.

The officer and Rami lay flat on the ground. Amica was standing over them. She had fired the first shots, using the Browning pistol hidden under her burka, the rounds ripping out through the fabric. Both men were dead; Rami's eyes rolled up, showing the whites.

I got to my feet. Daru was herding the customers into a corner, threatening them with his rifle. I stood alongside him. 'Great work, Daru, but change the magazine. An empty rifle is no threat.'

He laughed, his eyes wild with excitement, and tossed the empty magazine away. He took another from the soldier he had killed.

I walked over to Amica. 'Are you okay?'

She shrugged. 'He abandoned us and betrayed us. He deserved to die. Now let's get out of here.' There was a tremor in her voice.

'Daru, get the rest of the ammunition and weapons,' I said.

He draped himself with the soldiers' bandoliers and picked up the three Kalashnikovs. 'What about the others?'

'Take theirs too.'

'We can't take men's rifles.'

'We'll leave them in the snow outside.' I glanced back at Amica. 'We'll take the Toyota.'

'What if there's a checkpoint further up?'

'Then we'll just have to ram it. Daru, tell these people to stay here until dawn. If anyone tries to leave before that, we'll shoot them.'

He banged on a table with the butt of his weapon to get everyone's attention. It was a superfluous gesture. Every frightened eye was fixed on us. 'Leave this place before dawn and you will die,' he said. 'When the Taliban come, tell them a true warrior – Daru, son of Agha Shah Azuin – did this.' He spat on the officer's body to emphasise the point.

'I think they've got it, Daru,' I said. 'Let's go.'

I took the keys from the dead man's pocket and we backed out of the door. As I closed it, I fired a burst into the ground to deter anyone from following.

'I'll drive,' Daru said.

'Like hell you will. Twelve-year-old Afghan kids can do plenty of things but driving isn't one of them. Get in the other side. If anyone tries to stop us, start shooting.'

We kept the soldiers' Kalashnikov rounds but dumped the other weapons and ammunition in the snow. I let in the clutch and drove fast up the track, jolting over the ruts and boulders. The beam of the headlights was reflected by the particles of snow whirling around us, reducing visibility to a few feet.

'We'll get as far as we can in this,' I said, 'then ditch it and track Salan to the border.'

Amica shivered. 'The Taliban will follow us.'

'I know, but we've got a good start.'

The track wound across screes so steep that the Toyota seemed certain to roll over and tumble down the slope into the river far below us. Beyond the screes, it crossed a rock ledge clinging to a sheer cliff face. The ledge was barely wider than the vehicle and we crawled across in first gear, my heart pounding.

The way grew still more rugged and perilous. Boulders gouged at the underside of the truck, and even in four-wheel drive we slewed and slid on the icy surface. The bumper would strike sparks from the rockface as we skidded against it, and the next instant I would be fighting the wheel as we snaked towards the outer edge of the track.

At last the beams of the headlights stopped stabbing into the sky and swung downwards as we cleared the summit. We slalomed down the track, careering over the ice-filled ruts in a barely controlled slide towards the bottom. Almost at once the Toyota slewed sideways on a patch of ice and a sharp rock pierced the offside rear tyre. I heard the scrape of metal on rock and braked.

It was hard to imagine a worse place for a puncture. The gradient was steep, the ground rocky and uneven, and my fingers were clumsy with cold. More in hope than expectation I looked in the back of the pick-up and found a wheelbrace, a jack and a spare wheel whose tyre, although bald, was inflated. Daru and I packed the other wheels with boulders, then I stood the jack on a flat stone and began cranking it upwards, my hands sticking to the frozen metal.

The wheelnuts were so tight they seemed welded on. Only by standing and jumping on the arm of the brace could I move them at all. Three came free but the fourth was stuck so tight that I was about to give up and abandon the vehicle when the nut gave with a crack like a pistol shot.

I spun it free and Daru threw the old wheel into the ravine. I sent the jack and the wheelbrace after it – if we had to abandon the vehicle I had no wish to leave anything behind that might help the Taliban.

It had taken an hour to change the wheel, and dawn was breaking by the time we reached the bottom of the mountain and began to cross the plain. There was one more pass – the highest yet – between us and the border.

In the distance on the other side of the plateau I saw a wisp of smoke. As we drew closer I saw it was coming from a tent as black and leathery as a bat wing. There was no sign of Salan's red Toyota, but black-clad figures hurried from the tent as they heard the sound of the engine.

I put my foot down. 'Amica, duck your head. Daru, get the window open and the safety-catch off, but don't fire until the last minute. Give them no warning.'

As we sped towards the checkpoint, I kept the headlights full on and began blaring the horn. I was praying that the barrier would be less substantial than the gun barrel that had blocked our way earlier.

Armed men stood at either side of the track, but their posture showed their indecision.

Daru laughed. 'They don't know whether to shoot or salute.'

I kept silent, my eyes fixed on the thin line of the barrier. It bridged the gap between two huge boulders flanking the track and rested on an oil barrel in the middle. If the barrel was empty, we would smash it aside. If it was full of oil or concrete, we would go through the windscreen. 'Brace yourselves,' I said.

The soldiers had realised we were not going to stop. I saw them bringing up their gun barrels. Daru cursed me for spoiling his aim, but as the pick-up steadied he loosed off a burst. The soldier on his side dived for cover and the shots passed over his head.

The other one was taking aim when I jerked the wheel again. I saw him freeze for an instant, then there was a crack and a thud as one wing caught the oil drum a glancing blow and the other crashed into him. He tumbled over the bonnet, thudded against the corner of the windscreen and dropped to the ground behind us, leaving a red smear on the glass.

I heard more shots. Daru put his gun out of the window and fired a blind burst, more to spoil their aim than with any hope of hitting them. The gun jammed and he cursed, banging at the magazine to try to free it as bullets cracked around us.

I risked a glance in the mirror as we hit the rising ground and began to climb, and saw other figures spilling from the tent and putting their guns to their shoulders, but the firing died away as we passed out of range. 'I hope to God they don't have a vehicle,' I said, 'or we're really in the shit.'

The track became rougher. We took off over a ridge of rock and the suspension bottomed as we landed. We slid sideways as I fought the wheel and dropped my speed.

As the gradient increased, the surface deteriorated still further, forcing us close to walking pace. The pick-up ground upwards and the stench of hot oil and burning metal filled my nostrils as the engine laboured in the thin air.

Barely a third of the way up the pass I saw Salan's Toyota. It was empty. Beyond it the track narrowed and petered out, shrinking to the width of a footpath as it rounded the shoulder of the mountainside above a sheer drop.

I swore, banging the steering wheel with my hand, then jumped out. 'Come on,' I said. 'They can't be far ahead.'

I leaned in through the window and released the handbrake. Gathering speed, the Toyota rolled back down the track, then plunged over the edge and disappeared from sight.

A moment later, Salan's vehicle followed it.

Chapter 18

We struggled up the path, shivering in the cold. We were climbing in shadow, the sun still too low in the sky to light this side of the mountain. The track picked its way through narrow clefts in the rock and across screes so sharp they slashed the worn leather of my boots like knives. All the time, the river tumbled over its rock-strewn course below us, shrinking in size as we neared its source.

At each brow or bend we paused to scan the track ahead, but Salan's men remained out of sight. The path grew steeper and we half-scrambled and half-climbed, clawing at the rock with our hands. My breath came in gasps. There was no oxygen to be squeezed from the air.

My head pounded and my vision blurred. Even the weeks at 8,000 feet in the Jebel Akhdar and Konarlan had been no preparation for this. We were now at twice the altitude, close to 16,000 feet, and still climbing.

As we neared the summit, the wind shrieked around us and stung our cheeks with shards of ice. Our hands were white and numb. Our eyes blinded by tears, we crawled on our hands and knees the last few yards, the wind so strong we couldn't stand against it.

We took what shelter we could find among a cluster of boulders. To our right we could see the well-marked track leading down towards the border with Pakistan no more than five miles away. Beyond it the mountains rose sheer and forbidding to over 20,000 feet, in a ridge stretching several miles to the north-east.

Ahead of me I could see the remainder of the track. There was no trace of movement. It was deserted.

I stared in disbelief. Salan had had no more than a few minutes' start on us and had no reason to believe he was being pursued. Even allowing for the puncture, he could not have got so far ahead.

I scanned the mountainsides. To our left was a narrower line, a grey thread marking the little-used path over the watershed towards the next valley, still in Afghanistan. As I stared, I picked out three black figures moving down the track, well over a mile away. One of them carried a cylinder across his shoulders.

I looked back towards the frontier. We were five miles from safety, just one more group of refugees making for Peshawar. . . . But even as I framed the thought I knew what we had to do.

I looked at Amica.

'We don't have a choice, do we?' she said.

We turned our backs on the border and began to climb down the mountainside. Every step was twice as hard, because it was taking us away from safety, back into Afghanistan.

We moved fast, knowing that if pursuers reached the ridge behind us before we had found cover or left the valley, they would spot us from miles away, as easily as we had seen Salan. We were exhausted and needed to rest, but the loose slabs of rock afforded only the most rudimentary cover. We were all clumsy with fatigue – slipping, sliding and stumbling down the mountain – but I urged the others on.

The track was barely discernible among the scree. We stumbled to the bottom of the slope, undetected by the figures ahead of us. I had to fight the urge to turn my head and stare back towards the ridgeline, afraid I would see the Taliban turbans outlined against the sky.

There were no houses in this remote upper valley, only crude drystone goat pens and a ramshackle shepherd's hut, abandoned for the winter. We moved on, following the headwaters of another river but staying close to the side of the valley. The adrenalin that had fuelled us so far had ebbed away. All I felt was a numbing weariness and an overpowering hunger. I filled my bottle from the mountain stream. Water at least would be no problem. It was as clear as tears, but so cold it froze my teeth and set me shivering still harder as I drank.

A couple of miles down the valley, we came to a cave in the hillside, little more than a shallow recess screened by a mound of fallen rocks. Salan and his men were still moving on ahead of us, but I knew that we had to stop, eat and rest, if only for a little while.

We huddled in the entrance and shared out our remaining raisins and the last of the nuts the merchant had given us. We now had nothing left but two days' emergency rations for one man. It was precious little to share between three.

I pulled out the silk escape map and stared at it. 'Where are they heading for?' I said. 'We heard Salan talking about going to the frontier. Why didn't they cross at the border to Peshawar?'

When Amica raised her head, the hard glint in her eyes had

been dulled. I had never seen her look so weary. 'I don't know,' she said. 'There's nothing in this valley but the pass leading to Dir, and whatever Salan's doing, he's not going on the *haj* with Daru's uncle.'

As she spoke, Salan's words at the mule train came back to me: 'He will be truly blessed.' I remembered his men's laughter and I knew his plan.

'That's it,' I said. 'He's going to Dir.'

'To ship the Stinger out on the charter flight?'

'No, to shoot it down.'

'But that's crazy,' Amica said.

'Is it? A planeload of devout Muslims, shot down on their way to Mecca by an American missile? It would provoke a jihad that would set half the world ablaze. Salan won't even have to cross into Pakistan; jets taking off from Dir follow the southern slopes of the mountains all the way west. Remember what Dave Regan said: "You could wave to the Taliban from the windows — they'd be on the mountain tops looking down on you."'

I paused, still studying the map. 'We can box round most of the settlements, but there are two villages at choke points in the valley. We'll have to go through them. There's no way round, but we'll deal with that problem when we get to it.'

I looked at Amica. 'We know when Salan will attack and we know where — and we've got three days to get there. We have to destroy the Stinger and then cross the frontier. Even if it's guarded by the Taliban, these mountains are full of smugglers' tracks. And we still have the gold. We could bribe our way across.'

I patted my waist as I spoke, and then froze. I began clawing at my clothing. 'It's gone,' I said.

'What do you mean? It can't have. Who could have taken it?'

'Someone must have stolen it in the tea-house.'

'But how?'

'They could have cut the belt while I was asleep.'

Daru looked away as I glanced up. 'What do we do now?' he said.

I put a resolve in my voice that I didn't feel. 'We go on.' I faltered, knowing that I had lost the one thing that might have guaranteed our escape. 'What else can we do?'

'I can find us food,' Daru said, 'and blankets. There will be houses further down the valley.'

'No stealing,' I said. 'Not this time. I don't care about your hand being cut off, but the whole country will be looking for us. Anything that draws attention to us could seal our fate.'

'We leave now,' Amica said. 'We'll make what ground we can while daylight lasts.'

I knew she was right, but my heart sank at the thought of trudging on for more miles. 'Are you strong enough?' I said.

She smiled. 'Are you?' She put her hand on my arm. 'We can do it together. Share out a little more of the rations.'

I began to argue, but she held up a hand. 'Trust in Daru; he'll find us food.'

I divided a high energy bar between us, and we took a square of chocolate each. I felt as though I had never tasted such intense sweetness before. Then we moved on.

The sun was high in the sky now, and the ice underfoot was melting before our eyes, turning to slush. I slipped and fell, bruising myself on the stones and sinking to my knees in icy mud. I dragged myself upright and trudged on, grateful at least that the dull pain from my leg wound was easing.

Alone in that lunar landscape, we travelled for five hours before we saw another figure. A shepherd cradling an antique long-barrelled rifle left his herd foraging the dry grass among the boulders and walked towards us.

Amica and I stood in the background, our heads bowed, as Daru told our tale. We were refugees from the earthquake trying to reach relatives in Pakistan. We had no money and little food.

The shepherd immediately offered us a share of his stale naan bread and a raw onion. We each took a mouthful and passed it back to him. Daru thanked him and we moved on.

In the late afternoon we passed an isolated tea-house. We were cold, hungry and tired, and the smells of woodsmoke and cooking made it hard to resist – but tea-houses were too dangerous for us now. They were policed by the Taliban, and the customers also carried news of strangers and travellers far up and down the valleys.

About an hour before dusk we spotted a shack some distance from a small hamlet. 'We can sleep there,' I said.

'If we keep going, we could overtake Salan,' Amica said.

'We could, but in the darkness we might blunder into his guards or miss him altogether. When we do catch him, I want it to be when we're fresh and alert, and at a time and place of our choosing – the one place we know he's going to be.' I paused. 'It'll increase our chances of getting away as well. We can kill him and be across the border before anyone else can react.'

As I looked up and met Amica's eye, I knew she wasn't fooled. Neither of us expected to come out of this alive.

'If we fail, that plane will be shot down,' she said.

'But that's the risk we run wherever we attack him.'

We took shelter among the boulders, and watched and waited as dark fell. There was a flicker of light and movement from the houses, but we saw no sign of life in the shack. We waited until an hour after sunset, but as we stole down towards the shack a dog in one of the houses started barking. I heard a voice curse it into silence and a door bang. We kept our rifles at the ready, but there was no further noise.

I eased open the door. Inside was a single, windowless room. There was a powerful smell of goats, and a layer of dried dung a foot deep covered the entire floor.

We settled ourselves on the floor and I divided what was left of the night into three watches. I took the first and most dangerous one, and gave Daru the second so that Amica could get an uninterrupted spell of sleep. Her haggard face and black-rimmed eyes showed that she needed it even more than us.

She woke us an hour before daybreak, and we moved on at once, measuring each footfall to avoid rousing the dogs, then hurrying away down the valley. We now had exactly forty-eight hours to reach the frontier and stop Salan.

We were descending below the treeline now, and clumps of woodland began to appear, first rowan and spruce contorted by the wind, then tall stands of fir and cedar. Where the valley narrowed we saw the first large village clinging to the hillside. Each succeeding layer of houses was built directly above the ones below, rising to an almost impregnable bastion, more fortress than house, with square turrets and a rampart like a castle. The village blocked the valley. There was no way to pass without being seen.

Daru scouted ahead while we hid in the rocks outside the village. When he returned, his face was grim. 'There's a Taliban checkpoint in the square,' he said. 'They're stopping everyone.'

Amica bowed her head and stared at the ground in silence, but when she spoke, the spark was back in her voice. 'They're looking for three strangers — two men and a woman.'

'We're not splitting up,' I said. 'We'll be even more vulnerable.'

'We don't have to.' She pulled out the second burka she had taken from the ruined house. 'If one of you puts that on, we're a man and two women instead.'

'I will not wear it,' Daru said. 'A warrior does not hide beneath the skirts of a woman.'

Amica smiled despite her fatigue. 'Stop crowing and flapping your wings – you don't have to wear it. You'll have to speak for us with the Taliban.'

She handed me the burka. 'You must wear it.'

'A six-foot woman?'

'I'm almost that myself.' She gave the same tired smile. 'We could be sisters.'

'And when we're stopped?'

She shrugged. 'We're refugees. The whole country is fleeing war, earthquake, flood and famine.'

I thought for a moment. 'All right.' I stood up and struggled into the burka. Through the mesh covering my face I could see Daru's grin. 'Save the jokes,' I said. 'Let's get moving.'

The mesh fragmented my vision, and sound was muffled by the hood. I could see nothing to either side, just a blurred rectangle ahead. I had to swing my head in a strange, exaggerated manner to see anything other than the ground directly in front of me. I would have no warning of anyone's approach.

'We might as well be walking in the dark,' I said. 'I can't see a thing through this.'

Amica turned to look back at me. 'Stop complaining. Afghan women travel like this every day of their lives.'

We began to walk through the warren of narrow streets. Children with mongoloid features watched us from doorways as we made our way over the steep, slippery cobbles. Each time a man approached from the other direction, we paused and turned our faces to the wall. Every man passed us without a glance, as if we did not exist. Amica looked back at me. 'Now you are beginning to know what it is to be a woman in Afghanistan,' she said.

The street opened into a small square lined with the stalls of a threadbare bazaar. Groups of men sat talking in the open-fronted tea-house overlooking the square. A handful of traders squatted on the stone steps or sat cross-legged on the wet, cold ground with a handful of potatoes, onions or a few wizened tomatoes spread before them on a cloth. Barefoot boys sold single cigarettes, and a few tin and plastic novelties. A goat was tied to the leg of a stall on which a butcher was dismembering one of its peers. Chewing the cud, it was oblivious to its fate.

Just beyond the stalls, a row of black-garbed Taliban soldiers manned the checkpoint. Amica and I stood, heads bowed, as Daru approached them. The burka muffled the sound of their speech, but I heard Daru say *'faranji'* and point back to the way we had come.

The effect of his words was instantaneous; the soldiers turned and sprinted for their red Toyotas drawn up on the far side of the square. A moment later they screeched off up the valley, leaving the barrier unmanned.

We hurried past the square and threaded through the maze of streets to reach the far edge of the village.

'What happens when they find out you were lying?' I said to Daru.

'They won't. I told them we had seen *faranji* hiding in the shepherd's hut at the head of the valley. It will take them several hours. Who knows where the foreigners might have gone by then?' He smiled. 'Now I will find us food. Wait here.' He pointed to a clump of larches on a bluff overlooking the river.

'Be careful,' I said. 'We can't risk . . .' But he was already gone, running back up the street.

He returned apparently empty-handed, but as we stood up he winked and patted his jacket. 'Salan and his men stayed at the tea-house last night,' he said. 'There is much talk in the village about what they had with them. One of them stayed awake all night to guard it.' He smiled. 'The villagers think it is a great treasure or a holy relic.'

We found a ledge half a mile downriver, from which we could overlook the track while we rested and shared Daru's booty – two naan breads, a piece of stale goat's cheese and a pocketful of mulberries.

'How—?' I began, but Amica shook her head.

'Don't ask. It will only upset you.'

We sat for a few minutes after we had eaten, feeling the warmth of the sun soaking into our damp clothing, then we moved on down the valley. We paused every couple of miles to scan the mountains to the east of us for the break in the ridgeline that would signal the pass leading to Dir.

In the late afternoon we approached another village. Any hopes of passing by unnoticed were quickly dashed: a delegation of villagers, led by one of the elders, came up the valley to meet us.

'Should we run for it?' I said.

Amica shook her head. 'Villagers often do it to welcome travellers. It's a sign of hospitality and respect.'

I stayed next to Amica, two meek and respectful women in burkas, as Daru exchanged the ritual courtesies. Then the elders led us back to where the local warlord waited to greet us. He stood with legs astride, the inevitable Kalashnikov at his shoulder and crossed belts of ammunition on his chest. 'You are a welcome guest,' he said. 'There are few travellers in these troubled times.'

'There are Taliban soldiers on the road,' Daru said.

The warlord spat in the dust. 'Three passed not two hours ago, but they slunk by like the robbers they are. You will stay with us tonight.' It was more a command than a request.

'I thank you, but we have far to go,' Daru said, trying to ease past him.

The warlord blocked his way and threw an arm around his shoulders. 'And you will travel better tomorrow for food and rest tonight.'

My mind was racing. We were heavily outnumbered, and to insult him by refusing his hospitality would lead to a fight we could not win — but to accept would cost us eight or ten hours of the thirty-six we had left before the flight left Dir. We would have to march without pause all day and all night to reach the frontier in time.

I thought of the hours we had spent resting on the way and cursed myself, but there was nothing we could do now.

I caught Daru's despairing glance towards us and bowed my head in acceptance. At least, as the warlord said, we would travel faster with food in our stomachs and a night's rest behind us.

The warlord's house was built of massive baulks of timber plastered with mud and adorned with his hunting trophies: the huge, curling horns of wild rams and the skulls of wolves and bear.

I could hear Daru's voice filtering through to us down the corridor and the answering, booming laugh of the warlord as his wives led Amica and me to the women's quarters. They pestered us with questions, asking about our journey and for news from other areas. Amica answered for us, explaining that I was mute.

I had no knowledge of the etiquette of the women's areas, and was terrified that we would have to remove our burkas. If the warlord found out that a man had tricked his way into the quarters of his wives, I had no doubt that I would be castrated and skinned alive.

'Sisters, you have been many days on your journey. Let us

wash your clothes for you,' one of the wives offered. I shook my head vigorously.

'Sister, you are very kind,' Amica said. 'But we washed them only last night. Now tell me about your lord. Is he a mighty warrior?'

I kept my head bowed and my hands folded in my lap as Amica talked and the women cooked a meal. When it was ready we carried the food through and laid it before the men.

Daru sat with the warlord, his sons and a group of villagers who had gathered to welcome the guest. We women sat meekly in silence at the side of the room, our heads bowed, waiting for whatever scraps our lords might spare us from their table. We took them back to the women's quarters, where the warlord's wives and daughters fell on them without ceremony. I shovelled a few handfuls of rice and fish down before I noticed one of them staring at my hands. I hid them in the folds of the burka and ate no more.

As soon as it was dark, the women hurried outside, leading us to a corner of the field where they carried out their ablutions. It was not seemly for women to do this during the hours of daylight, in case they were observed by men. They squatted on a patch of ground no more than twenty yards from the bank of the river, where they washed their hands and faces, and drew their water.

We returned to the house, and the women settled themselves to sleep on the rugs and cushions scattered around the room. I lay down next to Amica, away from the others, and we whispered together, our heads so close that I could smell the warm, almond scent of her breath.

'One of the wives kept staring at my hands,' I said. 'I'm sure she realised I was a man.'

'I doubt it. If she had, her screams would have woken the dead.' She squeezed my arm. 'Don't worry.'

The lantern was extinguished, and I wrapped my arms around Amica. From elsewhere in the room I heard giggles and then a stifled moan of pleasure.

Amica gave a throaty chuckle. She leaned even closer to my ear and whispered, 'Even in purdah, Afghan men cannot control everything their women do.'

I was aroused both by the closeness of Amica and the sounds in the darkness. Through the thin cloth of the burka, I traced the outline of her face and the contours of her body. She placed her hands on mine, pressing them against her. 'And even the other women don't know our secret.'

I heard the rustle of her clothing and saw the soft curve of her breasts and the sheen of her skin. A moment later she eased my burka up and over my head. As I struggled to free my arms from the folds of cloth, I felt her hands caress my body. I lay there, biting on my knuckle to silence my own groans of pleasure, then reached down for her. I tasted her lips, kissed the hollow of her throat and slid down over her body.

We made love in silence. I fought down the waves of pleasure coursing through me until I saw her close her eyes and throw her head back, giving herself up to it. Then I too surrendered, oblivious of any danger, aware only of Amica and the force driving us together.

Spent, we lay still, locked in each other's arms. We lay in silence for some time, looking into each other's faces. 'What will happen to Daru?' she said at last.

'If we get out of this? He'll find his natural home in the West. He's completely amoral and an accomplished thief and liar; he'll be welcomed with open arms in the City of London or Wall

Street. He'll have made his first million before he's fifteen.' I paused, searching her expression. 'What about us?'

She did not reply, and when I touched my hand to her face, it came away wet with tears. 'Regrets?'

'Not for making love to you.' Her voice was so faint that I had to strain to catch her words. 'But regrets for love, and for loss, and for what might have been.' She kissed me once more, then one of the warlord's wives stirred and cried out in her sleep.

I pulled the burka back on and lay quiet, staring into the darkness.

We were woken before dawn, prepared tea, bread, yoghurt and mulberries for the men, then fought over what was left.

After dawn prayers, the warlord strode with us to the edge of the village, showing his protection of his guests. I thought of Daru's father who had done the same a few days ago. Since then, of all that group who had gathered in the village square on that occasion, only a handful of us were still alive.

The warlord faced Daru and touched his hand to his heart, but ignored Amica and me as we followed him along the track.

We walked quickly, refreshed and revitalised both by food and rest – and by the sight of the notch in the wall of mountains that showed the line of the pass we were seeking.

The track dipped and twisted, following the course of the river as it tumbled over rapids and flowed through empty plains. We crossed a ridge and entered a small wood, the track a dark tunnel beneath the trees.

As we emerged into the sunlight we found the way blocked by a barrier manned by two men. If they were Taliban, they lacked the distinctive black turbans, but they were well armed and their expressions were hostile.

Beyond the barrier the way split. The main branch carried on down the left bank of the river. The right-hand path led to a ford, and beyond it I could see the track snaking its way up the hillside.

I lifted my bundle from my shoulders, as if glad of the chance to rest. It was not seemly for women to bear arms, and my Kalashnikov was rolled inside my blanket. I rested one end on the ground and slipped my right arm into the bundle, feeling the cold metal against my skin. I slid off the safety-catch and eased my finger around the trigger, then raised the bundle again and cradled it across my chest.

The men's greetings to Daru were brusque and perfunctory. They demanded a thousand Afghanis to let us pass.

Keeping my head bowed in what I hoped was the correct attitude of deference, I scanned the rocks on either side of the track. I could see no other figures.

'Is this how a Muslim greets travellers?' Daru said. 'We have no more money. We are refugees from the earthquake, the last of our family. The rest are dead.'

'It is the will of Allah,' one of them said. 'But you must pay or you will not pass.'

Daru handed over the last of our money – 200 Afghanis. 'We have nothing more to give,' he said.

'Then you will pay with your lives.'

'We are under the protection of the warlord of Baran.'

The man shrugged. 'His writ does not run here. If you are under his protection, you are our enemy too.'

Daru's rifle was still slung over his shoulder. The guards held theirs in their hands ready to use, both of them with their eyes fixed on him, ignoring us.

I slipped the catch on the Kalashnikov to automatic and fired from the waist, swinging the rifle in an arc. The recoils pushed the barrel higher and it cut a diagonal line from the right hip of the first man to the left shoulder of the second. The first was killed instantly. The second man's hand closed around the trigger of his gun and he unloosed a burst into the sky as he toppled backwards.

The sound of the firing reverberated against the walls of the valley. We stood for a moment, our ears ringing from the gunfire. Then I began dragging the first body towards the river bank.

'Wait,' Daru said. He riffled through the pockets and pulled out a thick wad of Afghanis, before helping me push both bodies down the slope into the water.

As they were swept away, rising and falling, an arm broke surface like the branch of a sunken log.

I scattered some dirt over the bloodstains on the ground and kicked the ejected shells into the river. Then we ran down the track to the ford. It was barely shallower than the bed of the river itself.

'We must take off our clothes before we cross,' I said. 'Hold them above your head and at least they'll be dry.' I threw down my bundle, tore off the burka and tossed it in the river. 'There's no point in disguise now. If they catch us, they'll kill us.'

Amica stripped and threw her burka after mine. 'As you said, it's no use now. I've a coat and trousers in my bundle.'

Daru stared at her body saucer-eyed, then turned away as he took off his own clothes.

The shock of the water was heart-stopping. We were waist- and then chest-deep as we waded across. Something thudded against my leg. I looked down and saw the corpse of one of our victims bobbing against me before it swirled away in the current. I could feel the cold rising through my body as we forced our way through the water and clambered up the far bank.

I rubbed at my legs with the coarse blanket, trying to force some circulation back, then dragged my trousers back on. I tried to lace my boots, but my frozen fingers were clumsy and numb.

Daru was again staring open-mouthed at Amica.

'Rub yourself dry and get dressed,' I said. 'We don't have long.'

I crouched down and reloaded the clip of my rifle, then we hurried away through the forest, climbing the hillside as fast as we could go.

Chapter 19

We emerged from the first belt of trees on to a scree-covered hillside. The path was a wavering grey line, zigzagging up the hillside.

I think I heard the sound of engines first, and I looked back towards the river. A convoy of red Toyotas was approaching the checkpoint.

We turned and scrambled towards the sanctuary of the next belt of trees, and had almost reached it when I heard the crack of rifles. I flattened myself to the ground, the survival instinct stronger than the knowledge that we were out of range.

I looked behind me. The distant figures began to run along the track and climb down the river bank into the water. I forced myself to wait, counting them, before moving on. Twenty men crossed the river. I saw the first figures disappear into the trees with frightening speed, then I leapt to my feet and ran up the slope, urging the others on.

We climbed through the next belt of trees, crossed another stretch of scree and boulders, and dived into the wood beyond.

Then we paused to catch our breath, our chests heaving. 'We can't allow them to slow us down,' I said. 'We have to get to Salan before dawn.'

'We won't outrun them,' Amica said. 'They've travelled over these mountains all their lives.'

'Then we have to take them by surprise.'

We followed the track up through the wood, moving line abreast, crushing and trampling the undergrowth. When we reached the top, we moved left along the margin for fifty metres, then cut back down through the trees, working our way round to intersect our own track at the lower edge of the wood.

I'd expected the Taliban to move in a line, separated from each other to present a more difficult target, but they emerged from the woods below us in a double column. They clearly weren't expecting much opposition. Most of them held Kalashnikovs, but one had a grenade-launcher.

They barely paused before advancing over the scree towards us. Amica was behind a tree five metres away from me, Daru the same distance on the other side of the track. 'Hold your fire until you hear me shoot,' I said. 'Nobody fires until I do. Daru, take front left, I'll take front right. Amica, the next behind him. Fire short, controlled bursts. Save your ammunition; we'll need every round. As soon as you hear me stop firing, bug out fast to the top edge of the wood. I'll give you cover, then I'll follow.'

The Taliban moved forward, their eyes raking the trees, adjusting their stride to the terrain by instinct. As the lead pair neared the trees they swung up their rifles and fired. I ignored the shots. They were aiming up the broad track we had made, hoping to make us keep our heads down or trick us into giving away our position.

I slid the safety-catch off my weapon and heard a faint click as Amica did the same. I drew a bead on the pit of the stomach of my target and tracked him up the slope. I waited until he was no more than fifteen metres from me, so close I could see his eyes darting from side to side. Then I squeezed the trigger.

Amica's and Daru's guns echoed mine, and three men dropped. The grenade-launcher clattered on to the rocks in front of them. I swung my rifle and fired again as the remainder of the group dived for cover. My target disappeared behind a boulder, but I saw tufts of black fibre and a mist of red blown on the breeze.

Return fire smashed into the tree trunks, shredding the foliage around us. I fired another burst as one of the Taliban raised his head to take aim. He dropped out of sight and I stopped firing, ready to move out.

Amica wriggled backwards, turned and ran. I glanced left. Daru had sprinted forward out of cover. Shots ricocheted from the rocks as he stooped to pick up the grenade-launcher, then turned and ran, ducking and weaving, to the trees. I heard him crashing on up the slope, laughing as he ran.

I fired another burst to keep the Taliban heads down, then turned and ran after him. As I did I heard a whoosh and a roar. Daru had wheeled and fired the grenade-launcher. There was a massive explosion and a cloud of smoke and dust.

He threw the launcher into the undergrowth, then turned and ran ahead of me. We didn't even break stride at the top of the wood, racing on across the scree towards the ridge.

We dropped into cover, drawing breath as we reloaded. 'I think we got at least four of them,' I said, 'but that's still heavy odds in their favour.'

Daru laughed. 'Let's ambush them again and kill them all.'

I shook my head. 'Not here. They may split and come up

either side of us. In any event, they'll be more cautious for a while. We'll use the time to get some distance on them and close up on Salan.'

I looked at the bandoliers on Daru's chest. One was already empty, the other had only a few rounds left. All the rounds I had were on the gun and in a spare clip. Amica had even fewer.

The track zigzagged down a steep slope towards a lake the colour of agate. A few tufts of desiccated grass clung to the slopes, the only vegetation in acres of rock and bare earth. I ran down, jarring my knees and forcing the air from my lungs as I stamped my feet against boulders to break the speed of my descent.

Amica kept comfortable pace with me. Daru bounded ahead, sure-footed and nimble. We ran around the edge of the strange, green lake. The wind knifing through me barely seemed to ripple the surface, for beneath a thin layer of water it was solid ice.

I ran on, struggling for breath as we met the rising ground once more. The skeleton of a long-abandoned mule lay where it had fallen at the edge of the track. Patches of skin mummified by the cold, dry winds still clung to the bones.

I turned to glance back at the ridge. A row of black figures was outlined against the sky like crows on a wire. We were out of range for the moment, but they would overhaul us fast as they came down the mountain and we laboured up the other side.

Cold and weariness dragged at me as the gradient grew steeper, and I had to use my hands as well as my feet to haul myself upwards. At almost every step fragments of ice-shattered stone skittered away beneath my feet and tumbled down the hillside. A rock the size of my fist, dislodged by Daru, flew past my head, and I worked my way a few feet sideways, out of the line of his ascent.

The air grew thinner as we climbed, each foot- and handhold

a little more of a struggle than the one before. I had to pause, gasping for breath. The Taliban were more than two-thirds of the way down the other side of the valley, moving with alarming speed. I saw one trip and fall, rolling down the hillside. He came to a sudden stop against a boulder, but a moment later I saw him stagger to his feet and move on.

I turned and began to climb again, keeping my gaze fixed only on the next handhold above me, scared that if I raised my eyes to the ridgeline, the knowledge of how far I still had to go would paralyse me. I became oblivious of time, the cold, the wind, of anything but the pounding of my heart, the pain in my lungs and the roaring in my ears. Then there was a crack as a bullet smashed into the cliff a few metres to my left. I flinched, slipped and almost fell, then clutched again at a rock and swung myself behind it. The Taliban were at the foot of the climb, at long – but still lethal – range for their Kalashnikovs. I saw the muzzle-flashes as they fired again and more bullets whined around me.

I forced myself to turn and climb again, ignoring the ricochets. The wind and the extreme range meant they would hit any of us only by the greatest good luck. They must have reached the same conclusion, for a couple of minutes later the firing ceased and they disappeared from sight as they began to climb after us.

I could not stop myself from looking up. Daru was well above, almost at the ridgeline, Amica just a few yards ahead of me, climbing with a slow, steady rhythm. I tried to fill my lungs with the thin air and began to move upwards again.

The summit lay perhaps a hundred feet above me, but it was a steep, almost sheer climb. I grasped at a boulder as big as my body to lever myself upwards and felt it shift. I whipped my hand away and found a more secure hold. I climbed above the boulder, then braced my back against the cliff, took a firm grip with either hand, and began to push it with my feet. I let it rock backwards and forwards, gathering momentum, then pushed with all my strength. The effort sent pain stabbing through my wounded leg, but the boulder teetered and then tumbled over.

I almost followed it, and had to scrabble at the rockface to save myself. It gathered volume and speed, crashing over the scree, dislodging more and more slabs, creating fresh rockslides. I thought of the Taliban raising their eyes to see a wall of rock smashing down on them. Then I turned and began to haul myself up the final stretch towards the ridgeline.

It took an age to cross, and when I'd made it I lay flat, my whole body shuddering as I struggled to draw oxygen into my lungs. Amica and Daru were there, both sitting as they recovered from the climb. Even after I'd regained my breath there was a dull ache in my temples and a feeling of nausea I recognised as the onset of altitude sickness.

The track descended briefly into a hanging valley, then dog-legged to the right and followed the floor before climbing again to another ridge, still grey with frost and snow beyond the reach of the sun.

I could see a further ridge in the distance, covered with a thick mantle of snow. I dragged the map from my pocket. It was the summit we were seeking: on the far side was the frontier with Pakistan.

We would be climbing that 18,000-foot ridge during the cold of the night, in a wind-chill that could drop the temperature to twenty or thirty below zero.

By the time we reached the valley floor, everything was in shadow. I turned. Ten black-clad figures were descending the trail behind us. My heart leapt as I dared to think that the avalanche had carried the rest of them away. Then I saw three more figures picking their way along the razorback of the ridge, aiming to cut us off. It was not a move that I would have wanted to make in full daylight, let alone the gathering dusk, but if they reached the summit of the track before us, we would be trapped on the slope.

I called to the others and pointed. Before I could stop him, Daru had swung up his rifle and unloosed a burst at the figures on the skyline. They ducked for cover then re-emerged, inching their way along the ridge.

'Reload and don't waste your ammunition again,' I said. 'We must get to that summit before them.'

Ice was already forming on the crags as we climbed, making each hand- and foothold doubly precarious. The rasping of my lungs and the pounding of blood in my ears began again. Once more I was locked into the same grim, blind struggle, placing one hand in front of the other, closing my mind to everything but the few square metres of cliff in front of me.

In places the gradient eased and I could almost walk upright. Then it rose sheer again and I dragged myself upwards, willing more effort from my exhausted body.

Even Daru moved more slowly now. I risked a sideways glance: the three Taliban were still dimly outlined against the sky, moving ever closer to the notch where the track cut through the line of the ridge.

I urged Daru and Amica on again and redoubled my own efforts, my legs and arms quivering with the strain. I counted to 500, each number a movement of my hand or foot up the mountainside. Then I glanced to the right again. The Taliban were now invisible in the darkness.

I could just see Daru above me, outlined against the sky. He was hauling himself over a black buttress, the last sheer climb before the slope to the summit, when he lost his footing and slipped sideways. He crashed against a rock and I heard the grunt as the air was forced from his lungs. I let out a groan of my own as I saw the Kalashnikov slip from his shoulders. It fell and lodged for a moment against the rocks, then slithered down, spinning end over end, before dropping into the darkness far below.

I climbed the few yards to join him. 'My rifle,' he said.

'Don't worry about that; let's get to the top.'

He didn't move. 'My father gave me that rifle. He killed a Soviet commander with it.'

'We can't go back for it, Daru, we must go on. Are you hurt?'

He shook his head. 'Bruised, that's all.'

'Then come on, we must reach the ridge.'

He winced as he took his weight on his right arm, but began to climb again. I stayed close behind him, shepherding him over the buttress.

'Take my rifle,' I said. 'Watch the ridge while I help Amica. Don't shoot unless you're sure of a hit.'

Amica was at the foot of the buttress, her head slumped forward on her chest. 'I can't do it,' she said. 'It's too steep.'

'I'll help you. Don't stop now.'

'The frontier?'

'It's not far.' I took her arm and guided it to a handhold, then pushed and pulled her up and over the buttress. She crawled to the top and collapsed.

I waited as my own breathing calmed, peering into the darkness, watching and listening. I heard a faint clink and clatter of rock.

We were on the edge of a long, sloping plateau. There was no moon, but the sky above us was brilliant with stars and the line of the track showed faintly against the rock.

The wind cut across the plateau, knifing through me. I put

my mouth close to Daru's ear to make myself heard above it. 'I'm going to try and put a shot into those guys on the ridge. Give me my rifle back, you can take Amica's. Walk a thousand paces, then find cover and wait. You'll have to help her, she's very tired.

'The wind's blowing from me to you, so you should hear me coming. I'll call your name every few yards. If you hear someone coming and there's no other sound, it won't be me. Wait until they're close and then shoot them.'

I watched them walk away, Daru supporting Amica with an arm around her waist, then I moved back a couple of metres to drop below the skyline. Leaving just a chink for my eyes, I wound my turban even tighter around my face to keep out the cold wind and to hide the white of my face from the enemy.

I lay flat, my Kalashnikov trained along the ridge. There was no sound or movement from the track up the mountainside. If the other Taliban soldiers were still climbing in the darkness, they were well below.

As the minutes ticked by, doubt began to gnaw at me. What if they'd seen us cross the ridgeline, or had found another way down and were lying in ambush further along the trail? I was on the brink of turning and running to catch up with Amica and Daru, but there was no way down from the ridge except the track – or at least no way that a man could take in pitch darkness. I knew that if we turned and ran, the Taliban – fresher, stronger and more acclimatised to the terrain – would overhaul us before we could reach Salan.

I saw a trace of movement in the darkness – or thought I did. I strained my eyes and at last the shape moved again. I made out the curve of a head and the glint of a gun barrel. Somehow the lead man had crept to within ten metres, without me even seeing a trace of him.

I slid off the safety-catch, scared of the noise it made even though I knew the wind would snatch it away, then aimed, took a deep breath to steady myself, and gave the trigger a slow squeeze.

As the shot echoed in my ears I threw myself sideways and rolled down the slope a few metres. I saw two muzzle-flashes and heard rounds rattle from the rocks where I had been lying. I fired another burst at the muzzle-flashes, then rolled again. Once more two rifles replied.

I waited a minute for my ears to stop ringing, my eyes scouring the darkness for movement. I picked up a fist-sized rock and hurled it towards their last position. Even over the wind I heard the crack as it hit the ground.

Again there were two bursts, this time separated by twenty metres. Even in the darkness, the left-hand man was trying to work his way down the ridge to cut me off. I fired at him, rolled sideways, then ran down the track at a crouch, counting off the paces as I went. No firing pursued me.

I slowed to a fast walk as I reached the area where Daru and Amica should have been waiting. I called Daru's name, moved ten paces and called again. I did it over and over, counting off another 200 paces.

I hesitated, uncertain whether I had passed them in the darkness or whether they were still ahead, then moved forward again, called and advanced once more. Then I heard the clatter of a rock and saw a shape holding a rifle rise out of the darkness ahead. I was swinging my rifle up when Daru's voice hissed, 'It's me – Daru.'

'Jesus,' I said. 'I nearly shot you. Cover me while I reload.'

I crouched down, put the last clip on to the rifle and threw the empty one away. Amica was sitting behind a rock at the side of the track. I stooped down and took her hand. 'Are you all right?' I felt a slight answering pressure on my fingers. She raised her head and gave me a weary smile.

'It isn't much further,' I said. We both knew it was a lie. 'We'll give it an hour, then loop the track to see if anybody's following us.'

We moved on, shambling through the darkness across the rising plateau. Every step we took up the slope seemed to increase the intensity of the wind. I walked with my shoulders hunched, my gloved hands thrust deep into my pockets, but still my fingers were numb with cold. The track curved further to the east and the wind came straight at us, cutting into my face. We paused in the minimal shelter offered by a low outcrop of rock and shared out the last of our rations. There was no point in keeping them now.

I tried to drink some water but it had frozen in the canteen. I scraped up a few handfuls of gritty snow instead and sucked them for the moisture. 'Are you all right?' I asked again.

Daru nodded, but I had to repeat the question to Amica.

'Can we stop for a little?' she said, every word slow and slurred, her voice fading.

I stood in front of her, shielding her body from the wind with mine. 'No. The flight takes off at dawn; that's only a couple of hours away. We must keep moving.'

I rubbed her arms and back as hard as I could through her clothes, then we stumbled on again. Amica was moving slower and slower.

I looked back along the track and caught a hint of movement in the distance. I held Amica for a moment, crushing her to my chest, then took Daru to one side. 'Take her on ahead. Look after her. Don't let her stop or sit down. If she does, she'll die. I'm going to loop back and try to ambush them. Don't wait for me, keep moving. I'll catch you up.'

I swung round behind the rocks, crouched down and eased the safety-catch off the rifle. My right hand was so cold that I was afraid I wouldn't be able to feel the trigger. I eased off my glove and thrust my hand down towards the warmth of my groin. I left it there for a minute, feeling the temperature rise a little, then I pulled my glove back on and cradled the rifle in my arm.

The Taliban were moving with more caution now, making use of what cover there was on the windswept plateau. I saw them pause as they made out the dark shape of the rocks where I was hiding. Then they must have caught sight of Amica and Daru outlined against the sky, and they began to advance again.

I let them come closer — fifteen metres, ten, five — and even closer still. The leader was no more than three metres from me when I fired. I cut them down like a scythe — three of them crumpled and fell before I heard a click as the magazine emptied. Muzzle-flashes lit up the darkness and fire riddled the rocks around my hiding place, but I was already up and running.

I sprinted on, my lungs tearing with the effort. I ran for perhaps 200 yards, then had to slow to a walk, unable to drag enough oxygen from the thin air. I stumbled on, chest heaving, tasting blood in my mouth. I crossed a low ridge and saw Amica and Daru. They had reached the edge of the snowfield and were moving with painful slowness up the slope.

I shambled towards them. Alongside their tracks I saw other, older marks, half-filled with new snow. Salan and his men had come this way, not more than an hour before us.

I drove myself on, but beneath the frozen crust was a deep layer of powder, and at every step I plunged into it up to my knees. Several times I fell full-length and had to haul myself upright, my face frozen, my beard and hair matted with snow and ice.

Slow though my own progress was, I soon overtook Daru and Amica. I took her other arm.

'How many did you kill?' Daru said.

'Two, perhaps three,' I said. 'There are still others on our trail.'

'How many?'

'I don't know. Maybe six.' I looked back into the darkness. 'We're sitting targets against the snow.'

Daru nodded. 'Go on this time with Amica, I'll cover you until you're nearly at the ridge. If the Taliban come, I'll kill them.'

Before I could argue he had turned and was scrambling back. I lost sight of him as he reached the edge of the snowfield.

His words, I knew, had been pure bravado. There were no more than six rounds in the rifle. He might kill one or two, but the others would keep coming.

We crawled on. My lungs were bursting, my head pounded and waves of nausea swept through me. I had lost all sensation in my face, feet and hands.

Amica's skin was grey, her mouth hung open and her head lolled on her shoulders. 'Just a few more yards,' I kept saying as we staggered upwards, sinking to our knees in the snow, but each time somehow summoning the will to rise again. 'One step at a time, Amica. We'll make it, we'll make it.'

She no longer had the strength to reply.

We inched towards the top. Through the scream of the wind, I heard a burst of gunfire behind me. There was a long pause, then more shots. They whipped into the snow around and above us, but I dared not turn my head. I kept crawling upwards as I waited for the impact of a bullet.

The wind howled up another octave, a banshee screech drowning every other noise, and ahead of me I could see a fine spindrift of snow blown from the ridge.

Amica had toppled forward in the snow. I dragged her up and

pointed. 'We're there, Amica. We're there. A few more steps – you can see the ridge.'

Her eyes were unfocused and she sagged in my arms. 'NO!' I shouted. I slapped her face. Shock showed in her eyes. 'Move!' I said. 'We haven't come this far to lose you now.'

I seized her by the arm. She winced as my fingers dug into her, but she began to struggle up the slope again. We took a faltering step, then another, and another. I moved alongside her, pushing and dragging her whenever she hesitated, until she toppled forward and rolled through the snow at the top of the ridge.

I left Amica lying there for a moment and scrambled back to peer over the edge. A figure was stumbling up the slope behind us. I pulled the knife from my belt. The steel hilt touched my exposed wrist and froze to it in an instant. I gasped as I pulled it away, tearing a patch of skin with it. Lower on the snowfield I saw other dark shapes and muffled flashes, and I realised that the person just behind us was Daru. I sheathed my knife as he reached us, pulled him over the top, and he rolled down the other side gasping for breath.

Amica still lay where she had fallen. Her eyes were closed. I shouted at her and slapped her face again. Once more her eyes shot open. I almost wept with relief. 'Come on. We can't stop here, we'll die. Don't give up now. There's no more climbing. We can see Pakistan.'

I didn't mention the fact that Salan and his men were lying up somewhere on these slopes and we no longer had a single round to fire at them.

We slid down the slope, pausing every hundred metres to scan the ground ahead of us for any telltale sign.

The snow began to thin and black rocks pierced the frozen surface. Then we were clear of it, stumbling down a scree slope.

Snow still clung to the gullies on either side of us, but ahead the way was clear.

The stars were fading as the sky greyed. There were faint streaks of red in the east. The mountain fell away in a long, unbroken slope. I could see no sign of our quarry, but in the far distance, on a plateau several thousand feet below and to the east of us, I made out a pattern of geometric lines. Beyond it were the clustered buildings of a town. I stared again. 'That's the airfield.'

As I spoke I saw a white shape crawling across it. A jet was beginning to taxi towards the end of the runway. I saw it begin to move, accelerating away from us and lifting off into the dawn. It climbed straight at first, trailing plumes of black smoke from its engines, then I saw the sun glint from its wing as it began to bank in a long turn north and west that would bring it down the flank of the mountains.

It was then that I saw Salan. He had risen from the shelter of some rocks less than a hundred metres below us; his men were either side of him, a pace behind, all staring towards the aircraft rising into the sky. I could hear the distant murmur of its engines.

I reached across Amica, grabbed Daru's arm and pointed. 'Take the left man, I'll take the right. Can you use a knife?'

He nodded.

I pulled mine from my belt and gave it to him.

'But what will you do?' he asked.

'I'll bluff him with the rifle.'

'And if he doesn't buy it?' Amica said.

'I'll have to hit him with it.' I glanced at her and her eyes met mine. 'You wait here.' There was much more I wanted to say to her.

We moved down the hillside directly above them. There was bare earth and loose rock underfoot, but we had no time to measure our footfalls. The jet had levelled its wings and was now almost nose-on, speeding towards us, still climbing, as the thunder of its engines rolled around the mountainside.

A stone came loose beneath my feet and clattered away. We sprinted down the slope, abandoning any attempt at concealment. We were almost upon them when one of the soldiers turned, shouted a warning and began to swing up his rifle.

I had mine raised to my shoulder, but he ignored the threat and fired. I felt the bullet pass my head as I swung my rifle at his. It caught him high on his temple and sent him sprawling.

Out of the corner of my eye I saw the other soldier, slower to react, half-turn and then drop as Daru hit him. There was a glint of sunlight on steel as the boy raised the knife and brought it down.

The jet was almost level with us, and no more than two or three thousand feet away. Salan had not moved. The green launcher of the Stinger was pressed into his cheek, and beneath the thunder of the jet engines I heard a faint whine of the heat-seeking head. It was locked on and ready to fire.

The soldier I had hit was struggling back to his feet, but I ignored him and launched myself at Salan as I saw his finger tighten on the trigger. I felt a searing blast across the top of my head as I hit him with my shoulder. He crashed to the ground — but the Stinger was airborne.

I had knocked him sideways and the missile had launched low and wide of its target, but the seeker-head might yet re-lock on the jet's engines. I froze as the blinding white trail of flame streaked away and the jet seemed to hang motion-less in the air in front of me. Then the Stinger blasted past, its trail buffeted by the jetwash, and disappeared towards the sun. A few seconds later there was an explosion as it self-destructed.

As I dropped my gaze, I saw the face of Salan, contorted with rage. '*Kafir*, I will kill you at least.' He held a Kalashnikov trained on my heart.

I was still on my knees. Daru and the soldier I had hit were struggling together on the ground. I looked back at Salan and closed my eyes. Then I heard the roar of a gun.

When I opened my eyes, Salan was on his back, blood trickling from his chest. He was still alive, but his Kalashnikov had spilled from his fingers. Amica was holding the rifle of the soldier Daru had killed. She fired again, shooting the other one as he attempted to kick Daru away from him and scramble for his own weapon. Then she staggered forward and pointed the rifle at Salan's head, her mouth twisted with hatred.

He stared up at her.

'Do you remember me?' she said. 'How could you? I was only a woman in a burka. Yet I am the woman you raped and tortured the day the Taliban took Kabul. Your men raped me too, and murdered my husband in front of my eyes. Do you remember me now?'

He made an inarticulate, gurgling sound in his throat, his one eye still fixed on her. The rifle was still pointing at his head, but I saw it swing down along his body. I knew what she was going to do before she pulled the trigger. There was the crack of a shot and his groin disintegrated into a bloody pulp. An unearthly high-pitched scream came from his lips.

Still she stood over him. 'Finish him,' I said.

She continued to stare down at him, not even turning her head to acknowledge my words, but at last she took aim and fired again at point-blank range, sending another shot upwards through the bridge of his nose. He twitched once and lay still.

A wave of relief flooded over me. Amica swayed and almost fell, and I held her in my arms for a minute before running to help Daru.

He struggled to his feet, his face bloody and bruised, but he gave me a grin of triumph.

Then I saw a movement. My knees buckled as I saw dark figures slithering down the snowfield high above us.

Amica had slumped down, the last of her strength gone. 'Come on,' I said, lifting her to her feet. Daru and I took an arm each and stumbled down the track. My legs felt leaden and I tripped constantly over small rocks in our path. Each one sent jolts of pain through my body.

About a mile ahead of us I could see a huddle of buildings. Beyond it a dirt road snaked away down the valley, disappearing in the shadows below the line of the sunrise.

'Is that the Pakistani border post?' Daru said.

'I don't know,' I said. 'Please God it's not an Afghan one.'

We hurried on across another patch of scree. Amica slipped and fell full length, gashing her cheek, but we dragged her up and staggered on.

A wisp of smoke was rising from the frontier post. I imagined the samovar being lit, and the aromas of woodsmoke, hot tea and warm bread. 'Keep going. We're nearly there.' I glanced behind us. 'Faster.'

Amica didn't look round, but she heard the urgency in my voice and tried to increase her speed. The Taliban soldiers were no more than a mile behind us.

We broke into a stumbling trot down the rocky fields that separated us from the frontier post. Just beyond it I saw a gaudily decorated lorry parked at the side of the road. I ran on ahead, leaving Daru to help Amica the last few yards.

The two border guards were unshaven, their clothes creased

and stained, but I could almost have kissed them when I recognised their Pakistani uniforms.

One held up a hand as I ran towards him. 'Your papers,' he said.

'Please, you must hurry,' I said.

'The formalities,' he said. 'Paperwork. These things cannot be rushed.'

Daru and Amica staggered up to us. I looked back up the mountain. The Taliban were moving fast down the hillside less than half a mile away. 'Please,' I said.

He looked at me. 'You have money?'

Daru pulled out the bundles of Afghanis he had taken from the bodies at the checkpoint.

The man smiled. 'In Afghanistan, this is money. In Pakistan—' He simulated wiping his arse with the notes. The other guard laughed as he tossed them to one side. 'It is not enough.'

'Here.' I wrenched the watch from my wrist. 'You can have this too.'

He took it, looked at it, then back at me. 'It is not enough.'

The Taliban were 400 yards away.

Daru reached inside his shirt, fumbling with something. When he withdrew his hand, I saw the glitter of gold between his fingers. He gave me a sheepish grin. 'I am sorry. I am a thief.'

He threw two of the gold coins into the dirt. 'That is enough,' he said.

As the guards dropped to their knees, scrabbling in the dust for the gold, we ran past them towards the lorry.

The driver was dozing in his cab. We jumped in and I shook him awake. 'Drive,' I said.

Daru brandished a handful of gold coins in front of his bleary-eyed face. 'These are yours. Drive.'

Without taking his eyes from the gold for a second, the driver started the engine, released the handbrake and had the lorry in gear and rumbling down the track. 'Where to?' he said, his gaze still fixed on the gold.

Daru smiled. 'Take us to America.'